BOOK ONE

# THE WATCHER WARS

## T.C. EDGE

1

# Table of Contents

1     Legends...................................5

2     Spoils of Battle.........................18

3     Cloaks and Shadows...................31

4     Shadows in the Night.................43

5     A Hidden Enemy.......................52

6     Cull of Legends........................61

7     The World Opens......................70

8     Farewell to a Friend.................81

9     Fort Warden............................90

10    A Fantasy Realised..................101

11    A Plan Hatching.....................111

12    Unleashed.............................121

13    The Watcher Wars..................133

14    A Secret Pact.........................145

15    The Hidden Passage................156

16    The Training Cave...................164

17    Pushed to the Limit.................174

18    Stage Two.............................183

19    The Arena Awaits....................195

20    Knight's Terror.......................207

21    The Wars Begin......................216

22    A Legend is Born....................226

23    In Too Deep............................................235

24    Twin Threats...........................................244

25    Baron Reinhold.......................................256

26    A Connection Made................................265

27    The Secret Compound...........................275

28    Shrine to Evil.........................................287

29    The Seekers of Knight...........................295

30    Legacy...................................................302

31    Countdown.............................................309

32    The Looming Shadow...........................316

# 1

## Legends

I sit in the shadow of a large oak tree, looking out at the woods beyond. The quiet trickle of water reaches my ears, a small stream meandering its way down from the hills nearby. Birds sing their songs as they nest, insects buzzing in the warm afternoon sunshine. And behind me, a little way back, the sound of chopping wood filters through the forest, an endless symphony that I've endured my entire life.

Beyond the shadow, the grasses are verdant and lush, shining bright in places as the sun breaks through the foliage above. It's warm, even in the shade of the large tree trunk, the year entering its most oppressive and sweltering stage. In other parts of the country, I know, it's far worse.

I'm used to being in the shadow. It's where I fear I'll live my entire life, stuck here in these woods, tucked away into this quiet portion of the world. But it's not the shadow of the tree that I've grown accustomed to; it's the shadow cast by my parents.

It's a strange thing, really, growing up as the son of heroes. Across the lands, my father, and mother in particular, are legends. A couple of decades ago, when they were both only the tender age of 16, as I am now, they changed this country forever.

In a world that was once so full of inequality and injustice, they fought against the odds and won. They defeated a despotic ruler and, along with many other heroes, tore down the shackles and systems of the old world and ushered in a new one.

*The Golden Girl.* That's what my mother was known as across the regions of this country. She grew up with my father in the land of Agricola, a wide expanse used for farming and harvesting crops. Out there, hundreds of miles from here, they saw little respite from the scorching sun. The people there were known for their golden hair and deeply tanned skin.

And that's where my mother got her name.

But it wasn't what she looked like that caused a stir. It was what she could do. Things that, when I was just a boy, made me wide-eyed with wonder. When my father would sit by my bed, and tell me stories of my mother's great deeds, I hardly believed it possible. Not this quiet woman, who was just my mum. She hardly seemed special at all.

But she was special. She was a *Watcher*.

But not anymore…

The sound of crashing rumbles in the distance, of trees being chopped and felled. Here, in these woods, many people make their livings from the trees: growing them, chopping them down, and repeating over and over. It's hardly a life of renown. It's the sort of life I am terrified of living.

6

It's a very real fear, though. After the war, my parents came here to live a quiet life, away from the terrors that they'd seen. My father remains active, running the region as Governor. My mother, though, prefers to stay close to home, growing vegetables and fruits in our private orchard. I think she likes the peace here. She never wanted to be a hero.

I stand and stare out into the forest, stretching far and wide into the distance. I've hardly ever been beyond the boundary of these woods, my mother never allowing me free rein to explore. But that's never stopped me sneaking away at night, creeping out when I know she's sleeping. Going as far as I can into the woods and returning before dawn.

Each time, I go a little further. And each time, I wonder about going on, not turning back. About moving beyond the lands I've known my entire life, and exploring the places I've heard so much about over the years.

But I never do. I'm drawn back to the little cabin in the forest I call home; to the small school in the local town where I study, alongside only a handful of other boys and girls; to the quiet solitude of a life that seems so pointless.

Still in the shade of the tree, I take a step forward towards the light. Then another, and another, until I burst into the hot glow of the sun. A lull hits, the woodcutters taking a break, and in the sudden quiet I hear the gentle hum of my mother's voice as she picks fruit in the orchard nearby.

She always likes to hum the same tune as she

works, escaping into her own little world. I know, when she was young, she used to pick fruit for her own mother, filling in for her when she was too sick to work. My grandmother died soon after, when my mother was just 16. I suppose, picking those apples and pears reminds my mother of her somehow.

As I listen to her humming that familiar tune, another noise joins the fray; an engine, rumbling along dirt tracks. I turn right to see the shape of my father's old jeep slipping past the trees, pulling up to our cabin. He stops and gets out, and the sound of my mother's humming ends as they lock into an embrace.

I look at them quietly through the branches, and try to imagine what life must have been like for them when they were young. The brutal world they lived in; the adventures they shared; the things they saw and people they lost.

And, despite the suffering they speak of, I can't help but wish it had been me; that I'd been part of that world. Shaping it, changing it, leaving a legacy that will never be forgotten.

I turn from them, and begin walking in the opposite direction, casting my eyes through the trees. On my back, I feel the sting of a sharp end pinching at my flesh, and fling my backpack off my shoulder. Inside, my hunting knife sits awkwardly at an angle, the tip sharp even through its sheath. I draw it out and fix it to my belt, before continuing through the trees.

Not too far away, my best friend, Ajax, lives. He's

the only one around here who understands me, the only one who yearns for the same thing. His parents, Ellie and Link, trained with my mother as Watchers. They too saw the horrors of the world all those years ago. And they, like my parents, have chosen to live quietly here in these woods.

We meet often to go hunting. But it isn't deer and rabbits and squirrels that we seek…it's wolves and bears and cougars. Beasts that cause fear. Beasts that cause danger. Only in such a state of alarm do I feel truly alive.

I meet him at a small clearing, and find him launching his own handmade spear into a tree. Ajax is a little older than me, and a little bigger too. I'm hardly a shrinking violet, but he's got the brute strength of his father: a towering, powerful man.

The wood splinters as the tip of the spear hits, driving itself halfway through the tree. Ajax marches towards it and pulls it free with ease, before turning to me with a smile.

"You're getting good at that," I say.

I pull the knife from the sheath on my belt, and in one quick motion send it straight at the same tree. It cuts into the wood, barely missing Ajax as it passes. He doesn't flinch.

"You see that coming?" I ask.

"A bit," he says. "I'm getting better."

He pulls out the knife as I walk forwards, and passes it back to me. I slip it back into its sheath, and admire his spear. It's obvious he's been working on it more. Not just the blade itself, which is sharp as a razor, but the main handle. It's covered in intricate carvings depicting wildlife and grand structures. Structures in far off lands that we've heard about, read about, but never seen with our own eyes.

"I wouldn't take you for an artist," I say, gesturing to the finely carved shape of a bear.

"Not much else to do around here," he grunts. "Just takes a bit of practice."

We begin wandering through the woods, further away from both of our homes. Generally, we prefer to make sure that none of our parents know what we're doing. I know both our mothers, in particular, would forbid it.

"So, any bad dreams or anything?" asks Ajax casually as we stroll.

It's a pointed question, and carries much more weight than it would with anyone else. Because he isn't really talking about dreams. He's talking about visions, glimpses of the future. It's a power that all Watchers have…and one that, over the last few months, we've both realised resides within us too.

I shake my head in frustration.

"Nothing I remember," I say. "You?"

He shrugs. "Same really. I get flashes, sometimes. But nothing's clear. I think I saw a man accidentally chop his leg off with an axe…but, I don't know, maybe it was just a dream."

Ajax, I know, is frustrated too. Our parents were

trained specifically to develop their powers, and had theirs unleashed by some sort of machine that we certainly don't have around here. We have no such luck, and I can't even mention it to my mum without her telling me that her gifts were only ever a curse.

"You don't want them, Theo," she always tells me. "They'll only ruin your life. All you see is death and destruction each night in your sleep. It's no life for anyone."

It's why she moved here with my father in the first place, into these quiet woods where nothing ever happens. Where she can sleep in peace and live a normal life, take the medication that helps to suppress her powers.

Ajax's mother, Ellie, also takes the medication. She's the Principal at our local school, a small but bossy woman who has always been my mum's best friend. Only Theo's father, Link, continues to utilise his abilities, watching over the woods and the nearby towns for signs of danger.

When I asked my father why once, he told me that Link, above all others, always had a sense of duty; a feeling that whether a curse to him or not, his powers were meant to be used for good. So, he maintains a constant vigil over us all, keeping us safe from harm. It's something I agree with. If I truly do have these powers too, I want to use them for good…

But it's not really the visions that attract me. It's the other powers that only the most gifted Watchers possess: the ability to see partially into the immediate future, to see danger coming before it hits.

They call it seeing into 'the Void'. For years, as a child, I would sit and imagine possessing such abilities. How my mother, or Link, could run through a battlefield and never get hit by a bullet. How they could fight a dozen men and dodge every incoming punch and kick. Ajax and I would fight as kids, trying to see each other's attacks coming.

But we never did.

As we got older, we grew more aggressive in our bouts. Danger, and fear, we learned, was what helped to activate the powers. Once, when Link caught us sparring, he taught us a lesson I've always remembered.

"You have to learn to face your fears," he told us. "Watchers fear nothing. They train to fear nothing. Only then are you able to see danger coming. Only then can you see into the Void."

We were interrupted by Ellie, who reprimanded Link for filling our heads with such daydreams.

"There are no Watchers anymore," she said. "The training program has been discontinued."

That night, despite our parents' wishes, Ajax and I made a pact to do all we could do activate our powers. To train secretly in the woods together; sparring, hunting the beasts of the forest, putting each other into positions of danger.

Occasionally, we'd go to far, returning home with

broken noses or busted ankles. I'd be afraid to return home for what my mother would say. Now, when she finds me with cuts and bruises, she just looks at me with disappointment in her eyes, leaving my father to dish out the appropriate punishment.

But still, nothing has stopped us, and nothing will. More and more, we push ourselves. And more and more, we have begun to see the slightest signs of success; the barest hints that there is something stirring within, something fighting to get out. It's all we need.

As the afternoon sun continues its journey across the sky, we continue deeper into the forest, our steps turning lighter as we go, our voices growing silent. For such a large young man, Ajax is surprisingly light on his feet when he needs to be, his footsteps barely making a sound as he creeps through the shrubbery of the forest floor.

As we go, we pass by a lake, set within a wide clearing. At the distant shore, we see deer grazing and drinking at the water's edge. We crouch low, sneaking through the bushes as we grow closer. I stop, lick my index finger, and raise it to the air.

"We're upwind," I whisper.

Ajax nods and I see his hand grip tighter at the handle of his spear.

The deer continue to eat and drink, oblivious to our presence. One raises its head in our direction, its ears pricking up, before slowly returning to the grass. And slowly, silently, we move forward.

Soon, we're only a dozen or so metres from them. I look at Ajax, and he looks right back at me, and in a moment of understanding, we act.

Hunting knife in hand, I stand up and, in one swift motion, send the blade hurtling through the air at the nearest deer. To my right, Ajax does the same, his strong arm guiding his spear like a missile at the same animal.

Before it has a chance to react, both of the blades dive deep into its flesh. My knife embeds itself in the deer's neck. Ajax's spear tears straight through its midsection. In seconds only, the creature falls to the earth, dead. There is no need to finish the job and cut short its suffering, such was the accuracy of our throws.

I take no pleasure in killing the animal. I know it has to be done. Not only for its meat, which will serve both our families for days, but also the other use we'll make of the carcass.

Bait.

We set to work quickly, moving the deer's body a little way back from the water and setting it in a small clearing where the smell of its blood will permeate through the surrounding woodland. With the afternoon sun now beginning its descent towards the horizon, we step back, find a suitable tree, and climb up into its low branches.

And there, we wait.

A long silence hits. Together, we crouch in the foliage, unspeaking, listening closely for the sound of movement below. The herbivores grazing down at the water's edge have now vanished. The birds have gone quiet. Even the buzzing insects appear to have gone on hiatus, the entire forest descending into a deep, penetrating calm.

Minutes pass as the sun dips further down, casting its glow through the treetops. Gradually, the floor of the forest darkens a little, the world being covered in a shadow I know all too well. The water of the lake continues to glisten; little waves and ripples dancing with flashes of light reflected from above. Hues of orange and soft red begin to spread through the thicket.

And still, we wait in silence. Those minutes turn to an hour, that hour into two as the threat of total darkness begins to grow. I feel Ajax looking at me with his piercing brown eyes.

"Maybe we should call it a day?" he whispers.

I feel a tug of disappointment hunt me down. If we don't leave soon, they'll be hell to pay with our parents.

"A few more minutes," I mouth, turning back to the deer carcass, its meat already beginning to spoil in the sweltering heat.

Those minutes pass by quickly, and soon Ajax's eyes are on me again. Feeling defeated, we nod to each other, and prepare to climb down from the tree.

And just as we go, a rumbling, heavy growl reverberates through the woods. My eyes trace the source, and there, through the shroud, I see the form of a hulking bear emerging through the bushes. My heart rate spikes, my body priming itself for action. I look at Ajax once again, whose face is now lit with a devious and excited smile.

"Let's do it," he whispers.

And with that, we both drop straight out of the tree, hitting the ground with a thud.

The reaction of the bear is immediate. It stands up onto its hind legs, reaching its full height as it lets out a deafening roar. Standing next to me, Ajax suddenly darts off to the right. I begin moving left, the bear turning with me as I go.

Standing above the carcass, it continues to roar, stamping back down to the ground and kicking up dirt and dead leaves with its long, razor sharp claws; putting on a display of dominance that I cannot hope to match. I pull the hunting knife once more from my belt, and hold it firmly in my hand, staring at the monstrous beast from only ten or so metres away.

I stand there and watch it, waiting for it to make its move. My heart rate continues to soar, my entire body filling with adrenaline. And in that state, I feel the pulse of life run through me, feel something continue to activate at my core.

And then, suddenly, the bear begins to charge. A further jolt of adrenaline surges through my veins, priming me for action as this terrifying beast advances down on me. But I don't move. I just stand there, my mind focused on the danger ahead, my eyes locked with those of the beast.

Then, from the side, I hear the voice of Ajax calling wildly.

"Theo, run! Move!"

I ignore him. Instead, the faintest of smiles begins to rise on my face as the bear looms closer. I smile, and stand there watching, just as the sight of a spear comes surging from the right.

It cuts straight through the bear's neck when he's mere metres away, severing its jugular. The flow of blood is immediate, gushing from the wound as the bear stumbles and collapses, falling into a heap right at my feet.

I turn to my right, and see Ajax, eyes wild as he rushes forward.

"What the hell, Theo!" he shouts. "You didn't move! You got a death wish or something?!"

I shake my head, and my smile broadens. And immediately, he knows why.

"You saw it coming?" he asks breathlessly. "The spear? You knew it would hit…you saw into the Void?"

I look back down at the fallen beast, and say a silent thank you.

Then I look back at Ajax, and all I do is nod.

## 2
## Spoils of Battle

The world has grown fully dark by the time we set off on our path back home. After the excitement of the kill, however, neither Ajax nor I paid much attention to the clock.

In the clearing, the carcass of the great bear still lies, its body emptied of blood. A small stream of crimson winds its way down towards the lake, muddying the water under the glow of the moon.

I feel a slight tinge of guilt as I look at the beast, lured into the trap as it was. I banish the thought immediately, though, relegating it to the recesses of my mind. Out here, where bears are a constant threat to the people, there's really no space for it.

Some men are tasked with hunting them for that very reason. When they do, the custom is to take the bear's pelt as a sign of victory. I look to my side, and see Ajax now sporting the beast's hide across his shoulders; its roaring face sat atop his head. It still drips blood, trickling down my friend's cheeks. He looks altogether the ferocious man of the woods.

"Suits you," I say.

He shuffles under its weight.

"It's hot," he remarks. "Better for winter."

Still, he doesn't take it off as we turn and begin our journey home. His pride at felling the beast clearly overrides his discomfort.

On my back, my bag is now filled with the best meat of the deer. Ajax, too, has accumulated enough to feed him and his parents for the next week or so. I'm hoping that it'll be enough to appease my mother for returning at such a late hour.

The pelt, however, wasn't the only thing the bear gave us. Ajax, having killed it, deserved the most highly prized asset. That left me to fashion a necklace from its claws, which now hangs around my neck beneath my shirt. The rest of the carcass will make good eating for the wolves and other scavengers of the woods. Nothing will go to waste.

Our pace is a little slower returning home, dark as the forest floor now is. Occasionally, the moonlight filters down through the foliage above, giving light to the various clearings and breaks in the trees. Mostly, however, we have to be careful to not trip over some root or low-slung branch.

As we go, Ajax quizzes me further on exactly what happened.

"So, how far away did you see the spear coming? I mean, how long before it hit?"

"It's hard to explain," I admit. "I sort of saw the spear going into the bear's neck just after you shouted for me to move. It was weird…like a ghost version of the spear, white and blurred."

"So, you saw it just a few seconds before it actually happened?"

"Yeah, just a second or two. That's why I didn't move. I knew it was coming. You've seen the same before, right?" I ask.

Ajax nods as we continue through the brush. "Yeah, just a second or two, like you. You know my father can see, like, thirty seconds into the Void sometimes. Something ridiculous like that."

"That's crazy. So he'd have seen the bear being killed before we even jumped out of the tree!"

"I know. Imagine it. You'd be invincible!" he says, his voice eager.

We take a moment's silence to reflect, to let our imaginations begin to soak up such possibilities. Yet, right now, the sobering thought is that, for both of us, the possibilities are extremely limited. Without proper training, without fully releasing our potential, we'll never attain anything like what Link can do; what my mother could do before she decided to turn against her powers.

Yet still, to have seen into the Void properly for the first time is exciting. And as we walk and talk, a febrile energy spreads between us.

"Maybe your dad would train us?" I ask amidst the excitement.

Ajax is quick to shake his head. "I doubt it. I mean, maybe he'd want to…but mum wouldn't let him. And your mum wouldn't let you train anyway."

"Yeah, well, I'm not a kid anymore. I can do what I want."

Ajax huffs. "If only it were that simple. Let's face it, Theo, we're probably gonna be stuck in these woods for life."

I fix him with a stare. "Are you kidding me?! What, you're just happy chopping down trees the rest of your life now are you?"

"No, obviously not," he counters. "But come on, what else are we really gonna do. I mean, you've got some brains, unlike me, but you don't exactly put them to good use. If you wanted, you could work hard and do anything…"

"Like what?" I cut in.

"I dunno. Become an engineer, or a doctor or something. There are no Watchers anymore, Theo, so what's the point?"

"What about your dad. He's still a Watcher."

"Yeah, unofficially. He just doesn't take the meds to suppress his powers. I mean, it's probably not all it's cracked up to be, going around saving cats from trees…"

"He doesn't save cats from trees. He actually helps people. Didn't he save a family from a house fire the other week?"

"Yeah. But it's not usually that big a deal. I mean, look at our mums…they take pills to stop themselves having visions. They must do it for a reason. Really, do we actually want that?"

I stop in my tracks and stare at him. In the darkness, the moonlight leaks down through a small gap in the canopy, shedding a cool glow upon us.

"Are you serious with all this chat? I thought you *wanted* to be a Watcher?"

He shrugs and sets his eyes on me. "I do, but I'm just being realistic. You shouldn't go filling your own head with this stuff. You might just end up disappointed."

"God, you sound like my mother."

"Yeah, well, she's probably got a point. I mean, this is the great Cyra Drayton we're talking about here. She a legend for a reason."

"I know what my mum is, AJ, all right. Just don't dampen my spirits right now. Come on, this is a big night for me. And you, look at that damn bear on your back!"

I laugh to ease the tension, and he stands tall and proud under the glow of the moon.

"It does look pretty cool, right! And yeah, you're right too. Come on, we'd better get home before our parents send out a search party…"

Chuckling, we continue off into the dark woods, quickening our pace as we near home.

Before too long, I'm leaving Ajax at the same place we met hours ago, our cabins off in different directions.

"See you tomorrow at school," I say as he disappears into the darkness.

Alone now, I turn and begin making my way back to my own house. By now it's got to be pushing towards midnight, the position of the moon and stars giving me some indication as to that. After another few minutes, I make out the shape of our cabin through the dark silhouettes of the trees.

Inside, through the main window, I can see that the light is on.

*Damn.*

I take a deep breath as I press on, my feet cracking on twigs and old leaves, my pulse beginning to advance once again. It's strange, really, that the encounter I'm about to have with my parents makes me equally nervous as the one I just had with a nine foot bear.

Inside, I can hear the two of them in quiet discussion as I approach the front door. I know I could try to sneak in through the window to my bedroom, but that would be the coward's way out. No…I need to face the music now.

I reach forward, and begin turning down the door handle. Immediately, as the door creaks open a touch, I hear the conversation inside die down. I step in, and see two sets of eyes boring into me.

"What time do you call this?!" It's my mother, Cyra, who's first to speak.

"Night time," I say, trying to lighten her mood. I know it won't work.

"Don't get cute with me, Theodore Kane," she says. Her eyes peer forward at my wrist. "Why aren't you wearing the watch I got you?"

"It felt weird," I say, shrugging. "And it ticked too loud. It might scare off the animals."

Next to my mum, my dad, Jackson, stands tall, watching things unfold. If ever I do something wrong, this particular set up is usually the norm. Mum, reprimanding, dad supporting her. The standard 'good cop, bad cop' routine that I'm well versed in by now.

"I don't care if it ticks too loud. And you'll get used to the feel. Anyway, I know you can read the time from the sky, young man. Why are you so late?"

At this point, I take the opportunity to sling the rucksack from my shoulder. I lay it down on the small table in the rustic old kitchen, and open it up, showing off its wares.

"Ajax and me…we were hunting game. I guess we lost track of time and went too far into the woods. I'm sorry, mum."

She softens a little as she looks upon the bounty of meat.

"Theo, I know you like to hunt, but we can buy all the meat we need. You have school tomorrow. You should be focusing on your studies, not gallivanting out there with Ajax."

I hang my head in my well-worn routine of contrition. It usually wins her over.

Now my father takes his opportunity to step forward. He moves to the table and takes the meat out of the bag, before laying it down flat.

"It's a good haul, Cyra," he says. "The more free meat we can get, the better. Others around the villages aren't so lucky. We can pass some on…"

"Thanks, dad," I say.

He turns to me. "But that doesn't excuse you coming back this late, son. You need to keep a better account of the time. Wear your mother's watch, OK?"

My dad has a stern way about him when he wants to employ it. When he was a kid, he was groomed to be a leader, before being sent into the military. Ever since, he's led people through hardship. He knows how to command respect.

Once again, I nod and dip my head, trying to be as deferential as I can. I've learned it's the best way to keep the two of them sweet, so my next misdemeanour isn't quite so harshly dealt with.

It seems to appease him. He lifts his own wrist to his eyes and checks the time.

"Honey, it's late. I think we should let this one slide. But," he continues, turning to me, and lowering his voice, "don't let it happen again."

"I won't, dad. I promise," I mutter.

Hoping that's the end of it, I prepare to turn and sneak off to my room. My mother's voice stops me.

"What's that around your neck?" she asks.

I turn instinctively, and my fingers find their way up to the necklace of bear claws, hidden beneath my shirt.

"It's nothing…"

She steps forward, and pulls the necklace into the open, above the fabric. Her fingers examine the claws, see that they've been freshly taken from the beast's carcass.

"What is this? Have you…have you been hunting bears?!"

"No…of course not…" I stammer.

She pulls the necklace clean off me, and takes a closer look.

"We just found the bear dead, that's all…"

She rounds on me, her face like thunder.

"Theo, when will you learn! Why can't you just be happy? Your father and I fought for peace so that you could live free and safe. And you go off putting your life in danger like this?!"

"Well maybe I like the danger!" I retort, giving up the lie. "Do you have any idea how boring it is for me here, knowing what you two did? It's not fair."

"Fair? You don't know anything about what's fair, Theo! When we grew up, life really wasn't fair. People were assigned their duties for life. They were told who to marry and have kids with. They were given rations for their work, and if they couldn't work, they'd starve. *That* wasn't fair. And that's what we all fought to change. You have no idea how easy you have it. You think you want a life like that?" she says, shaking her head. "You have no idea what it was like back then…"

Her voice trails off, and a silence dawns. Then, without looking at me, she casts her eyes up to Jackson.

"I'm going to bed, Jack," she says. "The medication…it makes me tired."

With her ferocity gone, she moves off, deflated, and disappears into her bedroom. In her hand, she still clings onto my bear claw necklace.

For a while I stand there, heart thumping, wondering why she can't understand, why none of them can. Then my dad's soothing voice reaches my ears, saying the very words I never expect to hear.

"I understand," he whispers.

I look up at him, wondering if he can somehow read my mind. He has no powers like my mum; he was never a Watcher. But he's got an intuition that only a father can share with a son.

"You're young, you want to have adventures. Which boy of 16 doesn't? You hear our stories of the past, and they sound glamorous. Trust me, Theo, they weren't. Things were tough and brutal. Lots of our friends died."

He looks to the right, where an old picture is fixed to the wall. It's of a young man, only my age…the man who I was named after.

"You know where you got your name, son. Your mother was Paired with a boy called Theo when she was training on Eden. She cared for him deeply, and he died…saving both our lives. There were others, so many others. She's terrified that something might happen to you if you continue down this path."

"But nothing will. Nothing happens in this country anymore…there's no war."

He shakes his head.

"It's not just war. You seek out danger. You're trying to develop your own powers, we know that. But it truly is nothing but a curse. I've seen it first hand. You don't want that burden, Theo, you really don't."

"You don't know what I want. Maybe I just want to help, like Link."

"Link is a special case. He was born for this. That's not your path."

"You don't know that."

Once more, the room turns silent. I've had conversations like this in the past, but never this deep or heated. And never when I've been so close to attaining what I want. I feel like I'm being hindered at every turn, a weight hung over my shoulders, pressing me down. Like I'm shackled in this cabin, nothing but a prison.

"When you mother trained on Eden," comes my father's voice again, soft in the silence, "do you know what she faced?"

I shake my head, staring at the ground.

"She saw me die," he says gently. "Everyday, she went through simulations that felt real to her…simulations in which I was killed. And her mother too. Day after day, week after week, she had to suffer with seeing those she loved most die before her eyes."

Slowly, I look up into his eyes. They stare at me, filling with memories so clear I can almost see them myself.

"The others who trained with her faced other fears," he continues. "Fear of heights. Fear of snakes, or fire, or darkness. But your mother…her fear was losing me. She's had to carry those scars all her life, Theo. And now there's someone in this world she loves even more than me. You will never know how much she worries about you."

He moves to me, and lays his large hands down on my shoulders. They feel slightly different, the left landing a little heavier. Its silver, metal surface catches the light, bionic fingers capable of delivering a great deal more force than a regular grip. He lost his left arm at the elbow during the war. It's a constant reminder of the life he once led.

Standing face to face, we must look like mirror images of each other, only two decades apart. Same height, same build, same hair and eye colour; blond and blue, with the tanned skin so common in the region from which he hailed.

"For your mother's sake," he says, "let all of this go."

He waits for me to react. Slowly, I begin to nod and then say: "I'll try."

And with those words, he draws his hands back,

turns, and follows my mother back into their bedroom.

*I'll try,* I think to myself. *I can promise no more than that.*

# 3
## Cloaks and Shadows

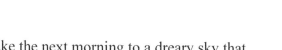

I wake the next morning to a dreary sky that mimics my mood. Hot, humid air clings at my skin, the woods around the cabin covered in a low layer of thick mist.

It's still early when I check the watch my mother gave me. I make sure to put it on before I leave my room, then head out into the kitchen to fetch some fruit for breakfast. My parents, notoriously early risers, are both already up; my father sitting at the table going over some files; my mother busying herself with some household chores.

I still find it odd seeing her, day after day, engage in such menial tasks after knowing what she did. My father, at least, continues to be actively involved in shaping the wooded region of Lignum where we live. How my mum can go from fighting wars to hanging washing is beyond me.

I grab an apple and banana without a word, before setting off out of the cabin. There's an awkwardness in the air that I want to escape as soon as I can, so I grab my school bag and make a quick beeline for the door before I can be drawn into any further debate.

Outside, the muggy air wraps itself around me as I work my way through the forest. We often get weather like this here in the early mornings, my walk through the woods to the local school frequently slowed by the mist. I give myself enough time to navigate my way through, however, and arrive in town as it begins to rise for the day.

It's a small place, barely a village really. A collection of buildings, many built from wood: some used for the various types of work people do around here; others used as homes. Mostly, the people here operate as they once did when people were assigned their duties. Back then, the people were planters and choppers and hunters. Now, nothing has really changed as far as I can see. The same people do the same work. Their children, for the most part, are likely to follow in their footsteps.

Our school is situated on the edge of town, overlooking the forest beyond. Each day, the sounds of the woods filter through the walls as we learn. The kids are well aware that they'll likely find themselves adding to the noise as soon as they grow up.

Ajax and I are in our final year now. It's a transitional period, a fork in the road, where the next stages of our lives are meant to start. Some will go straight to work out in the woods. Others will, if they're lucky, move to another more vibrant town or region and take up a vocational trade. Apprenticeships in things like engineering and medicine are available for those who get the right grades. They'll move off and continue their studies and work towards something better.

In our school, though, I can't see anyone moving from this place. There are only a dozen of us in our final year and, by my reckoning, they're all set to stay living with their parents and follow in the same trades. Maybe they'll move to another town in the area after a few years. Maybe they'll meet someone and settle down, maybe not. At least, in the past, people would be guaranteed a husband or wife based on their genetic compatibility. Now, we all have to go about finding one ourselves. Perhaps not everything has changed for the better…

As I reach the entrance to the school, I find Ajax already there. He sits outside, waiting for class to start, looking equally deflated as me. I can only assume that his parents gave him a similar talking to.

I take a seat next to him on the steps.

"Rough night?" I ask.

He nods. "Not sure wearing that bear hide home was a good idea…"

"You got the same treatment as me then?"

"Worse I reckon."

"You think?" I huff. With us, everything's a competition.

"Yeah," he says shallowly. "I was totally stupid…I forgot my mum's mum was killed by a bear."

"Oh…really? I, er, didn't know."

"Yeah, before I was born my grandma was killed by a bear in the woods near here. She was just a planter. I guess it was pretty insensitive."

"Well, you didn't do it on purpose, AJ. Anyway, I'd have thought a dead bear would make her happy. She's gotta hate them."

He shakes his head. "It's not about that. It's about the fact that I could have been killed, just like my grandma. I've never seen her so mad."

"There's a lot of that going around," I mumble.

"Yeah. Let's just forget it ever happened."

We sit in quiet contemplation for a while, before some of the other kids begin to arrive. Some are young, not yet into their teens. They play and giggle and dance their way into school, unburdened by the need for something more. As they get older, maybe their fire will begin to go out, like it does for so many others. Not many in the final year appear so enthused as they trundle in.

We set about our day, my mind constantly wandering elsewhere as I pretend to work. Even when I'm here, at school, I spend most of my time in the woods and beyond, fighting bears and wolves and exploring the lands that stretch far from the boundaries of the forest. It's always been a problem for me, my imagination taking me away from class, hindering the dull lessons I'm forced to endure.

Maybe I could do better. In fact, I know I could do better. I could get good grades and go on to live a life elsewhere. Maybe go to one of the more exciting coastal towns, or perhaps even the sea cities. Who knows, maybe even Eden itself, the capital sea city, where my mum trained long ago. My grandfather, Drake, is Vice President there. Surely he could put me to work. Not that my mum would ever let that happen, much as she hates the place.

When she was dragged off to Eden to train, it was the last place she wanted to go. For her, it's where everything started and ended. Now, it's been freed of the shackles of the man who burdened the world with such inequality, a man known all across the land – Augustus Knight. Back then, he held the title of High Chancellor, but really he should have called himself Emperor. It was he, and only he, who crafted the direction of the country.

Now, though, the political structure has been changed. There's a President and Senators who speak for the various regions and areas and major towns across the country. There are Governors, like my father, who sees to the day to day running of the places they live. There are even Mayors in the larger cities and towns, as well as other councils and government bodies that see to the running of this or that.

Power has been diversified. Where it was once held by one man, it is now spread among many. Men and women from all backgrounds, all ages, and all walks of life now have a say in how the country is shaped. That, really, is the legacy of my parents and those they fought alongside.

The day passes as it always does these days:

slowly. Little engages me here anymore. Lessons on practical things that will supposedly aid us in later life do nothing but bore me. The only time I find myself even remotely engaged is when we're taught about the history of this country. When we cover the recent history of the War of the Regions, all eyes turn to Ajax and myself. It's the natural response, I suppose, when your parents were so heavily involved.

Originally, I enjoyed the attention that such things brought. I'd be called upon to offer my own personal rendition of things, although really I had little to offer. Anything I've heard from Jackson or Link I could have read about in a book, or heard about in rumours and the stories that children tell.

Still, I'd be able to proudly talk about how it feels to be the son of Cyra Drayton and Jackson Kane. The kids would hang on my every word as I spoke, not only in class, but outside of it too. They'd hunt me down and ask me questions, always eager to know more.

But, as the years have passed, such attention has become a burden. The more I talk about the accomplishments of my parents, the more I want to achieve my own. Otherwise, what will become of me? Will I forever be destined to be known as Theo Kane, the son of legends? Nothing but a normal man, famous for being born from greatness.

The thought has grown more all-consuming as I've grown. Little satisfies me now except the prospect of leaving this place and escaping the shadow. When I'm in those woods with Ajax and my hunting knife, surrounded by wolves or facing a charging bear, I feel alive. When I sneak through the dark forest at night, imagining what it would be like to run away, I get an adrenaline surge that nothing else can bring me. And when I think about the powers that lie simmering inside me, working hard to break out, I want nothing more than to set them free.

By the day's end, I can barely recall anything I've been taught. I walk through the main school corridor with Ajax, wishing to return to the depths of the woods where the beasts lie in wait. The sight of Ajax's mum, Ellie, the school Principal, dampens that desire. She looks at the two of us with disappointment in her eyes, an expression I know all too well when I look at my own mother.

*They just don't understand.*

The weather has hardly improved as the day has gone on. It remains muggy and sticky, the heavy cloud cover above trapping in the humid air. I walk with Ajax through town, passing by the only vibrant area there is: the merchant and trading quarter. Mostly, the area is quiet, but at certain times of the month it livens up as traders come through town, selling their wares.

We move in towards the various carts and stalls that have been laid out for the afternoon, taking a particular interest in one that appears to specialise in knives and hunting gear. The rest, selling food and clothing and jewellery, don't have quite the same appeal.

Other hunters gather around our preferred stall, stocking up on new equipment that might aid them in their jobs and hobbies. They barter with the vendor, haggling over price. Such exchanges can often get heated, especially among the more burly men who take an interest in such things.

Ajax and I ignore them, though, and set about examining the knives on display. Some are finely crafted, less cumbersome than my own hunting knife. I'd love to find out what I could do with some of them, their lightness allowing me to throw further and with greater accuracy.

The vendor, freshly aggravated by a feisty exchange with one of the local hunters, spots me inspecting one of his finest knives.

"You there, boy, put that down. Don't touch what you can't afford."

I glare at him angrily. "How do you know what I can afford?" I ask.

"Because you're just a kid. And anyway, no one from a place like this can afford a knife like that. Now put it down and clear off."

I feel my fist balling by my side, and say a few calming words in my head.

Behind me, Ajax's sizeable paw taps me on my shoulder.

"Come on, Theo, let's get out of here. Forget him."

With a final, seething look, I turn and continue through the market. The vendor, however, has already moved onto his next battle.

Few of the other stalls carry any interest for us. I notice a stall selling necklaces and bracelets and other keepsakes, many of them made from natural materials mined from the earth or taken from animals. I consider fetching my bear claw necklace and selling it on. Ajax, too, appears to have the same idea when we pass a clothing stall filled with animal furs.

Neither of us, however, have access to the spoils we gathered last night. According to Ajax, his mum took immediate possession of his bear hide. My mum did the same. It frustrates us both that we're still treated like children.

Soon enough, we're growing bored and are ready to make our way back into the woods. It's still fairly busy around us, people coming down the dirt tracks leading into town to check out the local market. I spare a look back at the hunter's stall and see it still attracting plenty of attention. Among the crowd, I spy a small group of four dressed in light cloaks that obscure their faces. I remark to Ajax that it's an odd look, given the heat. He merely nods and shrugs, his mind clearly elsewhere.

Still, there's something about them that doesn't quite add up. I look at them for a few more moments before putting it down to the fact that they're clearly foreigners to these lands. Maybe tradespeople themselves who come from one of the warmer corners of the country, and for whom these parts seem wintry by comparison.

As we walk up the dirt track and begin working our way towards the woods, the sky cracks with a boom of thunder. I look up to see that the heavy clouds are ready to spill. Moments later, a deluge begins pouring, the heavens emptying. Behind us, people begin rushing for cover from the open-air market, the stalls themselves quickly protected by pop up umbrellas designed for this very threat.

I see the cloaked figures once more, calmly walking away. Amid the rush, they seem oddly unaffected by the torrent. I turn back to the woods and, at a brisk pace, move into the safety of the heavy canopy. The sound of rainfall beating on leaves and braches is deafening, but welcome. I've always enjoyed the natural song of the storm.

I part with Ajax at the usual spot. He tells me he's keen to get home early and study, a rarity for him. I suspect it's a reaction from the previous night.

Instead of going directly home, I spend a bit of time out in the storm, enjoying the fall of raindrops as they leak down through the canopy, soaking me to my bones. I wander back to the lake, deep in the woods, and watch the rainfall dancing on the water.

Along the shoreline, I spot the carcass of the bear once again, much of it now taken by scavengers. The red scarlet of its blood, dried into the dirt, is brought back to life by the rain. Together they form a cocktail that, once more, begins to flow down into the lake.

With my watch now tightly fastened to my wrist, I keep a close check on the time. I stay for as long as I can before returning home, the storm now beginning to wane. As the clouds part, the sky comes into view, the sun peeking down through gaps and sending bright shards of early evening sunlight through the forest. It's a beauty that, perhaps, I've started to take for granted. At times like this, however, I remember just how magnificent these woods can look.

When I return, I find that my mother has cooked deer for dinner. We sit quietly as a family as the last drops of rain tap on the roof, and eat. Eventually, my mum speaks, breaking the tension.

"Your father and I have been talking," she says.

I look up at her. Her eyes are hooded. I know immediately that I'm not going to like what she has to say.

"We think it's time that you started taking the suppressor medication."

I look at my father, then back at my mother, and shake my head.

"No. I won't do that."

"Theo, it's for your own good. If you keep trying to develop your powers, it'll only lead to pain. Trust us, as your parents, to know what's best for you."

"I don't really have any powers," I say. "I don't want to go on meds."

My parents share a look. I can see this isn't easy for them.

"It's just a precaution," says Jackson. "You won't

need to take as much as your mum. Just a small dose."

"But…" I start.

"No buts, Theo," says Cyra. "We've spoken with Ellie and Link, and we agree that this is best for both you and Ajax. We've made our decision."

I sit quietly for a moment, not speaking. I know that there's nothing I can say that will change their minds. If I try to fight it, they'll only be more convinced of their decision. So I do the only thing I can do – I agree with them.

"OK," I say eventually. "I'll do it."

They peer at me suspiciously.

"Good, son," says Jackson. "We're both proud of you."

I ask to be excused, and get permission. And as I sit in my room, stewing in anger, I wonder just what they can possibly be proud of me for.

For obeying their rules for once? For lying to their faces? For not working at school, and resenting them for keeping me locked here in this prison?

No, there's nothing to be proud of. And, really, that's the entire problem.

*And it's something I'm desperate to change…*

# 4

## Shadows in the Night

The next two days pass by at a glacier's pace. It's the weekend now, my time my own. Not having to endure school allows me the opportunity to spend too many hours in my own head, my anger stewing and festering like an open wound.

When I venture out of my room, however, I paint a calm expression on my face for my parents to see. I know it's no good me sulking around the house. That I can do on my own time, and in my own space.

I get on with the chores I'm given: tidying the gardens after the storm; fixing any wooden panelling that might have been damaged by the heavy winds; going into town to fetch some herbs and spices and other groceries.

When I've built up enough goodwill, I head off into the woods to do some more hunting. I promise my mum I won't go far, and that I'll only be hunting deer and rabbit this time. She nervously watches as I march off into the forest and disappear out of sight.

I hunt alone for the most part. For me, it's like stress relief, a way to take out my anger on the world. I spend several hours hurling my hunting knife at whatever I see; birds, lizards, even large insects feel the sting of my blade. I grind my teeth and only take what we might actually use. By the time I return home, I've collected quite a haul.

The next day runs the same as the first. My frustration builds and spills over, and I venture deeper into the woods than I have in a while. I reach a clearing at the summit of a hill, the valleys below stretching far off towards the horizon.

I climb the tallest tree I can find, reaching the highest vantage point possible, and spread my hand over my eyes to block the glare of the sun. From up here, way in the distance, I can just about make out the ends of the woods. Beyond, the earth flattens and grows more brown and orange, the beginning of the dustbowl that covers so much of the land.

The temptation to continue on hits me harder than ever, as I sit in the high braches of the tree and look out over the world below. It's a thought that's passed through my mind so many times now, always fading eventually as the reality of such a thing dawns. This time is like no other. I climb down from the tree and begin working my way back home.

That night, with another week of school looming, I sit in my room, unable to sleep. I hear a whisper out of my window, and squint into the dark woods to see Ajax hidden amongst the trees. It's late now, my parents in bed, so I silently climb through the window and join my friend in the shadows.

We walk off into the thicket, just a little way from

the cabin where my parents won't hear us talk, and take a seat on a couple of old tree stumps.

"I guess your parents told you then?" I say to him. "About the medication."

He nods. "What are you gonna do?"

"What do you think? I'm gonna pretend."

"Pretend to take the meds?"

"Sure, why not?"

"They'll make you. They'll give them to you when you have dinner or something. I know that's what my mum's gonna do."

"Well, I guess I'll be throwing up a lot then," I say. "I don't care what they say, AJ. I'm developing these powers whether they like it or not."

"Good," he says. "Me too."

A smile greets my face. "You've changed your tune a bit, haven't you?"

"It was a weak moment," he admits. "I dunno, the idea of just chopping trees all day doesn't fill me with much joy."

"Me neither. Anyway, I can't believe your dad agrees with this. I can see mine is on the fence…"

"Yeah…he doesn't, really. But you know what, it's my mum who wears the trousers over at my place."

The image hits me, and I can't help but laugh. Ellie is so small and diminutive, Link so hulking and brutal looking. He's got several scars cut across his face, and burn marks too from back in the war. If you didn't know him, he'd be pretty terrifying.

I take a deep breath, the night so quiet, almost eerily so. It feels good to know that Ajax is on the same page as me. If I lost him now, I don't know what I'd do.

"Anyway, I was thinking, we don't have to stay here," says Ajax. "Neither of us do. It's not like the old world. We can go wherever we want now. As soon as we leave school, we're free."

"I guess. But we need credits for that. We need to work…"

"Yeah, you think there's only work here? Even if we were both choppers, we could move to another part of the region. Anyway, there are no damn girls here. Whatever happens after school, I'm not sticking around long."

"Yeah, you're right. Even as choppers, we could work somewhere else and build our powers. And we wouldn't have our parents forcing pills down our necks."

"Powers and girls. That's what I want," laughs Ajax.

I laugh along with him, quietly though so as not to wake my parents. The reality, however, isn't quite as easy as that and we know it. Getting a place to live with no credits to pay rent wouldn't be easy. And with the sway our parents hold, it would be simple enough for them to prevent us getting work anywhere. In the end, they just need to trust that we're adults now and can make our own decisions. Perhaps, in time, that will come.

We sit for a while, the conversation turning back to the sorts of fantasies we've always discussed. We talk, as we do so often, about what it would be like to have the powers of Link. How we'd go off and be great warriors, heroes fighting for good, for the people. How we'd become legends like our parents, performing deeds that will be taught in the history books. It's the dream that slips into my head so often at night, something that's become so ingrained in my mind I've never wanted anything else.

I don't quite know how long we talk for. Half an hour, an hour, maybe even more. As we do, however, a mist descends over the woods, settling low on the forest floor. We both look up at the house, and a strange feeling of disquiet engulfs me. I look at Ajax, and his eyes narrow.

"Do you feel that?" I whisper.

Almost imperceptibly, he nods. The deepest silence I've ever encountered spreads through the trees, the light breeze itself seeming to freeze. I shut my eyes, and feel my heart begin to race. And then, when I open them, the forms of shadows appear in the distant trees, hidden in the mist.

Locked to that tree stump, I stare at the shapes in the darkness, appearing one by one near to my cabin. I count four of them, spectres in the dark, moving closer to my home, to the bedroom where my parents sleep.

To my right, I hear the sound of Ajax whispering:

"Fire. They're going to fire."

And as he speaks, I see it too. The cloudy wisps of bullets bursting from the tips of guns. Of barrels exploding with light in the dark, propelling deadly projectiles at the wooden walls of my parents' bedroom.

Together, we both stand, the attack imminent, our voices about to burst forth with some sort of warning. But we don't get a chance. Just as our lungs explode, so does the sound of gunfire, drowning us out as the still of the forest is consumed.

In the woods, the little lights flash, illuminating the culprits. I strain my eyes, helpless, and see the cloaks covering their bodies, hiding their faces.

*The people from the market...*

The bullets crack into the wood, splintering the panelling. I make a move to rush forward, but Ajax grabs me.

"Let me go!" I roar. "My parents are in there!"

I tear myself from his grip, and just as I do, the shape of a fresh shadow storms out of the woods from the left, rushing straight at the assassins. I hold my ground and see the form of Link charging forward, his hulking body gripping a heavy automatic weapon. He fires as he goes, the forest growing ever more deafening as a new gun enters the fray.

Suddenly, the four assailants turn on him, their attention away from the cabin. All four fire, bullets zipping and flashing through the blackness. Nothing hits link. Nothing hinders him. Onwards he goes, dodging the gunfire, firing back without breaking stride.

Breathless, Ajax and I watch as his father goes to work. Watch as the legend comes to life. Watch as all the stories we've heard of what he can do become real before our eyes.

I turn to see the assassins drop. Two of them fall quickly to the earth, their bodies filled with lead. Another takes shelter behind the stump of a tree, firing from behind cover. The final one, lithe and tall, stands his ground, moving as Link does.

I gasp as I witness the battle. *This other man is a Watcher too...*

For a few moments the two do battle, the third man behind the tree stump becoming little more than a bystander. The fight appears even, nothing hitting either from this distance. Clearly, they both see the bullets coming way before they fire. Clearly, this is nothing but a stalemate.

I see Link flick a switch on his weapon. Moments later, a larger projectile zooms towards the tree stump, hitting it and exploding into a ball of fire. The man behind gets caught in the blaze, his cloak quickly being consumed by the flame.

Smoke pours out of the flaming tree trunk, obscuring the view ahead. Suddenly, Link stops firing, the forest falling silent again but for the ringing in my ears, and the piercing screams of the man on fire. Link fires a final time, putting a bullet in his heart to end his suffering. Then, out of the blue, he turns to his right, and see us hiding in the trees.

"It's OK, boys," he says. "You can come out now. He's gone."

A brisk wind sweeps the smoke away, and we look to see that Link is right. The final attacker has fled, using the smoke as cover.

Staring in wonder at this legend come to life, my mind suddenly clicks into gear.

*Mum…dad…*

I storm towards the cabin, burst through the door, and head straight for my parents' room. I kick it open and immediately see blood.

On the floor, Cyra lies, blood trickling from her body. Jackson crouches over her, still in a protective stance.

"Mum…" I whisper.

Jackson turns around, his eyes lit with a deadly concoction of anger and fear.

"MUM!" I shout louder, rushing forward.

"It's OK, Theo," comes my father's voice. "It's OK…"

I fall to my knees and inspect her body. The blood is splattered across her chest and neck and the left side of her face. But her eyes are open, and there's a weak smile on her face.

Jacksons' hands cover her upper left shoulder,

blood seeping through the cracks in his fingers. "It's OK, son," he says again. "It's just a flesh wound. She'll be fine…"

My mum's good arm rises wearily from the wooden floor and wipes a tear from my cheek.

"Theodore…I'm OK, honey. Don't worry."

"Are you sure?!" I ask hurriedly, my voice brittle.

She nods, and with the help of Jackson, manages so sit up. Behind us, Link comes in, with Ajax at his side.

"Link, I can't thank you enough," says Jackson. "We'd all have been toast if it wasn't for you."

"I came as soon as I could," he says. "The vision was late, but I saw it just in time."

He looks down at my mother, her face a little pale as the blood drains from her shoulder. His eyes are hooded and stark.

"What's wrong, Link?" she asks weakly. "Has…something else happened?"

He nods. "I'm sorry, Cyra. I have terrible news."

The room goes silent. All eyes turn on Link.

He takes a breath and then speaks.

"President Stein is dead…"

# 5

## A Hidden Enemy

For a few moments, no one speaks. I turn to look at my mother, whose pale face has now turned ashen grey. In her eyes, I see deep pools of memory. I know that President Stein meant a lot to her.

"Aeneas," she whispers quietly, almost to herself. She looks Link in the eye, and her voice grows deeper. "How?"

"Details are sketchy right now, Cyra," says Link. "Your father called me…that's when I had the vision of the attack here. I didn't have time to hear him out."

Jackson stands up, his hands dripping with my mum's blood. "I'll call him now," he says. "Link, would you mind dealing with Cyra?"

Link steps forward. I know he's well adept at dealing with medical issues. His life is filled with such encounters, and he's often the first on the scene when treating wounds and injuries.

"Where's your medikit?" he asks.

"I'll get it," I say, wanting to help in any way I can.

I rush off into the kitchen, following my dad who

heads straight for the electronic interface near to the front door. It's one of the only pieces of advanced technology we have here, but is a necessity in allowing him to stay in touch with the various happenings across the region and the country at large.

As he begins tapping away, dialling into Eden, I grab the medikit from one of the kitchen cupboards and run straight back into my parents' room.

Link is already on his knees by my mother, inspecting the gunshot wound in her shoulder. Ajax, next to him, holds a bloodied towel in his hand, mopping up as much of the mess as possible.

"How's it looking?" asks Cyra.

"Pretty clean. The bullet's gone through, but it's splintered a little. There's some shrapnel inside that I need to get out. It's going to hurt."

Link turns to me and takes the medikit. Opening it up, he fetches the supplies he'll need, starting with a syringe filled with morphine.

Cyra shakes her head. "Don't waste it," she says. "I'll go without."

Link doesn't argue. Instead, he looks to Ajax and myself. "Boys, hold her down while I do this."

I move to her good shoulder and take a grip. She looks up at me with a small smile on her face for reassurance, as if it's me who needs it, and not her. Maybe she's right. She's seen far worse than this.

When Link sends the medical tweezers in through the torn flesh of her shoulder, she grimaces, but nothing more. No squeals of pain come out of her, no grunts of agony. She doesn't writhe or wriggle. She just lies there, still, until the job is done.

For a few moments, Link digs around, before drawing out a ragged piece of broken bullet and dropping it into the medikit. He returns once more to the wound to remove any smaller particles, before announcing that he's satisfied.

My mum takes a deep breath as he sets about sewing and cauterising the wound, first at the front, and then at the back. He's surprisingly quick and nimble with his large fingers.

"It's not the best job," he says when he's done, "but it'll do."

"Thanks, Link," says Cyra. "You're so often the life saver."

For a few more minutes, he completes the job, dressing the wound and setting up a sling for her arm. And all the while, as I watch him work, I know that he's keeping an ear out for any danger outside. For the remaining assassin, still out there in the woods.

Outside the room, the voice of Jackson filters in quietly. I help my mum to her feet and out into the kitchen, setting her down at the table. Link follows, moving to the front door and checking outside. He peers into the night and stays at the entrance, the most powerful guardian you could hope for.

Jackson clicks off the communicator and the monitor goes blank. He turns to us with a grave expression.

"As Link said," he starts, "the details are sketchy. But we do know one thing: President Stein was murdered…"

He moves to the door where Link stands, and looks out into the night.

"I've asked for an armed guard to come here. It appears that this was a coordinated attack. Link, I've got a military escort bringing Ellie here now. She may also be a target."

Link nods, eyes narrow. "Thank you, Jackson."

I look at Cyra, sitting at the table. Her face is pained, but it's not from the wound in her shoulder, or the impromptu surgery she's just endured. It's Aeneas Stein, the great friend she's lost. I know he was like a grandfather to her.

My dad moves over to check on her. I hear him whisper a few comforting words in her ear. Then he turns back to all of us, and raises his voice.

"There's more for you to hear. The attack on the President and the attack here were not the only ones." He pauses, shaking his head and grimacing in anger. "General Richter has also been killed at Fort Warden…"

I turn to my mother and Link and see their expressions deepen: Cyra's with greater sadness; Link's with greater anger. Both their eyes narrow, their heads shaking.

General Richter was another great leader during the war, helping to form and marshal the rebel army.

I met him once, many years ago when he came to our village to visit my parents. I remember how old he seemed, even back then, the war having taken so much out of him.

Jackson's voice comes back into the room, breaking the short silence.

"Both President Stein and General Richter were killed in their rooms as they slept. It doesn't sound like either of them suffered."

"But...how? I don't get it," says Ajax. "I mean, Eden and Fort Warden are so well guarded, aren't they? How could anyone get to them?"

"The details are still being gathered," says Jackson. "Both attacks appear to have been performed by single perpetrators. The guards and soldiers on protection duty for both of them have also been murdered. We are dealing with powerful enemies here."

"Like the assassins in the woods," I say. "One of them was a Watcher, I could tell."

All eyes turn to Link for confirmation. He nods gravely.

"Theo's right. Three had no powers. But one...one did. He had no trouble avoiding my bullets."

"Where did he go?" asks Jackson quickly.

"He escaped into the woods," says Link. "I would have gone after him but I thought it better to stay here to protect you all." He looks at Ajax. Clearly, he didn't want to leave his son.

"That was the right choice, Link. I thank you again for protecting my family. Do you think we should send out a search party?"

Link shakes his head quickly. "Not unless I'm included. Regular soldiers will be no match for this man."

"Right. Let's check the other assassins. The armed guard should be here soon with Ellie." He turns to Ajax and I. "Stay in here," he orders.

We wait a while as Link and Jackson go out into the silent, misty night. I stay at the table with my mother. Ajax stands in the doorway, looking out. Before too long, the two men have returned. It doesn't look like they've learned much.

"Who are they?" I ask.

"Hard to say, son," says Jackson. "They have no identification. We'll see what the scanners pick up when the soldiers arrive."

A little while later, the sounds of engines rumble through the silent forest. I step out to see a couple of military jeeps arrive. They stop outside the cabin, and Ellie steps out along with a small contingent of soldiers. She goes straight for Link and Ajax, hugging them both.

We all gather once more inside the cabin as the soldiers form a perimeter and begin checking the fallen assassins. Jackson gives a few orders to the lead guard before returning inside and updating Ellie on what's been going on. She moves over to Cyra and makes sure she's OK, before listening in.

As the discussion goes on, I sit back in the corner of the room, watching things unfold. Ajax sits silently beside me, watching as I am. And all the while, my heart throbs with a heavy beat, my body in a perpetual state of alarm. Despite the danger, it's a feeling I relish.

As the night lingers on, it's clear that none of us are going to sleep. I watch the assembled group of heroes and legends and see the past coming back to life. See history being written before my eyes. Something, it seems, is stirring in the shadows.

"All the attacks were timed together, within an hour or so of each other," I hear my father say. "This was highly coordinated by a group of very dangerous individuals. Each assassination attempt was on one of the key participants in the war. Each was led by a Watcher."

"You think that they're some of the old Watchers who served under Chancellor Knight?" asks Ellie.

"Could be. Not everyone has been happy with the way this country has changed. You cannot alter the landscape this quickly and not expect reprisals."

"But this is more than just reprisals, Jackson," says Link. "President Stein. General Richter. You. Someone is trying to destabilise things. I don't think this is over."

Link's words are prophetic. The rest nod, their eyes drenched in worry and concern. It's obvious that none of them believe that this is a one off event.

By the time dawn is beginning to approach,

there's a knock at the door. The lead soldier gestures for my father to join him outside.

"Governor Kane, I need to speak with you, sir."

Jackson rises to his feet and leaves the cabin. A few minutes later, he returns with the results of the brief investigation into the identity of the assailants.

"They're ghosts," he tells us. "The scanners have picked up nothing: no fixed abodes, no jobs, no next of kin, nothing. They do have many scars, though, from old wounds and injuries, and appear to be in their 40s. Probably soldiers loyal to Knight who have seen plenty of action in the past."

"But what about their old barcodes?" asks Ellie.

Back when my parents were kids, any young person beginning their life's duty would be issued with a barcode on their inner wrist. It was designed to quickly identify someone, and determine how much they worked and what rations they deserved. That was one of the first things to be wiped out when Augustus Knight's rule came to an end.

"They've been removed," says Jackson. "There's no way of telling what they did before, but I think it's safe to say they've been well trained and prepared for this mission. They just didn't count on Link being here…"

"And the others? You say there was only a single assassin?"

My father nods. "They acted alone, no help. That's what scares me the most."

Outside, the sun begins to rise up, casting a glow

that cuts in through the windows. A heavy mist remains on the forest floor, obscuring much of the carnage of the previous night, and the bodies that still lie in the dirt.

Suddenly, with dawn breaking, I feel a surge of weariness fill my head. I don't think I'll be going to school this morning.

Instead, under orders from Cyra, I move off into my room to get some rest. Ajax gets the same command, and together we fashion a bed of blankets and sheets for him to sleep on on my floor. Before I drift off, I hear him speak.

"You saw it too, didn't you? The bullets, before they were shot?"

I nod. "But we couldn't do anything about it. My parents could have died, and I just stood there."

"We didn't need to. We had my dad."

I turn over in bed, and feel a fresh resolve fill me. I don't want to rely on someone else to protect the people I care about, to protect myself. If those men had turned on us, we'd be dead right now.

And something tells me, this is far from the end of it.

# 6
## Cull of Legends

I wake in a cold sweat despite the sweltering heat. My body tingles and aches, telling of a fitful and restless sleep. Fragments of my dreams linger in my head, the attack on the cabin having played over and over as I slept.

I turn down to see that Ajax has already risen and departed the room. Quickly, I stand and look out of the window to see that the mist has cleared, and the sun has come out. Outside I see a couple of guards maintaining their vigil, staring out into the woods with weapons primed and ready for action.

Beyond my door, I hear voices in discussion. When I go outside, I find Ellie and my parents are still in the cabin. It's obvious by the weary looks in their eyes that they haven't slept. But there's more than that. There's a deeper desolation that suggests to me more bad news has filtered through as I slept.

When I ask what else has happened, it's my dad who speaks.

"Petram has also come under attack," he says. "The city Master has been killed."

"Troy…" I say.

Jackson nods sombrely.

"But…you told me he was a powerful Watcher? How could he be killed? Was he on medication?" My questions come out thick and fast. My dad deals with them calmly.

"Troy was a great man," he says. "He was always proud of his powers, but he's grown old. A younger Watcher could have bested him."

It's obvious that the news is still fresh, joining the rest and weighing down on all of their shoulders. Questions about how Troy could have died, above all others, linger.

"Was Athena not in Petram?" asks Ellie. "And what about Markus?"

Two more names from the stories I've heard and told, from the rumours that have spread across the country. Athena, the great warrior who trained under my mother in the city of stone. Markus, another distinguished military commander who was present on so many daring missions.

"Both are safe and alive," says Jackson. "In Petram the target was Troy. The assassin must have fled before he could make an attempt on Markus' life."

"And Athena?"

"She wasn't in the city. I doubt this would have happened if she was."

"But she's safe?" asks Cyra, concern in her eyes for yet another close friend whose life is now under threat.

"One of the few," says Jackson.

The front door opens suddenly, and Link walks in from outside. All eyes swing up to him.

"Well?" asks Jackson.

"No sign," he says. "Nothing at all."

The sight of a greater accumulation of soldiers outside suggests he's been in the woods, attempting to track down the assassin, or at least find some clue as to where he might have gone. Having tracked animals for years, I know that such a thing isn't so easy, especially when your quarry is given a head start.

"We're getting the same from everywhere. All we have are witnesses talking about men in cloaks, and a few unidentifiable corpses who could have come from anywhere…"

I can hear the frustration in my father's voice, and see it in his eyes. It's the same for everyone, mixed with confusion and concern. This coordinated attack, it seems, has come completely out of the blue. No one was prepared, no one saw it coming. Perhaps, after having peace for so long, they'd all begun to take it for granted.

The next few hours are a flurry of activity. Ajax and I are ordered to stay near the cabin within the cordon of soldiers guarding it. The others continue to get further updates from around the country, trying to figure out what to do next.

Word, I know, will already be spreading, putting fear into the people's hearts. Those who remember the War of the Regions will be nervously recounting memories of that time. Those young enough to have been born and lived free will be feeling the sting of fear for the first time.

Others, however, may find themselves with a different emotion rising up through their veins. One of excitement and interest. One of opportunity.

Outside the cabin, I stand with Ajax and look at the burnt tree stump, and the large patches of red scattered around it. The bodies of the assassins have since been removed, but the earth still shows scars of the attack.

"It looks no different from the site of a deer kill," I remark, staring at a stretch of blood-stained earth.

Ajax turns to look at the same spot. I see his dark eyes blazing in anger.

"You think you could do it," he growls. "Kill a man, I mean?"

"A man like that...I'd like nothing more."

"Same here. We're like brothers, you and I. Attack our family, and I'll tear your throat out..."

Ajax has the intensity of his father. He was born for the same thing. Not to be out here in these woods, chopping trees. He's wasted on that. And so am I.

As the day passes by, only my father leaves the safety of the cabin and its protective guard. Link, I know, will not move far from either Ellie or Ajax's side until something has been resolved. All the time, I can see him searching for any threat of attack, quietly searching the Void for imminent signs of danger.

Soon, darkness falls once more, and my father returns from his duties in the local towns. He takes a contingent of guards with him to assuage my mother's fears, not that any of them could do much were that Watcher to spring another trap. Around here, only she can do what Link can, but for the suppressor drugs that continuously flood her veins.

My father, though, was born to be a leader and will never stop in that duty. Just like Link was never going to be anything but a Watcher, my dad won't take a backwards step in the face of adversity. So, he will continue to go into the towns, continue to calm fears and ensure that the region is being properly run. At times like this, people like him need to stand up and be seen. Hiding away in the shadows in the coward's way out.

That night, we all eat together in the cabin. It's something we do occasionally, Ellie and Link and Ajax coming over to ours or us to theirs. Usually, we laugh and joke and, when appropriate, hear stories of the past; ones that are suitable for dinner time telling. That night, however, the atmosphere is very different.

The word from Eden, we hear, is that four guards were killed in the attack on President Stein. Another bystander was injured: a maid of the President's quarters. Link asks if she'll have anything to add.

"She's in a coma and isn't expected to get out of it," says Jackson. "All we know is that it was one man."

"Or woman," adds in Ellie. "It could be a woman."

"Could be," concedes Jackson. "Whoever he or she is, they were powerful enough to infiltrate Aeneas' home, kill his most highly trained guards, and escape without being seen. And it's a similar story coming from Fort Warden and Petram."

"They must be old Watchers loyal to Knight," says Link. "It's the only explanation."

"You served under him for a time," says Jackson. "You know what he had under his command, and most of them were gathered up after the war."

"Yeah, most of them," says Link, "but not all. There might be a few still out there."

"Maybe. But to coordinate an attack like this, after 20 years? It doesn't add up. Why the long wait?"

"So we get comfortable…"

Everyone turns to Cyra, who up until now has kept quiet. Her eyes have turned increasingly gritty as the day has worn on, her body fighting to repair her shoulder. The tan of her skin and the gold of her hair isn't so bright. Her blue eyes are no longer shining.

"Maybe they've been biding their time," she says, "waiting for the right opportunity. We think we're safe, but we're not. Maybe we never were."

"Then if that's the case, we hunt them down," growls Link. "I'll hunt them down alone if I have to. They've caught us off-guard. It won't happen again."

"We need you here, honey," says Ellie. "There's no one else who can protect us like you."

Link grits his teeth, and I see his eyes flash up towards Cyra.

"I'm not the only one," he says, his voice deep.

Once more, we turn to my mother. This time, her expression has dampened, and her eyes have been averted as she retreats into her shell.

Link doesn't push it. Instead, he turns his attention to a wider gripe he's clearly held for some time.

"The Watcher training program should never have been terminated," he says. "How many good Watchers have had their potential restricted and completely ignored? They could be out there now. They could have seen all of this happen."

"But would they?" asks Jackson. "You said it yourself, you only just saw the attack here in the nick of time. And what about Troy? And Drake, I know he's not on the meds, and he wasn't there to help Stein. If all of you couldn't have seen this, why would anyone else?"

"I don't know, Jackson, but more eyes on this could only have been a good thing. I never understood why the Senate voted to end the program. And now, look at where we are."

He looks down at Ajax and me, sitting quietly together at one end of the table, watching our fathers spar. I see pride on his face as his eyes greet us.

"These two boys have so much potential. They're out there, everyday, trying to develop their powers because they want to do good. And all you want is to keep them shackled here…"

His eyes turn again to my mother, who refuses to meet his stare. Then they move to his own wife, who rarely looks cowed. She does now as she speaks quietly: "We're just trying to protect them. You know that."

Link takes a long breath and lowers his voice.

"I understand that. Of course I do. This is my son we're talking about, and I would die to protect him. But denying someone their birthright isn't protecting them. It's hindering them. These boys were born for this, like I was. It's their choice if they want to follow that life."

"What life?"

Once more, my mother's voice whispers quietly into the room. But there's an authority to it that comes from her experience, from what she's seen and done.

"Being a Watcher is no life, Link. I don't want my son growing up as I did. We fought for freedom, and that's what I want him to have. These powers are a prison. For every person who can handle them, and live with them, there are countless others who they consume. Not everyone can be like you or Athena."

Another long silence descends. It's clearly a dispute that's been simmering for some time between Link and Ellie and Cyra, one that's been brought to the boil by the attacks. Jackson, acting mediator, brings his voice back into the debate.

"We're all tired," he says. "It's been a long day and an upsetting one. I think it's best that we all get some rest. Nothing is going to be resolved like this." He looks around the table, and I see heads nodding slowly.

"I'm sorry if I lost my temper," says Link quietly. "I care about you all, and I want to see you all safe. I suppose I'm just scared."

"But..." cracks Ajax's voice, "you never get scared, dad..."

Link looks at his son, and fails to raise a smile.

"I am right now..."

# 7

## The World Opens

I stand outside the cabin, staring at the small convoy of military vehicles parked on the dirt track. Several soldiers stand around them, talking amongst themselves. Others stand guard, a constant vigil being maintained around my family.

On my back, my rucksack is more heavily stuffed than it's ever been. Mostly with clothes, but with a few personal items of my own as well. My hunting knife, of course, was something I was never going to leave behind. I also made sure to retrieve my bear claw necklace from my mum's room and stow it away at the bottom of the sack. With everything that's been going on, and how distracted she's been, stealing it back wasn't a problem.

I hear a click behind me, and turn to see the door to the cabin being opened. My parents walk out with their own luggage, which is quickly taken by a soldier and stored in one of the jeeps. When he attempts to take my bag, my vice like grip makes it clear I'm not willing to part with it.

I can see my dad grinning at the sight. "All set, Theo?" he asks.

I nod excitedly.

"Right then, we'd better be on our way."

It's been several days now since the attack, a period during which I've had to endure the strictest curfew of my life. With the soldiers under orders to maintain a perpetual guard, I've been unable to get up to my usual tricks, slinking off in the afternoon or at night to continue my explorations of the area, or go hunting for some mild, midlevel adventure.

In the past, it's been only my parents' watchful eyes I've had to contend with. For the last few days, however, I've had dozens more keeping a lookout.

More than that, however, is the scanners that have been brought in and positioned at regular points around the cabin and nearby woods. Any sign of movement, whether from a bear or bird or bug, has been recorded and monitored by a technician, set up in a large tent just outside the house.

Never in my life have I been exposed to such an environment; soldiers coming and going as they change shifts, a mobile command centre set up right there in the woods outside my window. It's been busy and hectic and, despite me being unable to leave the house, the most exciting days of my life.

I suppose I should feel guilty about that. No one else appears to mirror my feelings, not that I show them on the outside. On the contrary, outwardly I attempt to display feelings of fear and concern, expressions that never seem to leave the faces of the others. In reality, I can't help but be enticed by the thrill of all of this, my dull world suddenly blazing into life.

When I look at the very real grief on my mother's face, or Ellie's face, however, I feel that pinch of guilt again. For me, those who have been killed are just names. For them, they are very dear friends, men they've known for years, men who they fought alongside to change the world. And with their loss has come the memory of a dreadful time, a time that has plagued my mum's dreams for years.

Yet despite all that, I feel a small smile rising on my face as I sit in the backseat of a military jeep and drive through the forest. When we stop at Link and Ellie's house, and Ajax steps in to sit beside me, I notice that he's holding a similar expression.

It's not that we're callous or uncaring. It's not that we're not afraid: for our lives, and the lives of our parents. It's simply that, today, we're both going to achieve something we've talked and fantasised about for years.

Today, we're going to see the world.

I feel like I'm nothing but a child again as I sit and look excitedly out of the window. The woods are the same, and yet different. The trees sway in the breeze like they always have, and yet this time they seem to be pointing to the exit. The sun cuts its shards of light down to the forest floor, illuminating our path onwards and out. Truly, as I sit and ponder what I'm about to see, and despite the fact that we're only leaving because of the dead, I feel more alive than ever.

We don't spend too long in that jeep, though. Before too long the woods are thinning ahead and we're approaching a military outpost that I never even knew were there. Had I only decided to venture this way during my many night time wanderings, I might well have stumbled across it.

The little base contains only a small contingent of buildings, all set around a central square. Inside that square, I lock eyes on a jet plane, sitting stationary on the ground. I have, on occasion, seen them pass by overhead, but have never been this close to one, and have certainly never been in one.

*That's about to change*, I think to myself with a grin.

As we pull up and get out, I'm sure to wipe that grin off my face. We're greeted outside by a pilot, who is quick to offer his condolences to us all for the recent spate of assassinations. I sour my face and drop my eyes as the man looks at me. Ajax does the same.

Then, my heart beams as he leads us onto the plane, up a short ramp and into the state-of-the-art interior. Everywhere there are comfortable seats and electronic tablets fixed to the backs of chairs and on walls. It looks more like a private aircraft than a military one, although the weapons affixed to its side suggest that it's more of a hybrid.

I take a seat in the back with Ajax, keen to shield myself from my parents' view. The rest take their own positions and sit in quiet thought. I look out of the window and see that the soldiers' job is done, their remit only to offer us protection here in Lignum. I'm sure, when we get to Petram, we'll be well guarded by others.

Because that's where we're going: the great city of stone. For so long I've wanted to see it, such a great fortress in the mountains. A place that harboured the rebels when they were at their lowest ebb. That offered them a place to train in safety as they plotted the downfall of Augustus Knight.

I wish, however, it was under better circumstances that I'd be going on this tour. I wish it wasn't death that had set all of this in motion. Tomorrow, we'll be attending the funeral of Troy, Master of Petram. Unfortunately, it won't be the last.

A solemn atmosphere descends as the pilot calls from the front, and the plane begins lifting vertically into the air. I hear the quiet hum of engines burning, and see the faint blue of their flame hovering beneath us out of the window. Slowly, we begin rising, and my heart itself lifts. I press my nose to the glass and watch as the soldiers grow smaller, the entire clearing showing itself amid the mass of trees.

Soon enough, I'm able to see across vast stretches of the region, the rolling hills cascading off into the distance. Then, with a sudden and exhilarating jolt, we begin rushing forward at a speed that sends my organs rolling into the rear of my body. Up we go, cutting through the sky at an angle, my fingers gripping tightly at the armrests.

I spare a glance forward and see the others sitting calmly. By the looks of it, it's only Link who doesn't particularly enjoy the sensation. My father looks back at me.

"Are you OK?" he asks over the din.

I can't stop the smile bursting on my face, the bright light shining from my blue eyes. I notice my mother looking at me too, and quickly turn away, leaning back to the window to continue watching the world below.

It staggers me just how quickly we gain height, zipping up into the heavens and the low hanging cloud. Villages that once appeared as thriving metropolises to me now appear as nothing but specs. Larger towns and settlements appear, wide roads cutting up the landscape below. I spread my eyes far and wide, trying to take in as much as I can, trying to lock it all into my memory. Because, really, I don't know how long all of this will last.

As we climb, however, the clouds deign to sabotage my view of the lands below, showing me nothing but a wall of white. I sit back and look at Ajax, who appears similarly disgruntled.

"Don't worry boys, you'll see plenty more," says Jackson. He gets a disapproving look from my mother for the comment.

The journey through the sky doesn't last as long as I'd expect. I know that these jets can travel at great speed, but locked inside that metal trap, smothered in thick cloud, it's impossible to gauge just how far or fast we're going. I curse the fog outside the windows as we go, although Link assures us that, from this height, we really wouldn't see anything anyway.

It takes only a couple of hours before I feel a

slight shift in the aircraft's momentum. Word comes from the front that we're about to descend, and gradually we drop out of the heavy, white soup.

When we burst from its shackles, my eyes pop wider than they ever have. I feel my breath caught in my lungs as I stare at the vast mountains, tipped in white snow, jagged peaks ripping into the sky and piercing the low clouds. Between the high peaks, deep valleys sit, littered with sections of woodland and little lakes and springs. Then, further down, lies the vast expanse of the desert floor, spreading towards the horizon. Orange and red hues hit my eyes, the barren wasteland known as the Deadlands surrounding this lofty mountain oasis.

But I know it's not barren, not lifeless. Out there, many people continue to fight the heat and battle on. Those who lived there before the war continue to do so, their lives unchanged. From the rumours that have reached my ears, I know that much of this land is still unforgiving and brutal.

We fly on for a little while, our speed continuing to slow, lowering ourselves further down towards the craggy rocks. Then, as we pass by a cliff, I spy the sight of a large open plateau in the high passes. At its front, a solid, man-made wall stretches from one side to the other, enclosed by the peaks. At its back, the wall of the mountain looms: hollowed out, thousands live within its impenetrable shell.

The plateau itself is filled with life. Buildings and people and vehicles litter the space. I see a marketplace in operation, but it's quiet, few traders allowed through the city gates at this time of lockdown. And at the back, above several arched entrances into the mountain, flags of the city fly at half mast, honouring their murdered Master.

We continue down, the jet coming to hover above a militarised area at the Western corner of the plateau. There, several helipads and landing platforms sit with helicopters and other aircraft upon them. One lies empty, waiting for us to land.

As we drop, I notice several men and women awaiting us; some dressed in fine livery, others in more rugged garments. Around them, highly trained soldiers form a cordon, heavily armoured and holding intimidating firearms.

Among the assembled group, one face jumps immediately out at me. Dressed in a finely cut black cloak, he stands at the front and centre, now the most powerful man across the nation. With President Stein now dead, my grandfather, Drake, has assumed the mantle.

With a little bump, we land. Moments later, the door opens and the ramp extends, and we all gather at the exit. Ahead, Drake stands, smiling warmly as he sets eyes on his beloved daughter. They embrace in a moment of mutual grief before my grandfather moves down the line, saying a few brief words to each of us.

When he finds me, standing at the end, he looks at me fondly.

"My, Theo, you've really grown up," he says, looking me up and down. "You're almost as big as your father already."

I glance over at my dad, tall and strong, and consider the comparison a favourable one.

"Hi, grandfather," I say. "Or, I suppose I should be calling you Mr President now…"

I flash a little smirk on my face, and he returns it. I don't see Drake often, but we've always shared a fairly light-hearted relationship. Despite his lofty position, I've always found that he's maintained a twinkle in his eye, one that he appears to reserve for me.

The smirk doesn't last long, though, and I realise that it's not the time to be making light of such things, not with President Stein so recently departed. His eyes quickly lose their sparkle, appearing a little less blue than I remember. His face, too, has grown paler and older, deep lines wrinkling his visage. In the two years since I've seen him, he appears to have aged a decade.

Along the line, the official greet continues as others step forward to meet our contingent. Some I don't know, senators and statesmen from the Deadlands and Petram who I've never met. A couple I do, however, their faces not known to me personally, but recognised from the books and stories I've taken to my memory.

The first to approach is Markus, formerly a Colonel in the war and now acting Master of Petram after the death of Troy. He has a sturdy, military way about him, taking my hand firmly and greeting me formally.

"It's a pleasure to meet you, Theo," he says. "You

have the look of your father."

"Nice to meet you too, sir," I say, slightly nervously. "I…I do get that a lot."

He nods courteously and moves off, leaving me to meet the final dignitary of the greeting party. I take a sharp intake of breath as I see her step in front of me, lean and tall and with sharp, keen features like that of a bird of prey.

"I've heard a lot about you, young man. My name is Athena."

A gristly, long fingered hand is extended before me. I take it and feel a firm grip squeezing tight. Dark eyes stare at me with an intensity that reminds me of Link. She, perhaps, is the only one as powerful as he is.

I look at her with slightly wide and unblinking eyes. I've heard so many stories about her, not only from during the war, but the many years after. Along with Link, Drake, and Troy, she was one of the primary Watchers who went and hunted down those who remained loyal to High Chancellor Knight. Her feats during that time have already passed into legend.

"It's an honour, Athena," I say, trying to sound as dignified as possible.

The barest of smiles breaks on her lips, but in her eyes I see no joy whatsoever. Instead, I see a deep darkness that tells of the great pain she's suffered over the years. Now, with the death of Troy, a fresh wound has been cut.

For a few moments, she inspects me, looking at me in a way I've never been looked at. Then she steps back and allows Drake to address us all.

"It's wonderful so see all of you again," he says, summing up. "The last few days, I know, have been difficult on everyone. But here, you are all safe. Rest well tonight. Tomorrow, we say goodbye to a dear friend."

With that, he turns, and together, we begin moving across the plateau and into the great mountain city.

# 8

## Farewell to a Friend

That evening I see things I've seen so many times in my dreams, places I've imagined over and over from the stories I've heard. But my imagination never did them justice. Never could I have fathomed the true size and scale of this place.

Inside the mountain, the great chamber of Petram stretches out into the depths, far back towards its rear rock wall. What once was merely a giant, cavernous space has now been developed into a thriving indoor city. I recall my father telling me of the chamber during the war, when it was filled with people sleeping rough, cordoned off into little areas where, if you were lucky, you might get a bed. Now, I see proper structures; homes and businesses scatter the rock floor, set up in a grid pattern of street blocks that appear like a maze before me.

There are people everywhere, the city buzzing with a strange energy. As we walk through the chamber, we find Markus at our side, educating us on the city's past and evolution over the years. Its population, it seems, has bourgeoned, many people moving here as the years have passed, not only from the Deadlands, but from the regions as well.

"As soon as Knight's Wall was dismantled, they

started flooding in," he tells us. "People across the regions never knew of this place. What they discovered was a free city, a haven up here in the mountains. They brought skills and trades with them, and the city has gone from strength to strength ever since."

I can understand the appeal. The regions, while free, still operate much as they once did. People still do the same work. There is still a great deal of social inequality. Up here, though, things seem more even, the quality of life better. It immediately seems like somewhere I'd like to spend more time.

We're taken through the chamber, and down a side passage leading deeper down into the mountain. The pathway descends as we go, the rocky walls turning more smooth and leading to a stairway. As we go, I notice armed guards lining the walls, and heavy doors blocking the route ahead.

Under orders from Markus, we're all allowed through, entering into a new chamber. It's much smaller than the main one, but still large enough to house several stately buildings, built right into the stone walls. It appears that this is where the more wealthy residents of Petram dwell.

Here, we're shown our quarters, all of us being put up in one large house with yet more guards stationed outside.

"We're not taking any chances," Athena tells us. "Your safety is our chief concern."

Athena, I know, acts as Link does in Lignum. She watches over the people in the city, her visions often taking her beyond the boundary of its walls and down the mountain to the Deadlands. I wonder how many lives she's saved over the years; how many people call her their saviour.

Our accommodation is luxurious, far more so than I'm used to. Ajax and I are put up in a nice, comfortable room on the first floor, with our parents in rooms down the corridor. The twin beds are large and soft, the air in the chamber cool. I suspect I'll sleep well here tonight.

We don't stay there for long, though, our little group separating. Link, it appears, is keen to catch up with Athena and talk about security. Jackson's main focus appears to be discussing the days ahead with Markus and Drake. Ellie and Cyra, however, look out at the city with glassy eyes, past memories flooding back in. My mother, I know, hasn't been back here in many years.

The night passes quickly, Ajax and I once more locked down here in this new chamber. I prospect anyone I can about the idea of exploring, but am once more denied, getting familiar reactions and words of caution.

"Now isn't the time," I'm told by anyone who'll listen. "It's too dangerous."

I'm getting bored of such restrictions, especially now, but don't push things. If there are more attacks, I doubt that they'll be directed at Ajax or me. If we were targets, the assassins could quite easily have dealt with us the other night in the woods.

Instead, we spend the evening in that chamber, discussing the day's events and what we've seen. When dinnertime arrives, we gather in a large hall and eat together, a grand banquet table set out for our pleasure. Despite the setting, there remains an uneasy atmosphere, knowing what tomorrow will bring.

Opposed to what I expected, I don't sleep well that night. What started as a refreshing cool turns to a biting cold, and no matter how many blankets I wrap around myself, I struggle to get warm. But it's not just the cold that keeps my mind from shutting down, it's the suffocating tension in the city. The place carries a sadness, a mourning for its great leader. On every face, in every pair of eyes, I see the same desolation.

The dawn brings with it a blanket of cloud that appears to have settled in overnight. We're all given warmer fabrics to wear to protect us from the cold out on the plateau, clothes that I don't own back in Lignum. I look up into the sky and feel the earliest signs of approaching rain, an incessant spray of light drizzle falling from above.

"It's like the sky is crying," I hear someone say. I turn and see that they, too, have tears drifting slowly down their cheeks.

I see the same everywhere as Troy's funeral begins. The central street of the plateau has been cleared, a small plinth erected at the front. On it I see the coffin of the former city Master, and behind it, the man who has stepped up to take his place.

I stand behind the main city dignitaries, Drake and Athena among them. To my left and right, my parents look out stoically, remembering the friend they've lost. And behind, a vast gathering of people fills every spare crevice, half the city emptied to hear Markus' eulogy.

He speaks with great sadness and yet great pride, and I feel like a fraud for taking up one of the prime positions ahead of him. My father's face remains stony as he listens. A single tear drifts down the cheek of my mother.

It's the first time I've seen her cry in many years.

When the service concludes, the coffin is carried through the mountain and into the catacombs at its depths. As Troy's body is set in its final resting place, I glance around at the many tombs and graves dug into the rock walls. I notice my mother staring at one with glistening eyes, and peer a little closer.

The markings on the wall simply state:

*"Here lies Theo Graves, who gave his life to save others."*

I realise, at that point, that her tears today have been split between those lost in the present, and those lost in the past.

The day is more sombre or bleak than any I've so far witnessed. Yet when the funeral ends, and the people return to the great chamber, the tension begins to ease. As has become tradition in the city of stone, music starts to play, and people begin to dance, and food and drink is served and passed around among the masses.

A further speech is made, this time by Drake. My grandfather stands above all of the people, as he so often has, and speaks with fond memories of the man he once considered his closest friend. He tells amusing anecdotes of their times in the Deadlands over the years, and sets about lifting the veil of grief that has suffocated the city for days. And when his short speech ends, he does so with the promise that Troy, Master of Petram, will be avenged.

"And so will General Richter," he calls out loudly. "And so will President Stein."

The mention of the other two names remind me that this is only the first day of mourning I'm set to see. Tomorrow, after so brief a time in this magnificent place, we're to move on and pay our respects to the great war general at Fort Warden. Then, it will be onto the one place I've always yearned to lay eyes upon above all others: Eden, the colossal city in the sea.

That night, I find myself for the first time with an alcoholic drink in my hand. To my surprise, it's my mother who hands it to me. She approaches down the busy street, her injured shoulder still wrapped up tight and arm hanging in a sling. In the other, her hand grasps a wooden cup, filled to the brim with brown liquid.

"I know I'm an old bore, Theo," she says. "And I know you resent me sometimes…"

I look into her blue eyes, bodies dancing and swaying around us, and drop my eyes into a frown.

"Mum, I don't…"

She shakes her head and cuts me off. "It's OK for you to feel like that. I understand. But I just want you to know how much I love you. You're the most important person in the world to me. I…I only want you to be safe and happy."

I open my mouth to respond, to tell her I don't resent her and don't think she's a bore, to tell her I love her too, but once more she cuts me off.

"Go and have some fun," she says, handing me the wooden cup of ale. "Have fun with Ajax. Talk to some girls. You deserve it."

She kisses me on the forehead, and wanders off into the partying crowd. And as I watch her go, I feel a stab of guilt for the way I am, for the adventure I crave, for the worry and concern I must put her through.

But, I do as she says. I laugh and joke and drink, feeling my head blur as I drink the toxic ale. I go from one corner of the main chamber to the next, exploring as much of it as I can with Ajax, but never venturing deeper into the mountain, the many passages guarded by soldiers.

A delirious energy consumes us as we're swept up in the wave of celebration. Everywhere, people talk of Troy and his adventures and feats, and we find ourselves hearing new tales that we've never heard before. And amid the clamour, our parents' names are spoken, and people notice us among them.

"You're Theo…and Ajax," they say. "You're the

sons of heroes!"

The people surround us and praise us, just like the kids do back home, giving us adulation and respect that we haven't earned and don't deserve. At first, I lap it up, soaking in their adoration. But then, as the questions start, I begin to feel the familiar sting of uselessness, the feeling that I'm nothing but an imposter.

"Can you do what your parents can?" they ask eagerly. "Are you Watchers too?"

"No, they're just kids," comes the voice of a burly man. "The days of heroes are done. The world doesn't need them anymore."

Inside, the blurring in my head clears immediately, the euphoria within me doused. The crowd begin to flock elsewhere, losing interest in us. I look up and see the reason: through the throng, Link walks, drawing all eyes to his mountainous frame.

They look at him in a way I yearn to be looked at. True wonder and fascination fills their eyes as he passes, standing tall above them. He approaches us, and suddenly I feel like I'm nothing but a child once more, shrinking into my shell.

"Ajax, Theo, it's time for bed. We have an early morning," he says.

I hear murmurs of laugher among the horde, sniggering as we're ordered off to bed as the party continues in full swing.

"But dad…" starts Ajax.

"No buts," cuts in Link. "The party's over." I spy more giggling eyes, the adoration I felt now turned to mocking. I glare around at them angrily, but no one cowers. *Why would they, to a boy like me?*

So off to bed we go, ordered there by a true hero. And as we climb under the blankets and try to get warm, we whisper together in the darkness, making a fresh new pact.

*We will never be looked at like that again.*

# 9
## Fort Warden

We rise the following morning at first light, my head aching a touch after my first taste of ale. I quickly take up my things and move outside of the house with Ajax to find the rest have already assembled. In addition to the party from Lignum, Drake and Markus will be accompanying us on our forward trip. Athena, who never knew General Richter quite so well, tells us she'll be staying in the city for the next couple of days, but will try to make it to Eden for the funeral of President Stein.

The city is quiet as we pass through the main chamber and out onto the plateau. I suspect that many will be nursing hangovers, the streets littered with rubbish from the party. Already, a small army of cleaners have begun sweeping up the mess and putting the place back in order.

Outside, it's a similar story. Clearly, the party extended out through the main arches and into the open air too. Here and there, I spy residents who may have taken things a little too far, drunkenly sleeping in doorways and up against walls.

"Good thing they have the day off," says Ajax with a wink, gesturing to one particular man curled up in the foetal position around a drainpipe.

I laugh at the sight and feel my own head throbbing. I can only imagine how much ale he must have drunk to put himself in such a state.

We move back to the landing platform and board the plane, before taking off vertically and shooting back up into the heavens. The morning has once more brought a covering of cloud, the view of the magnificent city quickly disappearing before my eyes as we rise.

This time, I'm not quite so bothered, tired and afflicted as I am. Instead, I fashion myself a pillow from a few items of clothing from my rucksack, and set about catching a few more winks.

To my surprise, I manage to drop off quickly, and wake to the sound of movement.

"Right, everyone, we'll be arriving soon," says Drake. "We won't be staying long, so leave your things on the plane."

He moves down the aisle and finds me at the back, rubbing the sleep from my eyes. He gestures to the window, and I follow his gaze. Outside, the cloud is gone, the sky a bright and dazzling blue. I scan the world below and see the red dust of the desert, contrasting beautifully with the colours of the heavens.

Then, my eyes find what my grandfather is referencing. Across the landscape, the skeleton of Knight's Wall stretches, its remnants still scarring the earth. Here and there, portions of it remain, even now the work still being done in dismantling the colossal structure.

"They've been working on it for decades," says Drake, taking a seat beside me.

"How come it's taking so long?" I ask him.

"Because it's a low priority, Theo. We can only provide so much manpower for the work. Most of it has been cleared, but we're years away from seeing the whole thing gone."

"Does it all need to go?" I ask. "I mean, couldn't you just leave some there, you know, like a reminder of the past."

He smiles at me. "It's an option," he says. "But the raw materials used in the wall are useful elsewhere. It's nice to be able to recycle it into something more profitable. So far, whole towns have been erected from its carcass."

I look back out of the window, and see a large military base down below. It grows larger in the window as we continue our descent.

"Is that it? Fort Warden?"

Drake nods. "It sure is. Your father trained there, back when he was your age. Did you know that?"

"He told me about it," I say, nodding. "He wasn't there long, though, was he?"

"Oh no…just a few months. It was a different time back then. Soon after, myself and your father and mother converged. It set everything in motion."

I look into his old eyes, so full of wisdom and memory. "It must have been exciting," I say longingly. "Changing the world like that."

He stands and smiles and lays his hand on my shoulder. "It was, Theo."

The plane slows further, and begins its vertical descent, once more dropping onto a landing pad within the confines of the military base. I stare out at the gathering of soldiers, an official party once more prepared for our arrival.

When the doors open, and we step back out, a wall of heat hits me. It's stifling and humid and so very different from what I experienced in Petram. However, while it's more akin to what I'm used to back home, it's a fair bit more oppressive. And being early morning, it's only likely to get worse.

Outside, though, the soldiers are dressed in their full regalia. They line up down the central corridor of the base, arms fixed sharply to their sides, faces staring forwards at their opposite man. I spy them closely to see that none move, none turn their heads to look upon us as we step into the dirt. Their discipline is highly impressive.

At the front, however, several do move. Another greeting party steps forwards, high ranked officials tasked with the running of the base. They greet Drake and Markus and Jackson particularly fondly, all three of them having backgrounds in the military.

Once the initial greet has been conducted, we begin moving through the base, down the corridor of men. As we walk, I peer out at the assembly, stretching into the distance, and the well ordered structures behind them. Everything appears as a machine before my eyes, everyone and everything fitting a specific role. It all looks so rigid and grand and intimidating that I begin to wonder just how the assassin managed to get to General Richter in the first place.

Unlike in Petram, however, our visit isn't going to last long. Our arrival, in fact, is the final piece in the puzzle needed to start General Richter's funeral. Almost immediately, and with military efficiency, the service begins as we make our way towards the other end of the base.

There, the body of the General lies in full military dress, not on a plinth this time but on a wooden stage, raised slightly from the ground. Beneath it, stacks of wood have been assembled, ready to be set alight. The custom in the military, I know, is for great leaders to be cremated, their bodies consumed by fire that's meant to symbolise the fire of war.

It is an honour, however, reserved for those who have seen battle. And General Richter has seen plenty.

No words are spoken this time. There's no eulogy to the man, no poignant speech sending him on his way. Instead, a salute of weapons fire shots into the sky, two dozen men standing side by side, firing on cue up into the big blue. Loud cracks fill the air, shattering the silence. Once, twice, three times they fire. And then, all goes quiet once more.

We stand in a line and watch now as several military commanders step forward with burning torches. As one, they reach ahead in unison, the fire quickly taking hold among the kindling at the base of the pyre. I watch as the flames rise up and begin grasping at the General's clothes, searing the exposed flesh on his old, wrinkled face. Quickly, however, the black fumes obscure him, riding the wind up into the air.

Down the line, I look at the others, and glance at the soldiers around us. Here, no tears are shed, no weakness shown. To a man, they hold fierce expressions, eyes hooded with anger. I see the same looks begin to spread among my own companions. I look at my mother, and don't see a tear this time trickle down her cheek. Instead, I see a coldness setting in.

No one moves until the flames have begun to die down. Only when they start to subside, and the black remains of General Richter lie before us, do we begin to move off. I turn around and see that the soldiers lining the central street still remain in tight formation.

Jackson notices me looking at them.

"They'll stay there until the flames are dead," he tells me. "Until there's nothing left of their General, they'll not move an inch."

"But that will take hours…"

"Many hours, yes. They'll be there long into the night."

"But we must go," adds in Drake. "We will leave them to their mourning. This isn't our world anymore, Jackson."

We move off in our little convoy, back up the

corridor of men, staring stoically ahead. And after only being in Fort Warden for less than an hour, we find ourselves back on the plane, rising to the sky.

"Do you have good memories of this place," I ask my dad as the doors to the plane shut, and he gets his final glimpse of the base.

He shakes his head. "No," he says. "This place was very different when I was here. It was under the control of High Chancellor Knight. Had Drake not taken me over on the Deadlands, I might never have learned the truth. I might have just been another pawn in Knight's game."

"And you and mum never would have got together," I say.

"Exactly," he says, smiling and running his hand through my hair. "And then you wouldn't be here…"

"And what a tragedy that would have been," I say, bringing a laugh from my father's throat.

I retreat once more to the rear of the plane and take my seat. Ajax comes and sits next to me, shaking his head.

"I don't get it, Theo. How the hell would anyone be able to get into that base to kill the General. Did you notice how many soldiers there were…"

"Well, put it this way: if your dad tried, do you reckon he'd be able to do it? I mean, we saw what he could do the other night, right?"

"Yeah, I guess. But I didn't know there was anyone else out there as powerful as my dad. Except maybe Athena."

I shrug. "Obviously they didn't clean up after the war as well as they thought. Or, I dunno, maybe other Watchers have been training in secret or something? We've both managed to see into the Void a bit. With proper training, who knows what we could do. There must be lots of others out there like us…"

"You think so?"

"It's only logical, AJ. Your dad was right the other night. The Watcher program should never have been shut down. They thought it was protecting them…but it's only made them weaker. I'll bet they'll consider starting it up again now."

"I hope so. But I'm not counting on it. Anyway, we'll stick with the plan, right? Now it's more important than ever that we keep training."

I nod and we lock our hands tight together. "Whatever happens," I say quietly.

For the next couple of hours, I once more find my eyes glued to the window. There's just so much to see as we pass over the regions, the weather holding out and displaying a full, bird's eye view of the land. At one point, I notice that we're flying lower today, descending as we approach the more active areas of the country near the coast.

Drake comes over to me once more to tell me he's instructed the pilot to lower his altitude so we can see everything more clearly. More than most, my grandfather seems to understand that, for Ajax and me, this is all very exciting.

The others, however, don't appear interested in the view below. Instead, they gather up at the front and continue to discuss important matters. Occasionally, I hear a few words drift to my ears, and realise that they're talking about the same things as Ajax and I, notably who exactly the assailants could be.

Logistical plans are also put forward and considered. I know that President Stein's funeral will take place in a couple of days, giving me a little bit of time in Eden. Beyond that, however, I don't really know what to expect. I'm sure that staying in Eden would be the safest course of action, although there's still the distinct possibility that whoever murdered the President is still there, hiding somewhere in the bowels of the sea city.

It's not exactly a comforting thought. Although, with the killers of General Richter and Troy, as well as the Watcher who attacked our cabin, still at large, there doesn't appear to by anywhere that you could consider completely safe.

Still, such concerns don't linger too long in my mind, overtaken as they are by the wonders I'm seeing. So despite wanting to listen to the conversation going on at the other end of the plane, I can't help but be sucked back to the window, my nose once more finding itself in constant contact with the glass.

Before too long, the sea appears, a blanket of deep blue stretching to the horizon. Along the coast, bigger cities and settlements than I've ever seen line up, many with a focus on fishing and trade. Below us, I also see a large military base. Unlike Fort Warden, it looks to be somewhat deserted, the army as a whole suffering from similar treatment as the Watcher program. After many years of peace, the military has been downsized.

It's the same principal as with the wall, the manpower not there to deconstruct it quickly. In this case, funding so many soldiers and building a large military force just isn't needed anymore. Clearly, the Senate have chosen to put their focus elsewhere.

In the distance now, I spy the high towers of New Atlantis, stretching up above the waves. The plane passes by so quickly that I hardly have time to take it in, the place once a free city even during the reign of Chancellor Knight. Now, it remains as it was then: a thriving trading post, and a haven for those who spend their lives on the waves.

"A place of neon lights and garish women," my mum once told me. "It's not somewhere you ever want to see."

"Speak for yourself," I had replied. "It's right at the top of my list!"

I'd been joking, of course, to get a rise out of her. But, really, it's not far from the summit. There are pleasures there that I would one day like to taste, a world so far removed from the quiet woods and whistling trees.

As New Atlantis fades into the distant blur, I know there's only one more stop on our aerial tour. I find myself moving over to sit next to Ajax to enjoy the moment together. We stare eagerly out of the window, waiting for the great sea city to come into view, the central point in all the great stories we've heard.

And there, through the mist, it appears, starting as nothing but a dot, but gradually growing before our eyes. The fortress city in the sea, fixed by giant pylons to the ocean floor, rising high and sinking low as it looks out in all directions, master of all it surveys.

Eden.

# 10

## A Fantasy Realised

The first moments on Eden are the most breath-taking of my short life. I sit next to Ajax, awestruck, as the giant platform fills the view through the window, its surface shining under the bright sun. On its extremity, a large door begins to open, and the plane hovers its way inside, setting itself down inside the hanger.

We all step out and move towards the exit. I feel my entire body shaking as the hanger door rises up, exposing the interior of the city. And even after everything I've seen over the last few days, I'm once more forced to rearrange the order of wondrous sights I've begun to compile in my mind.

That moment takes it: more striking than the interior of Petram; more cavernous than the mountain itself; more gigantic an architectural undertaking than anything I thought humans could achieve. Side by side with Ajax, we stare without moving at the giant buildings, the high domed roof, the strange white vehicles passing by before us.

It's like the opposite of Petram, a world built from the rock, high up in the mountains. Here, everything is mad made, sleek and streamlined and ultra modern. Everywhere are shiny surfaces and sharp edges. Metallic, urban colours spread far and wide, so different from the earthy greens and dusty reds of the mainland.

"You kids all right?" asks Drake. "Eden does have that effect on people when they see it for the first time."

We nod, jaws slack and slightly ajar, still staring out ahead. I hear Drake begin to chuckle, and the others join in.

"Just give them a minute, huh Drake," laughs Jackson. "Let them take it in…"

We're granted a few more moments of indulgence as several hovercars sweep in before us. Back home, you occasionally spot such vehicles passing through the woods. In general, however, the local residents prefer to use old, gritty jeeps, like the one our family owns.

"OK boys, that'll do," says Ellie, using her school principal voice. "In the cars please. You can look at the city from the windows."

Like zombies, we stagger towards the cars and climb through the nearest door, still ogling the city around us. I'm so preoccupied that I hardly notice the many city guards who have come to collect us.

I take more notice as we begin driving off towards the towering buildings rising to the domed roof. Here and there I see patrols of Eden soldiers, cruising along in cars and marching in formation. It's obvious that security here is extremely tight right now.

We drive through the city, down streets set up in the same sort of grid formation we saw in Petram. It's functional and easy to navigate, in this part of the city at least. As we move through the district, however, and arrive in the centre of the city, things turn a little more fluid. There are gardens and more beautifully constructed buildings, little side streets leading off from large squares. People stroll happily, many of them having the day off. Many others continue to work, running restaurants or cafes or other shopping outlets.

As we move through the centre of the city, people take notice of our little convoy. They stare and point and whisper among themselves, perhaps seeing Cyra or Link or Drake through the windows. For a time when security is such a problem, we're strangely conspicuous.

"Shouldn't we be sneaking around?" I ask Jackson, who sits in the front seat ahead of Ajax and I. "I mean, having us all together like this isn't that smart, dad. What if the assassin is around?"

"I'm not going to disagree with you, son," he replies. "But, I'd say we're pretty safe with Link and Drake with us."

I don't hear too much conviction in his voice.

We continue on, down side streets leading through the city centre, passing along the outskirts of the largest square in the city. At its heart is a large fountain, with many buzzing eateries and shops surrounding it. At one end, a large space has been cordoned off, and inside I see a stage being assembled.

"Is that where the funeral is being held?" I ask.

Jackson looks at the stage and nods slowly. "All large events are held here, whether good or bad. I should know…" he says, trailing off.

"Dad?" I say.

He shakes his head and retreats into his own thoughts. I turn to Ajax, who whispers to me: "The public execution, remember? Your dad was up there once, along with my mum…"

"Damn, of course," I whisper back. "It must be so weird seeing this place again for them."

Of course, it's my mother who will be having the worst reaction to returning here. Jackson comes here from time to time on official business as Governor of Lignum. Cyra, however, hasn't returned in many years, the memories of her experiences here too painful. The public execution, where she was forced to choose which one of her dearest friends would die, was only one.

But there were many others…

Soon, we're passing to the other side of the city, to a quieter residential district. The sight of a whole host of heavily armed guards makes it clear which building we'll be staying in. The convoy stops, and we all get out, before being led up into the building. The interior is dull and functional; the rooms largely empty when we go inside.

Ajax and I, of course, will be sharing together once more. When we go into our assigned room, we note that there's nothing but a single bed set up against one of the walls.

"Erm, we're gonna need another bed," says Ajax. "I like you, Theo, but not that much…"

Cyra hovers in behind us.

"Eve," she says.

From nowhere in particular, a soft and soothing female voice sounds.

"Good afternoon, Cyra," it says. "Welcome back to Eden."

"Nice to see you remember me," says my mother. "Can we have another bed in here, please."

"Of course, Cyra."

Immediately, a bed folds out from the wall on the side of the room.

"If you need anything else," says Cyra, "just ask Eve."

She gives me a kiss on the cheek before leaving the room.

"How cool is that!" says Ajax. "Shall we see what else we can get?"

For the next few minutes, we play with the resident city AI, asking Eve to provide us with all manner of things we don't need. Most requests, unfortunately, she's unable to complete, telling us the list of furniture the room can support, as well as the other functions of hers that we have access to.

After a few minutes, we become bored of her

monotonous tones and ask her to shut down. She does so without hesitation.

We spend much of the rest of the day in that room, once more locked away in a new temporary prison. We're told, as always, that it's for our protection, but all it's doing is making the both of us increasingly frustrated.

When we try to leave the room, we find that the door is locked. We ask Eve to open it, but it appears that doing so is one of the many functions that she cannot see through. Even if we managed to escape the room itself, however, we'd find no way out of the building, not with the substantial force of guards stationed down below.

Instead, we are forced to satisfy ourselves by looking out of the window. The view, however, leaves a lot to be desired, with little but the wall of the opposite building to look at.

The others see no such restrictions. We spy them, out of the window, going off to perform important duties. Cyra and Ellie pay a visit to the old Council Chambers, now given over as accommodation for the Senators. They have old friends there, others who rose up during and after the war into positions of prominence. Drake joins them, his own quarters situated in the same luxurious building. Now, perhaps, he'll be upgraded to President Stein's old residence.

Jackson, Link, and Markus, however, have other things to see to; namely checking over the security for the funeral and talking with the city's primary officers who oversee its safety. From the window, Ajax and I see all of them go off, leaving us there locked in that room like children.

Eventually, we get so frustrated that we attempt to physically detach the door, using all our might to try to wrest it open. When nothing works, however, a spark goes off in my head, and I rush to my bag, empty out my clothes, and pull out the hunting knife hidden in the bottom. As I do, my bear claw necklace comes out with it, dropping to the bed.

"Hey, you got it back," says Ajax, picking it up. "I didn't think Cyra would let you have it…"

"She didn't," I mutter, heading over to the door and unsheathing my knife. "I stole it."

"Really?" he laughs. "She probably won't care much now, I guess, with everything going on."

"Yeah, all that's small fry. Now come on, let's do something bigger. Help me with this, will you…"

He jogs over as I slide the knife through the doorframe near the lock. Thankfully, the doors here are thin, and the gap between the door and frame just about large enough to slip the knife right through to its base. I take hold of the bottom of the handle, and Ajax grabs the top.

"OK, on one…" I say.

Ajax nods, as my countdown begins.

"Three…two…one…"

Together, we heave with everything we have, muscles bulging as we pull back on the knife. I hear the sound of scratching metal, the door starting to strain. Then another sound comes, that of Eve's voice.

"Causing property damage is illegal on Eden," she says in a voice that's quickly starting to bug me.

"So sue me," I grunt, straining hard. "OK, AJ, let's go again. Three…two…one…"

Once more, we heave hard, and again the door begins to bend, the lock starting to weaken. I hear Eve telling us to stop, but don't listen.

"One more go!" I say.

With a final effort, the lock gives way, and the door goes tumbling open, sending Ajax and I flying off our feet and onto our backs in a heap. We stand up, high five, and dust ourselves down, before going to the doorway and looking out.

"Right, so now what?" asks Ajax. "We can't get out of the building."

"I know, never intended to. I just needed to get out of that damn room."

We look either way down the corridor, and then we both shrug.

"If we can't go down, we might as well go up," I say. "Let's see if we can get to the roof."

We move to the lift, and press the button for the highest floor we can access. When we step out, we start searching for some sort of access door to the roof. In my mind, there's gotta be one for maintenance.

After a bit of searching, we find just the right thing. To our great relief, this one isn't locked. We open it up, move up a short flight of stairs, and find ourselves passing through another door and out onto the flat roof of the building, several dozen floors up from the city's deck.

I take in a long breath of fresh air and begin wandering over towards the edge. We sit down on the small wall that runs along the boundary of the roof, dangling our legs off the side.

"You know, our parents are gonna kill us," laughs Ajax.

"Nah, they've got bigger fish to fry," I say. "Anyway, if they do, this was worth it. Would you take a look at that view…"

Ahead, the city spreads out into the distance. Sitting at its summit, there are few buildings taller than the one we're in, few obstacles blocking the paths of our eyes. We look from one district to the next, residential areas and parks and the great perimeter wall; the snaking tracks and walkways that pass between buildings here and there. Vehicles zigzag down streets, pedestrians going about their business. From corner to corner we gaze, soaking it all up, from the far side and the aircraft hangers, to the high domed roof above our heads, sparkling with the light of the early evening sun.

"You know, Theo," says Ajax with a smile. "I kinda like it here."

I stare at the centre of the world, at the place where Watchers were once trained and built, at the city where it all went down two decades ago, and begin to nod.

"Me too," I say. "I feel like I belong…"

# 11
## A Plan Hatching

"Are you kids out of your minds! What on earth were you thinking?!"

I knew it would come to this. We both did, Ajax and I. It's not overly surprising, either, that Ellie has taken the lead in reprimanding us. She does it as a day job at school, so why not here as well?

Next to her, Cyra stands, looking equally disappointed in us. Behind them, Link and Jackson remain quiet. I can, however, see the slightest sign of amusement in both of their eyes.

"Well...come on then? Out with it. What were you thinking?" continues Ellie when we refuse to answer.

Right now, I'm struggling not to smile. Such a thing would be close enough to a death sentence the way Ellie's looking at us, so I choose to keep my chin low and hide my face. Also, given that she's Ajax's mum, I think it's only right that he be the one to answer her.

Eventually, after a few more moments of silence, he does.

"We just couldn't stand it in this room anymore," he says. "We weren't going to leave the building…we just wanted to get to the roof and see the view."

"But you've caused property damage," says Ellie. "You can't go vandalising things like that, boys. We're going to have to pay for that now…"

"You'll do nothing of the sort." All eyes turn to the doorway, where Drake comes sweeping in. "It's an easy fix, Ellie," he says. "Let's cut the boys some slack on this occasion. They're only doing what comes naturally."

"With all due respect, Drake, I don't think vandalism should ever come naturally to a young man."

Drake turns to Link and Jackson, who continue to succeed in suppressing their smiles. "I'm sure you two had some similar run-ins when you were young," he says to them. "I know I certainly did."

Both of our fathers do a half shrug, half nod. Clearly, they're both keen to remain impartial on this one.

"These boys have been confined to one place after another for days now. They just want a bit of freedom. Sure, breaking the door was wrong, but there's no harm done really. Now, come on, let's make this right. Boys, apologise to your mothers."

Both Ajax and I offer a mumbled apology, trying to sound as contrite as possible.

"Right, that's that then. Now let's move on to more important business," continues Drake, sweeping away the issue. As his eyes pass mine, I notice the mildest of winks. I'm sure it's not lost on Cyra, keen as her gaze is.

Drake turns to our parents once more. "Would you all go and wait for me next door," he says. "I need to speak with you all about President Stein's funeral. But first, I need a moment or two alone with the boys."

Our parents defer to the authority of the new President. With a final glare of warning from Ellie in particular, they step out and leave us alone. When the coast is clear, Drake speaks.

"Take a seat on the bed please boys," he says.

We do as ordered, and move to the bed to sit down. He wanders over to the door and shuts it as best he can given the damage we inflicted.

"I'm sorry about the door, President Drayton," says Ajax earnestly. "It really won't happen again."

"Oh, no matter about that," he says as he returns, standing tall above us. "Broken doors are of no concern to me right now. In fact, I'm impressed by the both of you. I know how eager you are to explore, it's only natural. And," he adds, lowering his voice, "I know how much you want to develop your powers as well…"

His eyes bore into us, and a short silence begins to fall. I look at him with interest, trying to work out where he's heading with this. The look in his eyes causes a stir within me, my heart beginning to thud just a little bit harder.

"Is it true that you've both seen into the Void?" he

asks.

We both nod carefully.

"How far?"

Ajax and I look at each other. He lets me speak first.

"A second or two, maybe," I say. "We both saw the attack just before it happened back home."

"And all of this is down to your own training? Link tells me that you go into the woods often to hunt beasts, that you fight and spar together. Is that true?"

Again, we nod. "We've been doing it for a while," I say. "We feel it's our duty."

Now I see a smile begin to rise up on his face. Behind his eyes I see the cogs turning, something formulating in his mind. The look excites me. It's not the usual expression we get from Cyra or Ellie when they find out what we're doing. Drake appears to be on the same page as Link.

"I must say, you two impress me greatly. To do what you've done without any training is rare. It took me years to develop my abilities. Now tell me, do you want to be Watchers?"

Our reaction is immediate. "Yes, sir," we say together.

He nods, slowly, and begins moving back to the door, pacing slightly around the room.

"As you know," he says, "the Watcher program was abandoned soon after the war. I've always thought that to be a serious mistake…"

"But…you voted for it, didn't you?" I ask. "The Senate voted to abolish it?"

"The Senate, yes. Me…no. I was one of several who wanted to see it continued, developed even. President Stein was another. But this was a different time. We live in a democracy now, and Aeneas and I were hamstrung. So we watched on as the program was discontinued, and the military was weakened. I always suspected that something like this would happen."

He continues to pace, setting his path back to us. When he's right ahead of us, he speaks again.

"What I'm going to tell you, boys, needs to stay between us…"

I feel my heart tighten, my breath suddenly freeze. Neither Ajax nor I move, our eyes staring at the old legend before us. All we do is nod ever so slightly.

"Tomorrow, during President Stein's funeral, the entire city will gather in the central square. Everyone has been given the day off, and the lower levels of the city will be empty…"

He reaches into his pocket, and withdraws a small keycard. His hand extends towards me.

"Take this," he says quietly. "It will give you access to Underwater Level 3. Go to the South West quadrant, and search for the storage rooms. Look for one in particular – room U3-S21…there's an old machine in there that will help you."

"A genetics machine…" I whisper.

Drake smiles. "We need people like you. To protect the people, and protect yourselves. Good luck, boys. And remember, we never had this conversation."

With a final wink, he walks back to the door and leaves the room. I look down at the card in my hand as Ajax and I sit in silence for a few moments. Then we both look at each other, and I see that his eyes, like mine, are dancing with excitement.

The sound of movement outside in the corridor causes us both to jump. I instinctively pull the keycard behind my back, hiding it in case someone decided to come in. The sound of footsteps trails off as the culprit continues on down the corridor.

"You'd better put that somewhere safe," says Ajax.

"I was thinking the same thing."

I stow the card away in the most secretive pocket I can find on my jacket, thinking that my bag might not be the safest option. Given the way Ellie and Cyra reacted to our breakout, I wouldn't be surprised if they came in and rooted through both of our things.

A few minutes later, there's a knock at the door and a woman walks in. She's fairly old, short and fat, her hair and skin and eyes and just about everything else grey. Her expression, however, is bright as the sun, a smile ringing out on her face.

"Well, well, well, isn't this the most wonderful pleasure!"

I look at Ajax and frown. He looks equally confused by the interruption.

"Hey, lady, I think you've got the wrong room," he says.

"Oh no, absolutely not. I'm a close friend of both of your parents. I've know them for many years now." She reaches us and pulls us into hugs, one after the other. And then she says her name, and everything makes sense.

"My name's Leeta. Surely your parents have told you about me?"

"Leeta…you took my mum to Eden, didn't you?" I ask.

"Yes, your mum, Theo. And yours too, Ajax. It's so sweet that they gave you those names, they mean a lot to the people here. As do your parents, of course."

Like me, Ajax was named after another important man who gave his life for the war: Commander Ajax, who trained Link and Cyra and Ellie here on Eden, and who defected against Augustus Knight and helped seal his eventual fate. It's a hard name to live up to, his powers perhaps even greater than Link's.

And it's something that my friend has always considered a challenge…

Leeta inspects us a little closer, standing a good foot shorter than both of us. "And wow," she says, "aren't you such strapping young men! You both look so similar to your fathers."

"Erm, thanks Leeta. So…not to be rude, but why are you here?"

"Ah, well, I've been instructed by President Drayton to move you to another room. I, um, heard what you did to the door here. Boys will be boys, as they say," she laughs.

Immediately, I like her jovial tone and countenance. It's refreshing given the dour expressions we've had to contend with for the last week or so.

"OK, grab your things and we'll move you down the corridor."

As we move off, Ajax turns to me.

"Great, and there was me hoping we'd get to stay here," he whispers. "Now they're just going to lock us in again."

I slide the keycard out of my pocket, just enough for him to see. "I'm not sure that matters anymore," I return.

We move a little way down the corridor, and are provided with an identical looking room. Once again, only a single bed is set up against the wall. Leeta quickly remedies the situation by calling for a second. Eve duly obliges.

"So, you work for my grandfather now?" I ask.

"Oh yes, I'm his Chief Secretary. I was working with President Stein but…well…" She begins to trail off, blinking hard to stop any tears from falling, and plants a false smile on her face. "Things change,' she says. "It's your grandfather who I answer to now. I couldn't ask for a better replacement for dear Aeneas."

"I'm sorry,' I say. "He clearly meant a lot to you."

She nods forlornly. "He meant a lot to everyone here. A great man, a truly great man." She glances around the room to make sure we're all set up. "Excellent. Please don't hesitate to come to me if you need anything during your stay. It's so good to finally meet you, boys."

With that, she sweeps of out of the room, shutting the door behind her. I wait for a moment, expecting it to lock automatically, but it doesn't. I move over, pull the handle, and find that we're able to leave if we want to.

Ajax shrugs. "I guess our parents trust us now," he says sarcastically.

"More like Drake trusts us," I say. "Better him than anyone else."

We eat dinner that evening alone, just the two of us. Once again, we're kept to the same building, but this time allowed out of the room and up to the roof, providing we go no further. Our parents, important as they are, head off to official functions, dining with the Senators in the main banquet hall in the old Council Chambers.

With our dinner provided by Eve, we move up to the roof to eat, talking excitedly as we look out over the city. Our eyes focus particularly on the large perimeter wall, which extends around the boundary of the deck. Inside it, tram tracks cover its full circumference on most levels, providing quick passage to its various quadrants and regions, with lifts set at intervals, taking people into the depths.

"I wonder what it's like down there…on Underwater 3," says Ajax. "I mean, there's some weird science going on here. It's like another world from back home."

"A better world," I say. "People actually make a difference here. Back home, they just exist. I've had enough of just existing."

We stare together at the far perimeter, setting our eyes on the nearest entrance. Within it will be a lift. A lift that will take us down to the lower levels of the city when everyone is distracted. In a couple of days time, when the world is in mourning, we'll be celebrating.

Because finally, we're going to get our birthright.

Finally, we're going to unleash our powers.

# 12
## Unleashed

I stand side by side with Ajax amid the throng. Ahead of us, the large stage looms, the coffin of President Aeneas Stein on top of it. Chairs line up in front of his body, sat upon by the dignitaries of the city: the Senators and Governors from across the regions; the many Mayors and officials from the major cities; those who hold positions of prominence and power who have been touched by Stein's existence.

Only the most important sit on the stage. Such was President Stein's popularity, a whole host of others take up the first few rows of seating at the bottom of the stage. Among them, I see Athena, face coiled in a perpetual expression of stoicism. I knew she wouldn't miss it.

My parents take seats on the stage, though, along with Ellie and Link and Markus. Many of those who were present at the changing of the world, who took an active part in it, are afforded the most central seats. In the middle of it all, however, sits the new President, Drake Drayton, ready to stand and address the gathered masses; to give a long eulogy to the man loved by so many.

Ajax and I, to our delight, are not provided with

prominent seats. Not like in Petram, or Fort Warden, where we felt like frauds. Here, we're just one of the many, standing among the vast crowds, swallowed up by the throng.

It's possible that Drake had something to do with that. I can see him now, far away, eyes swaying over the people. They stop on us for the briefest of moments, giving us an unspoken cue to leave. And as he stands, and begins his speech, Ajax and I begin melting further back into the crowd, seeking to be set free from its clutches.

It takes a little while for us to extricate ourselves, partly because we never expected to be enveloped so deeply. When we arrived a while ago, there was already a great number of people waiting, keen to get the best positions in the square. Since then, however, so many more have gathered, the square full to breaking point, people spilling out onto the side streets and even around corners where they can't even see the action unfold. No other death could possibly have garnered such a reaction.

With a little effort, Ajax and I make it to the end of the gathering. By now, we're so far from the stage that we can barely even see Drake standing there. But we can still hear his voice, loud and clear on the microphone, extolling the many virtues and accomplishments of the man who took over at the death of Augustus Knight; the man who has overseen such a period of peace and prosperity.

Yet still, within his words, and within the crowd, a tension remains. Because for the first time in so long, something is rising from the depths and darkness.

The sight of soldiers only serves to exacerbate people's worries. Even though their presence should be comforting, the mere need for them suggests that danger is looming. That this day, this event, isn't considered safe.

They stand everywhere, some down in the crowd, others in lofty positions up in buildings. Snipers watch over from above like hawks, ready to take action if needed. Guards surround the entire throng, cordoning it off. Scanners and other devices are set here and there, singling out anyone who appears suspicious. And around the stage itself, a large bulletproof screen has been constructed, so clear it blends into the air and is barely visible unless you look for it.

Truly, this event is impenetrable, even for the most powerful of enemies.

When we reach the back of the crowd, we wander away casually. A few soldiers' eyes are drawn to us, but nothing more. It's possible they recognise us given our semi celebrity status.

When we're far enough away, we begin to improve our pace, our walk turning to a jog, our jog to a run. Soon enough, we're sprinting hard to get to the perimeter wall as soon as possible, passing through the quiet, empty streets, our footsteps echoing up through the buildings.

When we reach it, we rush through the nearest opening and see the tram tracks stretching away to our left and right. Nearby, a short walkway extends under it, giving safe passage to the other side. We take it, rushing on and towards the nearest lift. It lies open, as if expecting us.

We quickly take in the interior, before pressing the button marked 'Underwater Level 3.' The doors close, and the world suddenly jolts, my stomach going a little queasy as we drop abruptly into the depths. Within seconds, we shoot down past the 8 surface levels and 2 underwater levels in our way. Then, the doors open, and we're greeted by more silence.

We step out into the brightly lit space. Ahead of us, another tram track snakes by, giving quick passage around the level. The trams themselves, however, appear to be lying dormant today. A little way to the left, I see the front of one of the trains, sitting quietly and unused.

It matters not. We planned everything well enough to ensure that we'd arrive down at the South West quadrant, as advised by Drake. Now, it's merely a case of tracking down the storage rooms.

So, on we go, under the track and through the perimeter wall. Ahead, a corridor curves around to the left and right, brightly lit with yellow lights fixed regularly on the ceiling. On the wall ahead of us, however, is an electronic interface, used to provide information for the level. We begin tapping on the screen, opening up the map of the level, and searching for room U3-S21.

"There," says Ajax, spotting it amid the maze.

I click on it, and a set of directions appears, telling

us how to get there from where we are now. We take a moment to memorise it.

"Got it?" I ask. Ajax nods, and we quickly move off to the left.

A hundred metres or so along the corridor, we turn in to the right to find a large electronic door blocking our path. I retrieve the keycard from my pocket and enter it into the appropriate slot. The door whirs lightly, and a red light turns green, before the metal barrier slides up and out of our way.

"Easy enough," I say as we begin moving inward towards the centre of the level.

We make a few more turnings, lefts and rights, the corridors turning less brightly lit and well maintained as we go. Here and there, lights flicker or don't work at all. The place carries a dusty scent, suggesting that people rarely come down here.

Before long, we're checking each room closely, looking for the right one. It's Ajax, slightly ahead of me, who spots it first.

"Here! This is it," he calls.

I catch him up, and enter the keycard once more. And again, the door opens and slides up into the ceiling. Ahead, a dark expanse looms, a cloud of dust billowing out of it as it tastes fresh air for the first time in years.

I cough and choke and cover my mouth. And then, together, we step inside.

Behind us, the door slides shut, cutting off the

beam of yellow light and plunging the room into blackness.

"Er, where's the light switch?" asks Ajax. "Eve, turn on the lights will ya!"

There's no answer. "She doesn't operate down here, I guess," I say. "Check the walls near the door."

Somewhat ungracefully, we reach out with our hands and begin feeling around for any sign of a switch. After clumsily bumping into each other a couple of times, I feel my fingers close around something that feels right.

"Got it," I say, pressing on the button.

Immediately, the room begins to glow, lights heating up on the ceiling stretching to the back of the room. I shield my eyes from the sudden brightness as they gradually grow accustomed to my new surroundings. When I open them fully, I see a large room filled with boxes and crates and other unused equipment.

"Right, lets get searching," I say.

"But we don't know what we're searching for," says Ajax. "What does the machine look like?"

"We'll know it when we see it, AJ. My mum told me once it was just this large tablet thing that hovered over her, so look for something like that. Come on, let's split up."

I begin moving to the left, and Ajax to the right. Stacked up high, most of the boxes look too small to contain what we're looking for. Against the walls, high shelves stand tall, filled with old medical and scientific equipment, files, and electronic devices. For a while, I look around without any luck. Then, I hear Ajax calling from the other side of the room.

"Hey, Theo, come here…I think I found it."

I run over, passing more stacks of boxes, and find Ajax towards the far end on the right. He stands over what appears to be a medical bed of some kind. On it, there's a large, flat electronic screen, with a number of buttons on one side.

"Good catch," I say. "Now we've just gotta turn it on."

I run my hand over the top of it, wiping away years worth of accumulated dust. Over to the side, Ajax grabs a towel, handily packed into a nearby box, and begins rubbing down the screen. Soon enough, the main display has been cleaned, revealing a red power button.

"OK…here goes nothing," I say.

I press down on the button, and we wait. Very slowly, the screen begins to light up, glowing with a pale yellow light. From its corners, little burst of air cough out of the machine, sending sprays of dust with them. And, gradually, the scanner begins to rise up, hovering into the air.

Ajax and I look at each other.

"So, who's going first?" he asks.

"Be my guest," I say, not exactly wanting to act the guinea pig.

He considers it a moment, and then his natural bravado takes over.

"Fine, I'll do it," he says.

He climbs onto the bed, and lies down, putting his head in a mould at the end that appears to alter its shape to fit him.

"It's comfortable," he says, shuffling into position as I slowly move the scanner over his body. Soon, it's hovering directly above him. I can see him breathing slightly heavily, beads of sweat beginning to gather on his forehead.

"You ready?" I ask.

He nods, staring up at the light.

I reach forward and push the little green button marked 'start'. As soon as I do, electrical currents begin to flash on the screen in colours of red and blue and purple. They start gathering pace as the scanner begins its work, unleashing the potential within Ajax, opening up his pathways.

I look into his face, staring up at the rhythmic dance of the currents, and see his eyes begin to glaze over. I take a step back, looking for a seat, and satisfy myself with one of the many boxes nearby.

I know it could be a long wait. A normal person might only take a few minutes to be scanned. A potential Watcher, meanwhile, could take up to an hour, or even more.

So, I move back, and I sit and watch as Ajax's eyes begin to close, falling into a trance. Occasionally, his eyes flicker behind their lids, his body twitching as it would when engrossed in a deep, dark dream. I wonder, right now, just what he might be seeing. *Is he having visions? Are his powers being awakened?*

It's strange to think that this was common practice two decades ago. That every school leaver would endure this test, known as the 'genetics test', to determine if they had any secret, hidden abilities. Of course, back then, no one really knew what Watchers were. It was only during the war that they came to prominence.

When my mother underwent this test, she had no idea what to expect. She thought it was a waste of her time, but in the end it revealed what was locked inside her. And now, here I am, having to do all of this in secret, sneaking down here into the depths of Eden to do what used to be done to every 16 year old across the country. It's strange how times change.

As I sit there, I wonder just what's going on up above. Drake told me that the service would last for quite some time, over an hour and a half at least. Afterwards, he said, there would be a party like there was in Petram. An opportunity for the people to celebrate Aeneas Stein's life, rather than mourn it.

Soon enough, the people will be eating and drinking once more, raising glasses to their lost leader and cursing the person who took him from them. Telling stories of his deeds: from his time as an Eden Councillor, long ago during the reign of Knight, to his long incarceration in the sea prison of

Tartarus, hell on earth. No one quite thought he'd last this long, old as he was during the War of the Regions twenty years ago. The fact that he managed two decades as the first President of Eden is yet another feather in his wonderfully adorned cap.

As I sit and think, I notice Ajax beginning to stir. His eyes flicker once again, this time opening fully, and his body starts to come back to life. I quickly move over to the scanner and turn it off, pulling it away from him.

"How do you feel?" I ask, looking into his dark eyes.

He takes a moment to compose himself, and then answers with a smile.

"Strong," he says, grinning and tightening his fists into balls before his eyes. "I feel strong."

"Did you see anything? Any visions?"

His eyes narrow. "Fragments," he says, wracking his memory. "I'm not sure what I saw…"

"OK, we can talk about it after. Come on, my turn."

Wearily, he stands to his feet, and I take his place. The bed moulds itself to my slightly smaller frame, and I take a deep breath as Ajax moves the scanner into position above me.

He raises his eyebrows. "You're gonna love it," he says.

Then, he flicks the start button, and the same dazzling show of lights begins. I stare up at it, mesmerised, and the rest of the room suddenly begins to fade away and darken. For a few moments, only the lights are visible, zigzagging their way across the screen in random formations, the blues and reds and purples painting a beautiful, spellbinding tapestry.

I'm quickly hypnotised by the show, my eyes beginning to shut. As I fall behind my eyelids, I feel my heart racing with excitement.

*This is it. This is what I've been waiting for...*

I fall into dreams, sights flashing before me. Like Ajax said, they're nothing but fragments. I focus as hard as I can, trying to recall what I see, knowing that when I fall out of the spell of this strange machine, my memory may well be lost.

It's colour that first comes to me. Orange and red and yellow; the dusty hues of the Deadlands. Then, movement: fists being thrown, men fighting, weapons drawing blood. Now noises reach my ears, echoing chants and cheers that come from all around me. And just as I see it all and hear it all, it fades once again, morphing into something else.

Other colours now start to descend, darker colours of black and grey and green. I smell a scent of decay, of chemicals, of stale air. Images form before my eyes, sharp edges of metal tables, medical utensils lying atop them. I see tubes and beakers and other equipment, some small, others large. Inside the larger tubes are shadows surrounded by sickly green liquid. It's all a blur, so indistinct. And as I try to focus, try to see more, everything once more fades to black.

I come out of the spell, and the dazzling lights glow before me again. Beyond the scanner, Ajax looks down at me eagerly. I see his mouth moving, but it takes a moment for his words to form in my ears.

"How was it? How do you feel?"

He moves the scanner away, and I sit up and take a long breath. And through my veins, I feel a tingling, buzzing energy. I smile as he did and ball my fists.

And then I repeat the words he said to me: "I feel strong."

# 13

# The Watcher Wars

As I stand from the bed, and we begin making our way back through the level towards the lifts, I check my watch and find that it's been nearly two hours since the funeral began.

"They'll probably be looking for us if the whole thing's over," I say.

Our response is to quicken our step and rush a little faster, discussing what we saw under the scanner as we go.

"It was weird," I say, panting. "People were fighting, like warriors. Hand to hand combat and using weapons like swords and spears and stuff. I heard a crowd cheering and chanting, like I was in some sort of arena."

I notice that Ajax is listening intently as I speak. He stops me halfway down a corridor.

"I saw the same thing, Theo," he says. "What do you think it is?"

I shake my head. "I don't know, but it was clearly over on the Deadlands. If anyone's gonna know, it'll be Athena. Let's go find her."

We continue on, rushing towards the exit, as I tell

Ajax about the strange science lab I saw as well. This one he didn't see, although I have little to tell him beyond seeing a few utensils and tubes.

"Maybe it's just one of the labs down here?" he says, shrugging.

"Could be," I say. "Although, I don't know…it seemed like it was really run down, kinda dilapidated in places. I think it's somewhere over on the mainland."

"Well, wherever it is, you know what this means, right?"

I nod. "It means that we're taking a trip outta here," I say. "And I don't think our parents will be with us…"

We're quickly at the lift and rising back through the city, stepping out onto the deck level. When we arrive, we find that the sounds of partying have begun, the noise of celebrating drifting over towards us on the air.

We rush as quickly as we can through the streets, the noise growing ever louder as we go. Soon, we can see the backs of the crowd, already beginning to spread out away from the central square, off to toast their fallen President in their own way.

Many, however, will remain in the square until the early hours, just as they did in Petram. When we reach the square, music has started to play, and the tears have already begun to turn to laughter; mourning and grief to celebration of a life well lived.

Right in the middle, the esteemed members of Eden and the rest of the country talk together in little groups. Among them, I see Athena, stony faced as always, talking with an elderly member of the Senate.

"Right," I say, " there she is. We should go talk to her."

"You think that's a good idea? I mean, do we want her knowing what we've done?"

"We have no choice. If anyone's gonna know about what we saw, it'll be her."

"Fine. Let's go."

We begin fighting our way through the crowd once again towards Athena and the other city luminaries. I scan the people ahead, searching for our parents, but don't see them anywhere. Only Markus remains, locked within a group of men wearing military dress.

As we approach, a couple of guards step in front of us.

"I'm afraid this area is off limits, boys" they say, looking at us suspiciously. "Go and mingle with your own people."

I see Ajax glare at the man, looking down on him. It's funny, us being called boys when we're both so much larger than them.

"These are *our* people," he says angrily. "This is Theo Kane, grandson to President Drayton. I suggest you let us through."

The two guards look at each other, and a moment later burst out laughing.

"Really...wow. Well then, through you go, sir," one says sarcastically.

I can sense the anger in Ajax, his fist balling. Now wouldn't be the wisest time to lose your temper.

Thankfully, a timely intervention from Markus eases the tension.

"Hello boys," he says, walking past the guards. "Do you want to come in and meet some of the Senators?"

The soldiers look at each other again. This time they're not laughing.

"Let these young men through, please," says the Master of Petram. "They're pretty much royalty."

The two guards look cowed and back away, avoiding the burning gaze of Ajax. We walk through, past several more guards, and through a small, barely visible door set up within the bulletproof screen that surrounds the stage and nearby area. I look ahead to see that President Stein's body has been removed, most likely taken off to its final resting place in the main city graveyard.

"Do you know where our parents are?" I ask Markus as we move into the crowd.

"They had some urgent business somewhere," he tells us. "They rushed off soon after the service ended with your grandfather. I didn't get a chance to ask where, I'm afraid."

For the next half an hour, Ajax and I are forced to meet a bunch of government officials: Senators and Governors and city leaders, some of whom I've met before, but most of whom I haven't. In the main, they're polite and courteous, as you'd except from men and women who hold such offices, but also rather dull. Or maybe it's just the fact that I'm desperate to talk to Athena, my eyes constantly turning to her to make sure she's still there.

At one point, Ajax whispers to me: "why don't we just ask Markus about what we saw? He's from the Deadlands too."

It's not a bad shout, but I'd call it a back up plan. Markus, while a very important man and someone who's spent their entire life on the Deadlands, isn't a Watcher. He might not quite understand what we're getting at.

As more distinguished guests come to meet us, I find myself getting increasingly antsy. When I look over to see Athena wandering towards the exit, I have no option but to extricate myself.

"Sorry," I say, cutting of an old Senator mid-sentence, "but I really have to go…"

I hear him mutter something about me being 'rather rude' as Ajax and I gallop over to the exit just before Athena escapes.

True to her nature, she doesn't look at all startled as we jump down in front of her, cutting off her way out. She probably saw us coming a mile off, her expression hardly changing as she lays eyes on us.

"Ah, Theo and Ajax. Good to see you again," she says smoothly.

The two of us shuffle with nervous excitement, hardly able to select the right words.

"Well, what can I do for you?" she asks, peering at us with interest. "You appear to have something to ask me, so spit it out."

I take a deep breath, and then blurt out: "Can we trust you…to keep a secret?"

Her frown deepens. "I'm not up for playing games, Theo. Tell me what you want or don't. I can't make you any promises."

I stand my ground for a second. It's long enough for her to get bored and begin to move off. My voice calls her back.

"I saw something," I say, a little too loudly. She turns and looks at me as I creep back towards her. "I saw something, and so did Ajax. Something out on the Deadlands…"

Her interest is now ours. She looks to her left and right, and leans in, lowering her voice.

"What did you see?"

"We don't really know," says Ajax, drawing her eyes and joining the conversation. "People fighting…with their fists and weapons…"

"Spears and knives and swords," I add in quickly. "Like gladiators. They were fighting. And…" I say, glancing at Ajax, "…so were we."

The change in her eyes is subtle, but significant.

They begin to glare a little harder, grow a little fiercer. And then, from her lips, she whispers three words: "The Watcher Wars…"

Suddenly, everything else around us seems to go quiet. The din of the party suddenly goes mute, the sea of bodies blurring into one.

Ajax and I stare at her narrow eyes as they look off into the middle distance. Then, suddenly, they come to again, swaying back to us.

"How did you see this?" she asks sharply. "You've had no training. You can't have seen that far."

We don't answer, but we don't need to. Athena's famous intuition kicks in, reading our expressions. It's been said that the most powerful Watchers are able to see the truth in someone, draw it out just by looking at them. It's an instinct that they develop over many years, one that the people say allows them to read minds.

Whatever it is, Athena is using it now.

"You've done something," she says quietly. "You've activated your powers…"

"We went to the science level," says Ajax. "We…we found a genetics machine there. We thought it was our duty."

He stops short of mentioning Drake's role in it all, remaining loyal to our promise that the conversation would stay between us. In truth, I doubt my grandfather would mind at all, but it's good that Ajax knows how to keep his mouth shut.

"You were just down there? During the funeral?"

"Yes," I say. "We just had the visions now. What does it mean? What are the Watcher Wars?"

Once more, her eyes slide left and right, checking that no one is hovering too close nearby.

"I shouldn't be talking to you about this," she says. "Your parents wouldn't like it."

"Please, Athena," I say. "If this is a vision, then it's going to happen anyway. We might as well know what we're getting ourselves into…"

My words have the effect I desire. She considers them a second, and then begins nodding.

"Years ago," she starts, her voice quiet and slow, "people started fighting for money on the Deadlands. It's nothing new, something that's been happening for centuries all over the world. It grew over the years, and now it draws big crowds from around the area. The rich come to watch for sport. Those with nothing to lose enter in order to win money. The tournament can be brutal…very brutal."

"But why is it called the *Watcher* Wars?" asks Ajax.

"Because it's Watchers who always win, at least in recent years," she says. "Soon after the war ended, the tournament grew bigger, more popular. Trained Watchers would enter and take the spoils, no longer forced to do their duty. More and more came from all over. Now, it's filled with them."

"You mean, there are lots of Watchers out there still? But the program was abolished…"

"Has that stopped you?" she asks us. "How old are you now?"

"We're both sixteen," I say.

"Then your powers are only just surfacing. Imagine if you trained now for many years, how powerful could you become? Drake never had official training. I only trained with your mother in Petram, Theo. And look at us. It doesn't take fancy technology and training to make a Watcher. It takes desire, and focus, and courage. There are many more Watchers out there than the people here realise."

"But why haven't you spoken of this? Have you told our parents? Have you told Drake?"

"Oh, Drake knows. He's been supporting me for years."

"Supporting you? In what?"

She looks as though she might have stepped over the line, given up more information than she wanted to. For a second she goes silent, and then fixes her gaze on us again.

"Training Watchers," she says. "I've been training Watchers for years…"

I stare at her, dumbfounded, not quite believing what I'm hearing.

"You've been training Watchers, all this time?" whispers Ajax.

She nods, her jaw set firm. "I believe as your father does, Ajax. The Watcher program should never have been terminated. Drake wanted to develop it, so did President Stein. I wasn't going to let so much potential go astray, so I said I'd train new recruits. I'd take on that mantle."

"But...the ones who killed President Stein, and Troy, and General Richter...did you train *them*?" I ask.

Her eyes darken, and she slowly shakes her head.

"I only train people with good hearts," she says. "I don't think anyone I've trained would do such a thing."

"You don't sound sure," says Ajax.

She stares at him ferociously. "I'm sure," she growls. "Whoever did this wasn't one of mine. I don't know who they were, but I'll get them. When they surface again, I'll get them."

There's an intensity in her voice that sounds so much like Link. I know she must feel guilty for letting Troy get killed in the city she's sworn to protect. And now that I know there are other Watchers out there, it makes even less sense that the assassins would get through.

Ajax and I share another look, and nod in a moment of understanding. Then, I turn to Athena once more.

"Train us," I say. "We have so much potential...Link and Drake have said that before. Please...if we're going to be in these Watcher Wars, we need to be trained."

A long moment passes that seems to last an age. I

see the slightest shaking off her head, a battle going on inside her. I sense the same old reservations coming, the same excuse: that our parents, our mothers in particular, won't let us; that she'll need to get their permission first.

And, as expected, that's what she tells us. It's the same old story, blocking my path again and again.

"I'm sorry, boys," she says with regret, "I cannot train you."

I feel my teeth biting down hard as she calls a close to the conversation and wanders away, back through the crowd, not giving me a chance to respond. Ajax's voice reaches my ears, cursing under his breath.

"I was sure she'd agree," he grunts. "Now what are we going to do?"

A moment of clarity hits me. I've had enough of being told 'no'. Enough of being treated like a child. I don't care what Athena says. I don't care what anyone says.

I turn to Ajax and smile.

"What are you so happy about?" he asks.

"I'm happy, because Athena's going to train us..."

"Erm, she said no, Theo. Didn't you hear?!"

"I don't care what she said. You and I, AJ, are going to Petram anyway."

And with that, I see a smile rising up his face too. We're in this together...and no one is going to stop us.

# 14

## A Secret Pact

With the party only just beginning to get into full swing, Ajax and I stand amid the throng and whisper quietly between each other. We don't quite know how, but we're going to need to formulate a plan to get the hell out of here, ideally without anyone knowing.

"Once we get to Petram," I say, "Athena will have no choice but to train us. She'll see just how serious we are then."

As we stand there, we spot our parents coming back towards us through the crowd. They carry weighty expressions on their faces that suggest that they've got more bad news. Thankfully, they've clearly been too preoccupied to know what we've been getting up to.

"Ah, there you are, I'm glad you're still here," says Cyra, faking a smile. "Are you having a good time. Nice to get out of that room, I'll bet?"

She's acting weird, nervous almost. Her eyes are hooded and a little manic, as if she's just seen a ghost.

"Um, yeah mum, it is."

She gives me a hug and a kiss and shuffles off

again, Jackson taking her place.

"What happened?" I ask. "Markus said you rushed off on some important business?"

"We went to the hospital," he says. "The maid – the one who saw the assassin in Aeneas' residence – she woke from her coma. We went to see if she had anything to tell us."

"And did she?" we both ask eagerly.

"Just a basic description. She said he was wearing a cloak; that he swept through the place like lightning. The guards never stood a chance."

"And did she see his face?"

Jackson nods. "Briefly," he says, his frown deepening. "She only managed a few words before she passed out again. Thin lips. Dark hair. Grey eyes."

"Could be anyone," says Ajax. "It's not much to go on."

"There was one more thing," adds Jackson, looking a little confused. "I'm not sure, she was delirious…but I think she said he was just a boy."

"A boy?"

He nods. "None of it makes any sense."

I look back over to Cyra, and see the slightly haunted look in her eyes. "What's up with mum," I ask, staring at her. "She OK?"

Jackson's eyes swing over to her.

"She's fine, son. It's just…the description the

maid gave, it reminded your mother of someone."

"Who?" I ask.

My dad turns back to me. "Augustus Knight," he says.

*Knight...I wonder if his shadow will ever cease to loom over her.*

The celebration continues, but it's clear that, unlike in Petram, our little group aren't going to be partaking amid the main population. This time, I don't get to drink any ale, and I don't want to. In a strange twist of irony, all I want to do right now is return to my room so Ajax and I can craft our plot in private.

Instead, we're invited to go to the Senators' Chambers just across from the square, where Drake is hosting a more private wake for President Stein. Flanked by guards, many of the main attendees of the funeral begin moving off towards a tall, ornate building with a high arched doorway leading into a wide foyer.

As we go, I see that several of the VIPs aren't coming along; their attention needed elsewhere perhaps. Among them is Athena, who I spot once again a little way off, stepping into a hovercar and moving off South through the city. I suspect she'll be heading back to the hangers and then back to Petram.

We pass in under the arches and into the open entrance hall. This building used to be the Council Chambers, each floor given over to the privacy of a single Councillor. Now, however, it has been reconstructed, with the floors split between several Senators instead. The thinking, I believe, was that these men and women didn't require such space. Essentially, it was merely another way to show that the gap in equality among the rich and poor, the unimportant and powerful, was being slowly closed.

Still, it's immediately obvious that the building maintains its luxurious dressings. Ahead, a staircase leads towards the first floor, large wooden double doors ahead. As far as I know, beyond those doors was where President Stein lived.

That's not where we go, though. Instead, we move into lifts on the left and right that lead up through the building. Up at the top is where the Senate meets to discuss its business, right at the summit of the city where they can gaze out over it. On the floor beneath, however, there's a large banquet hall used for important events. Today is one such evening.

So up we go, towards the top of the city once again, stepping out into a spacious, wide room that's well adorned with artwork and tapestries and fine dressings. It appears as though a buffet style wake is being held, waiters ready with food and drink to be passed among the dignitaries.

Ahead, Drake is there, already in conversation with several men and women. Immediately, Ajax and I find ourselves running towards the window to take a look down. Here, we're even higher up than before, the entire city spreading out before us in every direction. I strain my eyes into the distance and see what I assume to be Athena's hovercar just reaching the aircraft hangers.

*We should be with her*, I grumble to myself.

The private celebration for President Stein is nothing like the party for Troy over in Petram. It's formal, quieter, and far more sombre. Those who knew the man well take turns to make short speeches, Jackson among them. Cyra, though, chooses not to step into the spotlight, her eyes still a little hooded and stark after her rendezvous with the maid.

I stand there with Ajax, and we whisper ideas back and forward, considering our next move. Occasionally, we're drawn into another conversation, having to meet other officials from across the nation. Mostly, however, we're left to our own devices, our parents themselves seemingly distracted by the latest news that came out of the hospital.

"We have to get out of the city," I say. "Once we're back on the mainland we can slip away unnoticed."

"What, drive to Petram?"

"Sure, why not? I can drive, my dad taught me. You got any better ideas?"

He thinks for a while but then shakes his head. All of this is new to us.

"I guess not. It'll take a while, and won't be easy."

"Nothing worth fighting for is easy, AJ. Dad tells me that all the time."

"OK, so we just need to get out of the city then," he says. "How are we gonna do that?"

"Guess we'll have to convince our parents that we wanna go home."

I look over at them now, standing here and there. Ellie and Cyra stand together, talking with some of the Senators. Jackson appears to be bending Markus' ear over something or other, probably security concerns. Link, though, stands alone, off to one side. When I scan the room, I find him staring straight at us, eyes unblinking.

I quickly avert my gaze and whisper: "I think your dad might be onto us, AJ."

Now it's his turn to scan the room and locate his father. "Don't look…" I say as he does so. "It'll make it obvious we're up to something…"

Unfortunately, it's too late. From across the room, Link begins marching towards us. His dark brown eyes stare as he comes, face cut up by scars. In moments like this, I can't help but cower a little under his presence, under the power that exudes from him.

"What are you talking about?" he says as he reaches us, his voice deep.

"Not much, dad," says Ajax cheerily. "Just the view. Take a look, it's amazing…"

"Cut the nonsense, Ajax," he says. "I know what you've been doing today. Don't think I'm blind to it."

We both make pathetic noises of ignorance,

glancing at each other and then back at Link with wide, innocent eyes. They're clearly not fooling him.

"I can sense something new in you," he says. "Your powers aren't just bubbling below the surface anymore. They…they've been unleashed. Now tell me what you've done?"

We both fall silent. Like Athena, Link is able to see right through us. Standing to the side of the room, he must have been working us out, must have seen a change in us somehow. I know there would be little point in lying to him now, but still, neither of us speak.

Thankfully, we don't have to. From the side, out of the blue, comes a new entrant, his wrinkled visage appearing from the gathered crowd.

We turn to see Drake sweep in, his own eyes peering close. He, too, will be well aware that we succeeded in our mission. He'll be able to sense such a thing himself.

"We all need to talk in private," he says to us immediately. "Come with me."

Ajax and I exchange more looks as Drake begins moving across the perimeter of the room towards a door. We shuffle in behind him, my eyes glancing back over at the rest of our parents to make sure they're not looking. When we reach the door, Drake opens it quickly and the four of us disappear inside.

The room is featureless and largely empty, fitted with nothing but a table and a few surrounding chairs. As we enter, it's Link who is first to speak.

"Drake, what exactly is going on here?" he asks. "Don't think I haven't noticed...something's up."

Drake looks at me, seemingly ignoring Link, but in reality giving him his answer. "Theo, you have something of mine," he says, reaching out his hand.

My fingers slip into my pocket, and out comes the keycard. I pass it back to Drake, and Link has his answer.

"You gave them access to the lower levels..." he says.

"I did," says Drake. "And I can see, boys, that you found the genetics machine just fine. All went well, I assume?"

We both nod. And then, I take a leap of faith.

"We need to go to Petram," I say sharply. "We need Athena to train us..."

A frown deepens on Link's face.

"Petram? What are you talking about? Athena wouldn't train you."

"We know," says Ajax. "She told us that herself."

"Someone is going to have to fill me in here," says Link, growing slightly aggravated. "Why would you even ask her?"

"Because," says Drake, " she's been training Watchers for years. We needed them when the Watcher program was abolished. President Stein and I put her up to it, and she was only too happy to oblige."

Link's reaction is cool and calm as the news registers. He begins nodding slowly, his jaw firming up.

"Good," he says. "It should never have been abandoned in the first place."

"And that's why you're in here, Link," says Drake. "You understand what we've been trying to do. We had to keep it secret in case the Senate found out. We couldn't legally continue the program, so we've done it all under the radar. Very few people know."

Now Drake turns to Ajax and I, peering into our eyes.

"What did you see under the scanner?" he asks.

"The Watcher Wars," I say quietly. "We're both going to be there...whether we like it or not. We need to be trained."

It's clear from Link's confusion that he hasn't heard of the Watcher Wars either. When he asks, Drake simply says: "I'll fill you in later."

Then he turns back to us. "And Athena said no, when you asked her?"

"She said she'd need to clear it with our parents."

We look at Link, who I suspect will be on board with it. It's not him, though, who Athena was referencing.

Drake begins shaking his head, taking charge in his typical, assertive way. "No, forget that. I'll deal with Athena. You just need to get to Petram as soon as possible. How were you planning on getting there?"

My face lights up. "Car," I say. "We'd need to get back to the mainland and then drive, I guess."

Drake's head continues to shake. "No, that's no good. It'll take you ages and you might get caught. You need to fly, I'll see to it."

"Drake," cuts in Link, "shouldn't we think about this? I'm not sure I'm comfortable sending my son off to Petram. And these Watcher Wars, whatever they are...they sound dangerous."

"Oh, they are dangerous," says Drake. "Any war is dangerous, Link, you know that better than most. These two young men are no longer boys. At their age, you were battling Watchers one-on-one. Now it's their turn."

My heart races as Drake speaks, the adventure I crave just around the corner. He leans in a little closer to us, and lowers his voice a touch.

"When you're there, at the Wars, keep your eyes peeled," he says quietly. "I sense there's more going on here than we realise, and you have a part to play in unravelling this mystery. This is a mission, boys. Don't let me down."

His words are cryptic and veiled. They send my heart beating harder, my breathing growing a little more shallow. I stare right back at him, as does Ajax to my side.

"We won't let you down, sir," we say. "We'll do

whatever we can to help."

Drake and Link look at us with pride.

"This stays between us," says Drake. "No one else can know the truth. We'll tell the others that you're being sent to Petram for your own safety, under the protection of Athena. Link, you know what you have to do. It's time for you and I to go hunting."

"But Drake, you're President now..." says Link.

"Exactly. Who better to fight for the security of this country than me."

"And what about these new Watchers Athena has trained?"

"None are as powerful as you or I," says Drake. "This is our duty, Link."

"What about mum and dad, and Ellie?" I ask quickly. "If you two go off, who will protect them?"

Drake begins to smile. "Oh, I think they can protect themselves," he says. "Your mother, Theo, has started to come off her meds..."

# 15
## The Hidden Passage

Ahead of me, the hanger doors begin to rise up once more, revealing the jet within. Behind, the city looms, magnificent and powerful, and yet stifled by fear and a lingering sense of grief. It's given me more than I could have hoped for, but now the next stage of my journey is set to begin.

After the wake at the summit of the Senate building, things moved quickly. I knew that convincing Cyra and Ellie to let us leave would be a tricky prospect. When Drake announced his plans to have us go to Petram for our safety, they clearly didn't like it.

"They'll be safer away from you," he said to them, calming their fears. "These assassins aren't after Theo and Ajax. They're trying to wipe out those involved in the war. If they're going to be safe anywhere, it will be under Athena's watchful eyes."

His calming words and logic appeared to appease them both somewhat. Eventually, after a little more persuasion, they agreed that, perhaps, we'd be safer elsewhere, particularly with both Link and Drake going off on a mission to try to track down these men.

That night, my mother came to me in my room.

"Would you mind giving us a moment, please Ajax," she said.

Ajax left, leaving us alone.

She sat me down on the bed and looked me deep in the eye.

"I'm sorry if I've been weak," she told me. "And I'm sorry if I've held you back. When this is all over, we can talk about your future properly, Theo. Please, don't do anything stupid when you're in Petram."

I assured her I wouldn't, once more lying to her face. Despite her relentless reservations about me developing my powers, a part of me wanted to tell her, warn her of the truth, of what I was about to do. But I didn't. I kept my mouth shut, as Drake told me to do, and merely told her that I'd stay secret and safe in the mountain.

She left me with a final hug and a kiss, her eyes growing a little steelier. Before she reached the door, I spoke the words I knew she longed to hear.

"I love you, mum," I said. "I know I don't tell you enough, but it's true."

She smiled, and I saw the hint of a tear beginning to build in the corner of her eye. But before it could fall, she turned and disappeared, leaving me alone once more.

That was last night, and now as I stand with Ajax, about to board the plane to Petram, she's nowhere to be seen. My father, too, is absent, the both of them saying goodbye that night, not wanting to draw any attention to our departure.

Because really, this is all meant to be a secret, our journey to Petram off the books. The fewer people who know, the less likely any assassin will know of our whereabouts should they decide that we're targets too. That was the way Drake sold it to our parents. In truth, our journey is off the books for another reason…

We have the jet to ourselves as we rise up into the sky, shooting through the outer walls of the city. Drake's private pilot sits in the cockpit, his lips sealed. I look down at the wondrous fortress in the sea, part of me sad to be leaving it so soon. The more prominent part, however, feels a constant swell of excitement bubbling up within me, my veins filled with adrenaline at the prospect of what's to come.

Ajax and I sit and discuss the events of the last few days as we go, our fantasies now starting to come to life. He tells me that Ellie, too, has gone off her meds.

"More eyes looking for danger can only be a good thing," he says.

Mostly, we talk about the revelation of the Watchers, that there are many more out there than anyone seems to know about. Personally, it baffles me as to how an assassin managed to get into the city and kill Troy, especially if there are Watchers there.

"Yeah, well, you heard what your grandfather

said," says Ajax. "These Watchers aren't as powerful as him or my dad. Most of them only have blurry visions and can't see much into the Void. A powerful Watcher would have been able to get through."

"Yeah, but who's that powerful? And the guy who killed President Stein…the maid said he was just a boy. I don't believe that."

"Why not? Cyra, Athena, my dad…all of them could have done that back during the war when they were young."

He's got a point.

"Yeah…as long as they were just normal guards, maybe. But who knows, Stein's personal guard might have been made up of Watchers…the ones trained by Athena."

Ajax shakes his head. "I doubt it. It would look a bit suspicious if he had Watcher guards when the program was voted out by the Senate."

"But how would anyone know? A Watcher is just a normal person on the outside. Unless someone sees what they can do, you'd never know the difference really."

He shrugs. "I dunno. It's like Jackson said…none of this makes sense. All we can do is focus on ourselves right now. I'm just wondering how Athena's going to react when we arrive."

We know, of course, that Athena has been briefed already by Drake, instructed to take us under her wing. Having told us 'no', being ordered to change her decision only hours later must sting a little bit. I don't get the impression that Athena is the type of woman who likes being told what to do.

The flight passes by quickly, the jet zipping high up through the sky to maximise its speed above the clouds. Mostly, there's little to see below this time, the majority of the journey spent in the upper atmosphere. After only a few short hours, I feel the now familiar change in motion and altitude as the aircraft begins to cut its way down.

I hover near the window, gazing out once more as we enter the soup. A few minutes later, after a short bout of turbulence, we exit the clouds and the high passes of the Deadlands greet my eyes again. I smile on instinct at the towering mountains and jagged peaks, the earthy oranges and reds of the Deadlands spread out beneath us.

It's only just late morning still, the sun continuing its climb. Down there, on the dust, the heat will be searing, a constant hardship that the people who live out there continue to endure.

"I wonder why anyone would choose to live on the Deadlands," I say, looking out. "Why not move to Petram, or further East to the regions. It can't be much of a life…"

"They're used to it, I guess," replies Ajax. "That's what Markus said. Those who lived there before the war still do. They'd probably hate it in a big city, or in the woods of Lignum. You kinda get used to what you live with. You kinda learn to love it."

I look at him, and wonder if he's missing home a

little bit. The trees and the lakes and little, winding streams. It's strange how quickly things have changed in the last week or two. How busy our quiet world has become. Maybe there's a part of him that misses it all, a part that's homesick.

There's no time to dwell, though, and no space for such thoughts. The two of us are soldiers now, and we have to do our duty. Somehow, I get the feeling that competing at the Watcher Wars isn't the end game for us. That, maybe, all of this is only just a catalyst for what's to come…

And as I sit and think and look at the mountains, my mind turns back to the other sights I saw under the scanner. The strange lab, the caustic smell of chemicals, the shadows in the tubes. I didn't mention it to Drake, too blurred and indistinct as it was. But, sooner or later, I know that I'll find myself in that place too…

A sudden jolt frees me from my daydreams, and I refocus once more on the world below. For the second time in days, the city of stone appears before me, coming to life through a heavy mist. This time, however, we don't drop down onto the plateau, but begin moving around the mountain to its rear.

There, on the other side of the towering bastion of rock, I spy a smaller entrance cut into the mountainside. Slowly, we drop, the jet hovering on its blue flames, expertly guided forwards by the pilot. The cave, which appeared small from above, grows larger, the jet easily sliding into the cliff and setting down on a flattened stone floor. In the distance, I see a tunnel stretching into the darkness, and out of the shadows, a figure walks.

A hiss sounds suddenly, and the door of the plane begins to open, a ramp extending out to the rock floor. A cool sweep of air rolls inside, chilling me to my bones. I pick up my rucksack, my hunting knife and bear claw necklace stored safely inside, and follow Ajax out into the cave.

Almost immediately, the plane begins to rise again, drifting off out into the bright light at the end of the tunnel. Taking the blue light of its engines with it, the cave is plunged into a deeper darkness, only the sun's rays giving any illumination to the entrance.

We turn back to look into the depths, and hear footsteps coming towards us. Words, too, filter down to our ears, echoing around the cold walls, just as the tall and wiry frame of Athena emerges before us.

"Well, boys, it seems you have some very powerful friends," she says, a rare grin on her face. "I hope I don't regret agreeing to this."

"You won't," I say loudly, my voice bouncing down the tunnel and repeating over and over.

"No?" she says as she looms closer, gazing at us through her fox-like eyes, "I guess only time will tell..."

I see Ajax looking around at the walls and ceiling and into the distance behind her.

"What is this place?" he asks.

"A secret way into the mountain. Drake told me

that no one was to know you were here, not even Markus. I hope you're able to keep your mouths shut, and do everything I tell you."

Her fierce eyes glint in the dim light, catching the sun as it appears behind us. Ajax and I look at each other, and try our best to mimic her expression.

"We'll do whatever it takes," we say. "We're not afraid."

"Give it some time," she says, her grin deepening. "Maybe you will be…"

And with that, she turns and begins walking back into the darkness, the two of us hurrying to follow behind.

# 16
## The Training Cave

The mountain is cold. Colder than anything I've ever experienced. We're led down into its depths, a place of no natural light, the rocky tunnels only sparsely illuminated by fixings on the walls. Through the maze we go, winding our way down. Here, on this side, the place isn't developed. Its corridors and caves are natural and rugged, not carved and made homely. There are no heating systems or houses or home comforts at all. It's a desolate, cold, and silent place, far removed from the main chambers up above.

We encounter no one as we travel. There's no sound but for our footsteps and breathing, and the occasional dropping of loose stones in the distance. We reach a wider chamber and Athena moves over to the far wall, her body blurring into the darkness. Moments later, she flicks a switch and the cave lights up, brighter than the tunnels that have led us here.

I look out, and see stocks of weapon affixed to one of the walls. Not only guns, but knives and spears, swords and shields. I see body armour and various protective garments used for fighting and battle. I see gloves and headgear used for hand to hand combat. On the other side of the room, dummies are laid out on the floor, used perhaps for firing practice. And right in the centre of the cave, a rudimentary white line has been painted onto the floor in a large circle about half a dozen metres in diameter.

She walks back over to us, speaking as she comes.

"This is where I trained, many years ago," she says. "Ellie and Jackson and Cyra made such a difference down here, training soldiers and the occasional Watcher." She looks at me directly. "Your namesake, too, played a big part before his death," she says. "Theo Graves was a talented Watcher too. He taught me a lot before he was taken."

It's another place from history that I've yearned to see: the training cave for so many soldiers who helped defeat Augustus Knight's army. It looks smaller than I expected, and far more basic. Nothing like the high tech training facilities on Eden.

Athena appears to read my thoughts once more as I peer out.

"We have only basic provisions here," she says. "This isn't like the Grid, where Cyra and Link and Ellie trained. My methods are not the same as what they endured. Do you know where a Watcher derives their strength?" she asks.

"Fear," says Ajax firmly. "They need to master their fears," he says.

She begins nodding, pacing before us, back and

forward.

"Yes, Watchers need to learn to live with fear. If you can't face what you're afraid of, then you'll never learn to focus and use your powers. But there's more than that. As I told you on Eden, it takes desire and courage. You have to really want it, otherwise you'll just turn and run away. I've trained many Watchers, and so few reach their potential. It's very easy to give up, when the going gets tough."

"We won't give up," says Ajax. "We've been training for years already. We relish fear."

I nod to his side, agreeing with every word he says.

"Good," says Athena. "Then we shouldn't have any trouble."

She stops walking, and the room goes silent. And then, from nowhere, she turns and flashes forward, sniping at us like a snake from the grass. We instinctively back off as she comes, weaving from one side to the other. I see her fists curling into balls, her arms coiling and ready to strike.

My heart-rate spikes, and I see the tiniest hint of her attacks coming. But not enough. Nowhere near enough.

Her fists swing, connecting with my jaw first, and then Ajax's a split second later. And only moments after she turned and came at us, we both find ourselves sprawled across the cold, hard, rock floor, our jaws aching and the wind knocked from our lungs.

Wheezing, I turn up, my head spinning a little. I feel the trickle of warm blood beginning to spread from a crack in my lip, my eyes slightly blurred as I stagger to my feet.

Ahead, Athena stands firm, callous eyes reviewing us.

"Did you see me coming?" she asks.

"A bit," I mumble.

"A bit is not enough. Let's try again."

"Wait…"

She doesn't. Even faster than before, she shoots back into us. I see only a blur through my eyes, feel the hard shape of her fist plunge itself into my stomach. Any air that was left inside me is pushed out as I stagger to my knees, gasping.

She takes no notice of my suffering. Another strike connects with my jaw, rocking my head to one side. Then another on the other side, pushing my head the other way. In a furious, frenzied attack, Ajax and I are battered like we've never been before. In all the bouts we've shared in the woods, thinking we were pushing each other to our limits, nothing ever came close to this.

And as my eyes fade into black, and my body drops to the floor, I know that this is only the beginning. Truly, Athena's methods are different to what has come before. It's easy to understand why so many people give up.

I wake on that same floor, lip swollen, head aching. A strange smell of chemicals darts up my nose, bringing my brain to life, and my eyes open sharply. In front of me, Athena kneels, holding some sort of pen to my nose that gives out the terrible scent.

"Welcome back," she says, standing. Ajax, already having been woken, comes over and helps me to my feet. Both of our faces are swollen and bloodied, eyes sunken in partial defeat.

She looks at our expressions and shakes her head.

"I've seen looks like that too many times before," she says. "If you can't handle it, don't waste my time."

"We can," I growl, my voice catching slightly in my throat. I repeat it again, deeper this time. "We can."

"We had no warning," adds Ajax. "How were we to know…"

"Watchers don't get warnings," says Athena, cutting him off. " That's lesson number one. You need to be ready at all times, no matter what. Perhaps now, you will be."

We both nod but don't speak.

"You two have a lot to learn. You will eat, drink, and sleep in this place," she says. Her eyes point to a small alcove dug into the cave wall. "There is a basin full of water in there. Go soak your faces, and get some rest. I'll be back tomorrow."

We turn achingly and gingerly make our way over

to the alcove. Inside, next to the basin, are two wooden beds with no bedding. Athena's voice reaches us a final time, over near a passage leading up and out of the chamber.

"Do not leave this place. Do not try to explore. If you do, I'll expel you from the city. This is your home now, so you better get used to it fast."

With those words, she disappears into the darkness, her footsteps echoing down from the passage above.

Ajax and I share few words after she leaves. Frankly, there's not much to say, and opening and closing my mouth only causes my head to ache further. I go to the basin and dip my hands in the cool water before dousing my face. The sting on my lips and cheeks is immediate.

Next to the basin I see a couple of small towels. I pick one up, soak it, and lay it down on my forehead as I lower myself onto the uncomfortable, wooden bed. Without saying another word, I feel my eyes beginning to shut in the shallow light of the cave, my head spinning as I drift into an uneasy sleep.

The spinning continues behind my eyes. And with it comes further flashes of battle; of fists flying and swords cutting; of men and beasts in deadly combat, fighting for their lives for the pleasure of the baying crowd. Inside my mind, it's a little clearer this time, and when I wake in the darkness, I know why.

Visions are obscured by distance, both through space and time. As you get nearer to the vision becoming reality, it will begin to reveal itself. Now, here on the Deadlands, I know I must be closer to the Watcher Wars in space. But the real question I have is: how long before I find myself there amid the carnage?

I stew on that question in the darkness, my head aching terribly. On the other side of the small alcove, Ajax snores lightly, his sleep seemingly undisturbed. I sit, and I wonder whether I'll be ready in time. When I find myself face to face with a man who wants to beat me, hurt me, even kill me…will I be able to look him in the eye and do the same to him?

Killing animals is one thing, bears and wolves and the monsters that roam the woods. But a man, someone's father and husband and brother and son, that's something else entirely.

In that weak moment, the thought invades me briefly, but I don't let it settle. This world of ours isn't fair, despite everything my parents fought for all those years ago. It's still unforgiving and brutal, a world where the cream rise to the top, and the rest linger beneath their feet. And when I stand in that arena, face to face with my enemy, I'll do whatever it takes to come out the victor.

*Whatever it takes.*

I don't get any more sleep that night, the cave bathed in a deep dark that's only penetrated by a single solitary light that relentlessly glows on the high ceiling. The main lights are set to fade over time, only blazing back to life when the switch on the wall is flicked.

It's cold too, something I know I'm going to have to get used to. Without any bedding, I'm forced to sleep in my clothes, using others as blankets and sheets. I suspect it's another device of Athena's to make us more uncomfortable, to break us down quicker. Only when someone has been broken down can they be rebuilt.

It must be several hours before the sound of footsteps once more filters down from the passages above. Moments later, the room begins to glow again, and I see Athena standing by the switch on the far end of the cave. I glance down at my watch and notice that it's still early morning.

"Get up," comes Athena's voice. "We have work to do."

Ajax stirs, wiping the sleep from his eyes. We quickly rise in our clothes, and I look into Ajax's face as light fills the room. His bruises appears to have already gone down, the beating he suffered at Athena's hand barely visible. I look down at my own reflection in the basin, and find that the same effect has taken place.

"There's medication in the water," Athena informs us. "It helps to hasten the healing process for minor wounds and injuries." She smiles a devilish smile. "It means that you can take more punishment," she says. "Now come here, and face me."

I drag my weary body to the middle of the cave. Athena walks to the wall and fetches some protective garments: headgear and gloves and padded body armour.

"Put these on," she tells us. "It's not good me knocking you out so easily."

Her words are half goading, serving to prod at both our egos.

"I'll go without," says Ajax. "I don't need it."

"Suit yourself," she says.

Seconds later, Ajax is once more nothing but a pile of limbs on the rock floor, wheezing and groaning.

"He'll be out of commission for a while," Athena tells me. "This isn't a test of manhood, Theo, it's an order: put on the protective gear."

I do as she says, hiding my more vulnerable body parts beneath soft padding. When she comes at me again, and I try my best to see and avoid her shots, they offer me some shelter from her powerful, relentless blows. Yet still, after a sustained and punishing barrage, I too find myself back on the floor beside my friend.

I hear Athena standing above us, disappointment exuding from her every pore.

"I expected more from you," she says. "Cyra and Link would be ashamed."

Her words strike through me, and my heart begins pounding. With a sudden energy, I rise from the floor and turn the tables on her. Defence becomes attack as I throw everything I've got, my fists flying fast…but not fast enough.

Not a single shot hits. She moves like water before

me, so fluid and athletic, shifting her body position with ease and grace as my fists hit only air. I grow more frustrated, laying it all on the line. Behind me, I hear Ajax rising to his feet, adding his own fists to the fight.

Now there are four limbs flying at her, but it hardly makes a difference. I catch her eyes and see almost boredom in them, as if she's off elsewhere, thinking of something else. Then, suddenly, they come back into the room, and in a flash, she sends her left hand at me, and her right at Ajax.

We both hit the floor with a collective thud, blood dribbling from our noses.

"Better," she says. "You have some fight in you. Now, stand up, and let's go again."

I stay on a floor for a split second. I look at Ajax, and he looks right back at me, and despite everything, we both smile through our grimaces.

And then, we do as our master orders.

We stand, and we go again.

# 17
## Pushed to the Limit

I stand in the white painted circle in the middle of the training cave, facing my opponent. He stands an inch or two taller than me, his frame a little wider and more muscular, his dark brown eyes staring at me as they have many times before in a situation like this.

Ajax and I have faced off more times than I can count over the years. From a very young age, we would spar in the woods, pretending to be our parents and the heroes we grew up learning about. Mostly, during those younger years, Ajax would win. Not only because he's slightly bigger, but because he's a bit older too, so was always just that one step ahead in terms of his physical maturity.

Over the last year or two, however, I've begun to catch up. We're both young men now, and whilst he maintains that physical advantage, I've got him on speed and agility.

As we begin circling each other, I see a small smile lighting in the corner of his mouth, his dark eyes shining. I return the look as Athena watches on from outside the circle.

"First one to step out loses," she says. "Now stop

flirting and get on with it…"

Her words bring the fight to life. Suddenly, from nowhere, Ajax charges in towards me, fists rising to strike. Our heads are protected by padded headgear, but that's all. No gloves on our fists, no protection on our bodies. Over the last week, we've moved right past that.

He comes forwards, and when he moves to strike, I see his fist coming. I feel a surge of adrenaline, of pure joy, at the fact: every time I see even partially into the Void, I feel completely and utterly alive. I dodge under the attack, and send forth my own. Ajax, though, is ready for it, his progress being just as good as my own down here in the darkness.

He moves and parries, striking back at me when he sees an opportunity. For a few minutes, we enter into a rhythmic dance, neither of us connecting properly, both of us managing to move just in time before any attack hits home. Outside the circle, Athena watches on silently, reviewing our every move.

Soon enough, we're both panting hard, sweat starting to drip down our faces. I've discovered that fitness is important to a Watcher. When you begin to get out of breath, you start to lose focus, and your mind can wander. In such a state you're more vulnerable, your ability to see deep into the Void diminished. So, as Ajax and I continue to spar, a few hits begin to land, our abilities being stretched and tested.

Eventually, it's me who falters. Heart pounding,

lungs burning, I miss a side attack. The connection is a good one, Ajax's fist hooking across my head and sending my brain spinning inside my skull. After that, I have no chance, and am quickly tossed from the circle.

I hit the floor with a thud and smash the ground with my fist. Ajax comes to me and helps me to my feet. Mostly, our bouts have been fairly even, although he's probably one or two ahead.

"Close one," he says, pulling me up.

Athena walks over, hands behind her back.

"Better," she says, "but not good enough. You won't make it far in the Watcher Wars like that…"

"And when are they?" asks Ajax. "It would help if we knew when we'd be there."

"I don't know," says Athena. "The Wars are illegal, and not heavily advertised. They spring up quickly and disappear just as fast. When they get near, word will come to me. Until then, focus on your training."

We both nod, realising that any backchat doesn't go down well with Athena. She's a woman of few words and doesn't like her authority to be questioned. I have several scars already that can attest to that fact.

We spar several more times that day, our focus still on hand-to-hand combat. Mostly, we split our time between fighting each other, and fighting Athena. Each time she steps in front of us and invites us to attack, I feel the sting of her fist before she even strikes. Her beatings continue to be severe, often leaving us bloodied and bruised on the floor when she goes off to attend to her other duties.

Each night, we douse ourselves in the healing water from the basin and climb onto our wooden beds. Each night, I drift off quickly into a deep sleep, my body so weary from the day's events. And each time I wake, I feel stronger, every fibre inside me growing harder. Soon enough, when Athena steps before us, I relish the pain and suffering, the taste of blood on my lips. Because I know that every beating I take is crafting me into a more powerful weapon.

Day by day, I see it. I see the fierceness begin to descend in my own eyes when I look upon my reflection in the basin. My youthful face is already growing older, little scars that may never fully heal starting to appear. After a couple of weeks in that cave, I look like a different person. And I like what I see.

I see more flashes of visions in my sleep, but not only of the Watcher Wars. Other things come to me, blurred and hidden in mist. I hear the sound of a woman shrieking in terror as a man attacks her with a knife. I watch on from the side-lines, unable to help, as a man and his young son are set upon by bandits somewhere down in the desert. Night after night, I see cracked images of terrible things, my sleep now peppered with the sort of horrors that my mum wanted me to avoid.

And as the days and weeks pass by, I begin to understand more fully what she was trying to protect me from; why she wanted to keep these powers locked away inside me, never to be unleashed. Sleep, now, is a place of nightmares set to come true, my mind filled with terrible things happening to good people. And the worst thing about all of it is that I can do nothing to help.

That, really, is the curse of the Watchers: that most visions will never be clear enough to be prevented. A random shack where a man kills his wife. A poor young girl drowning in a lake. A hunter being set upon by a pack of hungry wolves somewhere out in the wilderness. There's nothing I can do to prevent any of them.

When Athena comes down each morning, I tell her of what I've seen. She listens to the atrocities with a flat and detached expression that anyone else might consider heartless. But I know she's not. She's spent her life trying to help others from such things. And as much as anyone, she knows that most she can do nothing about.

"That's our fate," she tells me. "We see these terrors but can't always stop them, as much as we'd want to. Unless there's some obvious signs as to when it takes place and where, there's nothing we can do, Theo."

"But shouldn't I try?" I ask. "Try to find clues, to search harder? I want to help these people…"

She lays a hand on my shoulder in a rare show of comfort. "Of course…always try. But know that, whatever you do, most of what you see will come true. And that's not your fault, Theo. There's nothing more you can do."

I get no respite in that cave. In the days, we fight, my mind constantly focusing, trying to see deeper into the Void. At night, my visions come to me more frequently, pain and suffering now filling my sleep. Sometimes, I speak with Ajax about what I've seen, and he does the same. Occasionally, he's seen the same as me: a case of domestic murder somewhere down in the nearby Deadlands; a rockslide that buries a house and the occupants inside. Together, we try to piece together some clues to stop these visions from becoming reality. Not once do we succeed.

I begin to realise just how brutal this world of ours really is. Back home in Lignum, life was calm and easy. The people seemed good, mostly happy in their lives. But who knows what was going on behind the scenes. Who knows how many terrible things Link saw that he wasn't able to prevent. Now, I see it night after night: the awful things people will do to each other, the terrible accidents that will befall them.

Our faces darken down in that cave. Our eyes sink deeper into their sockets, the smiles beginning to fade. Soon enough, when I see my reflection, I see the same look that Athena carries, that so often dominates Link's face: a look of hardness, of gritty eyes and a stony jaw.

There's no joy to be had there in the darkness. When our parents trained on Eden, they'd face their fears in the Grid day after day, seeing them become a reality before them. When they trained, they'd do so using virtual reality, their ability to see into the Void tested and developed by technology. Down here, we have no such luxuries, no fancy equipment to accelerate our learning.

But we don't need it. Athena's methods are different. Pushing us to our physical limits, she tests our resolve again and again. We have no time to socialise, locked in this cold, damp cave. We don't get to go to comfortable rooms each night, or walk around the deck level of Eden, taking in its beauty. Unlike our parents, we don't get to eat nice foods and spend time with our friends. We eat the basic rations Athena brings to us, drink the water she provides. Sometimes we work on empty stomachs, thirsty and tired and cold. We get to breaking point, so many others before us having walked away and quit, but soldier on, unwilling to give up.

And in those more desperate times, with our days full of beatings and our nights full of terrors; hungry and dehydrated and cold to our bones; we begin to change. And as we change, I see a change in Athena too. She no longer goads us, no longer talks us down. She looks at us with a measure of pride as we evolve before her eyes.

And now, when we stand in front of her, ready to fight, we look at her as she looks at us: cold and hard and fearing nothing.

Her strikes appear clearer before me now, the white precursors of her fists easier to avoid. When Ajax and I fight her together, we're able to make her sweat, get her panting and moving. When I fight her alone, I still suffer the beatings, but they're not so easy to inflict, Athena taking longer to land her blows.

And after several weeks in that cave, I manage to land a punch of my own on her for the first time. Freeing myself, I focus on nothing but her, the world around me blurring. Her attacks glow white in the dim light as I duck and weave. And in one moment of clarity, I thrust my hand at her with a speed I've so far been unable to achieve. I see her eyes bulging as the attack comes, seeing it just a split second too late. She moves, but not enough, and I feel my knuckles pressing into her firm jaw.

She staggers back a little, feet moving close to the white line. But she doesn't step out. Not Athena.

Her eyes lift to me, narrowing. And then, a smile rises on her lips.

"Good, Theo," she whispers. "Very good."

She steps towards the two of us, the bout concluded, and begins nodding.

"You may make good Watchers yet," she says, looking at her two apprentices. Then she turns to look at the various weapons lined up against the wall: the spears and swords and knifes and guns. "I think it's time we moved onto stage two," she says. "Rest well tonight, tomorrow things are really going to heat up."

And with those words echoing a little around the walls, she walks away again up the main passage.

# 18
## Stage Two

"I've gotta say, it feels good to be holding a spear again," says Ajax, gripping tightly at one of several spears lined up against the wall.

He lifts it into the air and thrusts it straight at one of the dummies, well over a dozen metres away. The tip blasts right through the dummy's chest, bursting it apart.

"Wow, that thing really flies," he says. "It's much better than my one back home…"

Ajax, of course, wasn't able to bring his favoured hunting weapon with him, large and conspicuous as it is. Not like me and my hunting knife, which has found itself in my hand on many occasions over the last month.

Under strict instructions from Athena, however, I haven't used it until now. She was adamant that we only progress onto using weapons when we were ready, and that all of the spears and knives and guns over on the wall were not to be touched. Other than a couple of weak moments, when we took them up and inspected them more closely, we've done as ordered.

Right now, it's the knives that catch my interest.

There are a number of them of different shapes and sizes. I pick up a particularly small and sleek one, light as a feather in my hand, and send it at the head of the same dummy Ajax has just demolished. The blade embeds itself into the centre of the forehead, just as Athena comes walking in from the tunnel.

"Impressive," she says. "You have excellent aim. I wonder how you'll be able to do when it really matters, though. Stationary dummies are one thing; moving people are quite another."

"I've killed countless animals with my knife," I say, lifting it from its sheath on my belt. "Moving targets aren't a problem."

"Perhaps not," says Athena. "But beasts and people are two very different prospects. Come, try to hit me."

I frown at her, my knife poised in my hand.

"I'm not sure…" I say.

She smiles confidently. "Come on Ajax, you too. Grab yourself a spear. Anything you want. Hit me."

Ajax shrugs and picks up another spear, even lighter than the last. We look at each other for a second. Athena, I know, can run through a battlefield dodging bullets. Dodging a knife and spear is an absolutely piece of cake for her. And yet still, it feels weird to be thrusting a blade in her direction.

However, we do as she says, and together throw the weapons as fast and hard as we can. She merely swerves around them both, letting them clatter into the back wall.

"More," she says. "Put your heart into it. You need to get used to using weapons on other people, and not just wildlife."

Standing by the line of weapons, we pick up more spears and knives and throw them at our mentor. They join the rest on the floor, some lodged into the rock, as a pile soon accumulates.

"Grab the guns. Shoot at me."

Once again, I feel a little tentative as I pick up an automatic rifle. I've shot guns in the past, but only rarely, and never at a person. I raise the barrel of the rifle in line with Athena's body, and find my finger reluctant to pull down on the trigger.

"Stop wasting my time," comes Athena's voice, "and shoot the damn weapon."

The deafening sound of gunfire fills the chamber, battering my eardrums. Bullets flash on the back wall, breaking off pieces of rock and ricocheting around the cave. In only seconds, hundreds of rounds have been sent at her, and none have got close.

As we shoot, I watch as she moves forward towards us. By the time we stop, leaving nothing but a loud ringing around the chamber, she stands barely metres from us, her face a picture of calm. It's a staggering display of power, unlike anything I've ever seen.

"How did that feel?" she asks as the ringing begins to subside. "How did it feel to shoot at me like that?"

Ajax shrugs. "A bit weird, to shoot at a person. But…I knew nothing would hit you. I guess it would be different with someone else."

She begins nodding. "Oh, it would, but when you're faced with a life or death situation, you have to be willing to take the necessary action. Never hold back from pulling the trigger, not when facing an enemy. You have to be ruthless to survive. It's the only way."

She wanders back to the wall, to the pile of spears and knifes we threw, and picks up one of each. She comes back to us, handing the spear to Ajax, and the knife to me.

"Ajax, go and stand over there," she says gesturing to one side of the cave. "Theo, you go there." She points to the other.

Knife in hand, I walk towards one of the rock walls. When I turn, Ajax is about twenty metres away from me, Athena standing slightly off to the side between us.

"I want you to try to hit each other with your weapons," she announces. "You're able to see into the Void well enough now with fists and physical attacks. It's time to see what you can do when your life is really under threat. Now…throw."

Holding the lightweight knife in my hand, I look at my best friend across the cave, raising the spear above his shoulder into its typical throwing position. For a few seconds, neither of us do anything as a series of concerns rush through my mind.

What if he doesn't see my knife coming? It's lighter than his spear, and I can throw it faster, much faster than a fist. What if he doesn't dodge it in time, and it hits? What if he stumbles on the uneven floor? What if I kill my best friend?

No such concerns for my own wellbeing enter my mind, but I can see that Ajax is wondering the same thing. Once again, Athena's harsh voice splits the air, calling for action.

"Throw the weapons!" she calls. "Have faith in each other's abilities."

Ajax and I lock eyes again. *Have faith...I have all the faith in the world in him.*

I throw the knife, and don't hold back. And in the same motion, Ajax does the same. And just as the spear leaves his hand, I see its ghostly shape coming towards me, a typically accurate shot for him. It comes at my chest, and I step quickly to one side. A few moments later, the physical shape of the spear follows in behind, filling in the white space and firing towards the wall. It hits, and clatters, as the sound of my knife doing the same echoes from the other end of the cave.

I look up, immediately, to see Ajax has stepped to the same side as me.

"You see, wasn't that easy," says Athena, clapping. "Now imagine those knives and spears coming ten times faster. And imagine dozens of them coming at you at once. Then you'll have some idea as to what you'll be facing at the Watcher Wars."

As that first week using weapons progresses, we begin to learn just what she was talking about. Taking it in turns, Ajax and I dress in full body armour and find ourselves standing on the far wall of the chamber. Ahead of us stands the other, with Athena alongside, automatic weapons in hand.

When it's my turn, I hear Athena counting down, and feel my entire body pulse harder than it ever has with anticipation.

"Five…four…" she shouts. I know, at 'one', those two weapons will fire.

Yet it's not on 'one' that I see their ends burst with bullets, lighting up as they spray their fiery death upon me. As Athena shouts 'three', the bullets are already coming, white wisps drilling through the air. Lines fill the cave, glowing in the dimness, most coming straight at my body, some missing by an inch or two.

By the time she calls out 'one', I'm already on the move, stepping left to avoid the incoming barrage. The two see me moving, and spray the next wave across me. Soon, there's nowhere to go but up and down, weaving in and out between the lines. Some come before others, filling in and cracking into the back wall. Others stay white for a little while longer, the bullets yet to be sent from the tips of their guns.

The attack is so different from anything else I've faced, the barrage relentless. Soon enough, I feel a couple of bullets hit me, cracking into my chest and knocking me back. I stagger down and the firing stops.

Athena comes over and helps me to my feet.

"You did well, Theo, until you got hit. The body armour will protect you, but only so much. When you get hit, you lose focus. When you lose focus, you're more vulnerable to attack. If we'd have been trying to kill you, we'd have closed you down by now and done so. Watchers are not invincible, remember that. Our bodies are just as brittle as the rest, and when a bullet hits, it shows no mercy."

We suffer injuries as the days continue to pass. Any time a bullet hits body armour, it leaves a heavy bruise underneath. When we begin training with swords and shields, cuts are suffered, some of them deep enough to require stitching using a strange medical stapler. Soon, more visible scars appear on our arms, Ajax suffering a particularly nasty one across his face that makes him look even more like his father.

The night it happens, he inspects it closely in the basin, knowing his face will never be quite the same again.

"Well, you were always the pretty one," he says defiantly. "Mum's not gonna like this when she sees it…"

The mention of Ellie brings thoughts of my own parents back to me. Mostly, I've been too busy down here to think about them, my days spent training and my nights filled with visions. Yet that night, having left Eden many weeks ago, I begin to wonder just what everyone else is up to.

"Do you think they're safe," I ask Ajax.

He nods, sitting on his wooden bed, wincing as he slowly dabs his fresh new wound with healing water.

"We'd have heard if anything had happened," he says. "Maybe those attacks were a one off."

"Or maybe they're just biding their time again. Waiting for security to slacken."

"Yeah, well they might be waiting a while. I doubt anyone's going to relax until they're all caught and put in the ground."

He's probably right, but still it's only natural for people's guards to drop just a little as time goes by. With my mum now off her medication, however, I feel a little more confident that her and my dad will be safe back on Eden. Then again, having not used her powers for so long, it's hard to say how effective they'll be. There's no precedent here, no way of knowing what long term effects the suppressor medication might have. She might never be as strong as she once was.

The hottest topic for us, however, is the fate of Drake and Link. We wonder together in quiet moments whether they've seen any success, tracked down any of the assassins, or simply caught wind of another upcoming attack. Somehow, I sense that little will have been achieved, the assassins too good at covering their tracks.

"If they could get in and out and kill Stein and

Troy and Richter without anyone stopping them, I'm sure they won't be that easy to catch," Ajax says. Clearly, we're on the same page on that one.

As the days press on, and no news comes, it begins to grow stifling in that cave. We begin quizzing Athena more frequently on what it's like up in the city.

"Are the people scared?" we ask. "Is security still tight?"

She gives us short answers, such is her way, and then tells us what she always does: "Focus on your training. Nothing else matters to you right now."

Unfortunately, it's not as easy as that, the isolation beginning to take its toll. With our powers growing, we begin to consider the idea of sneaking up into the main chamber at night, going out onto the plateau to get some fresh air. Athena's movements have been ingrained into us now, her arrival at the cave each morning almost always at the same time.

"We could go and come back before she even knew it," I say. "I'm starting to go mad down here."

Ajax, however, is the voice of reason.

"You know she won't take kindly to it, Theo," he says.

"She won't know," comes my reply.

He raises his eyebrows. "You really think that? You really think we can fool *her*?"

I grunt loudly in the cave, and throw a knife at a dummy, cutting straight through its neck.

"If only we knew when these damn Watcher Wars were…surely they've got to be close by now!"

"Why are you so eager to get there?" he asks. "You really think you can win?"

"It's not about winning," I say. "It's about doing *something*. The world's going mad up there and we're locked down here. I want to help…"

"And so do I, but the best way to do that is to keep training. Look, if you want, we could go up the passages to the secret entrance at the back…get some fresh air there? How about that?"

I take a deep breath, Ajax's calming words helping to soothe the temporary feeling of inertia that's risen inside me. And together, we turn and begin moving up through the long, dark passages, away from the chamber that's been our home, our prison.

When we reach the wide tunnel, leading towards the secret exit to the mountain, I see the fading light shining outside. It's early evening, the sun setting beneath the high mountings, painting the tunnel entrance with a warm orange light. Just seeing it helps to ease the growing restlessness inside me.

That night, we spend several hours up at the tunnel opening, sitting right on the edge and looking out over the world below. As we lower our bodies down and let our legs dangle over the precipice, I realise how far I've come. There, I feel no fear whatsoever of falling down, my mind now attuned to the danger of such a thing. I wonder if there's anything that scares me now…

We sit and talk quietly, our voices carried off on the wind, and let the strong breeze flow across our weary faces. And as the light fades, and the world goes dark, we watch as the moon rises, as the stars begin to sparkle, one by one.

It's a beautiful sight, and something we both needed.

"It gives you some perspective, doesn't it," says Ajax, "seeing a view like that. You realise just how small you really are."

I nod but don't answer. I've spent my life being small, just a son to legendary parents. Now is my chance to be big, to set down my mark, show the world who I really am. And it's the Watcher Wars that will give me that opportunity. That's where it will all begin.

We return to the darkness of the cave during the dead of night, back into the chamber that has carved us into weapons of war. Immediately, I miss the cool breeze on my face, the sight of the black peaks spread across the sky. And over the next few nights, we go back up there, to the edge of the mountain, to taste the cold, clean air again.

We do so night after night, the trek becoming a daily pilgrimage, a way to balance out our days and keep us sane. And as our training continues to intensify, Athena pushing us harder and further than ever before, we find ourselves craving the evenings, wishing for them to come faster.

We sit there one night, the evening growing late, gazing silently up into the stars. And as we do, the silence is broken, light thuds echoing from behind us. We turn and stare into the darkness to see the shape of Athena emerge, walking briskly and more hurriedly than usual.

Immediately, my heart constricts. *Has she come to deliver bad news? Has there been another attack?*

We stand from the edge and move towards her, not quite knowing what to expect. She steps right into the light, and the words spill calmly from her mouth.

"It's time," she says, scanning us both. "The Watchers Wars are coming…"

## 19

## The Arena Awaits

The dawn is still only just beginning to bloom when Ajax and I stand at the secret entrance to the mountain, looking down at the world below. On my back, my bag is packed with the worn and rugged clothing I've been wearing over the last few weeks and months. My hunting knife, however, finds itself proudly fixed to my belt, my bear claw necklace now hanging around my neck. I thought both were appropriate given where we were about to go.

Next to me, Ajax looks at the striking red glow pushing up from the valleys below. "It looks like blood," he says. "Do you think we're ready?"

Truly, I don't know the answer to that question.

"I guess we'll find out," is all I say.

As we wait, the loud hum of an engine begins to sound, brought to our ears on the wind. It grows louder before, suddenly, a jet plane hovers into view before us. We step to one side as it moves into the tunnel and sets itself down. The ramp descends, and Athena stands in the doorway.

"Come on," she says. "We have no time to lose."

It's been several days now since she announced to us, in this exact spot, that the Watcher Wars were coming. Ever since then, our minds have been set on the single task of finalising our training as best we can, stretching ourselves to our physical and mental limits. Not once did we return here at night to look out over the world below. Every single waking minute has been dedicated to honing our skills.

We quickly step up onto the plane and take a seat as it begins to rise up into the heavens. As we go, Athena gives us our brief.

"I've spoken with Drake," she tells us. My ears prick up, my eyes widening.

"Is there any news?" I ask quickly. "Have they made any progress?"

She shakes her head. "That's not what we spoke about. He told me he wants you two going to the Watcher Wars alone. I cannot be seen with you."

"You're…not coming?" asks Ajax.

"I'm afraid I can't. My presence would draw too much attention, and Drake wants you incognito. Remember, you have a mission to do. Keep your ears to the ground, and your eyes peeled. Understand?"

We nod together, eyes turning to steel.

"Good. Now remember, the Watcher Wars are different every year. Each time they appear, they come with different challenges, and more competitors. They've been growing increasingly brutal. You may be required to fight to the death. Remember your training, and do what you have to do. That is your mission."

"We'll do whatever it takes," grunts Ajax.

She smiles and nods. "I believe you will."

The jet flies for a while, descending down through the mountains and into the sweltering desert of the Deadlands below. I look out at the sands and rocks and craggy peaks, the place so desolate and unforgiving. I know that, out there, it'll be hotter than any place I've ever been. In the arena, that's sure to present us with a challenge that other competitors will have dealt with before.

As we drop, Athena gives us more details and advice. The Wars are taking place far to the West of Petram, in a stretch of land known for its jagged rock formations and deep canyons cut into the desert. Many of the people there still live in those canyons, settlements and villages built into the rock walls where they get some respite from the heat.

We're to be dropped off nearby to continue our journey alone. The sight of us stepping off a jet like this would be far too conspicuous, so before too long the jet is slowing and descending towards the desert floor at an appropriately empty spot.

"There's no life around here, Commander," calls the pilot from up front. "Shall I set her down?"

"Yes, Captain," says Athena. "Make it quick."

The pilot does as ordered, the jet quickly losing altitude and landing on the rocky floor with a bump. Immediately, the door is being opened and we're stepping into the searing early morning heat. It hits us like a wall as we enter into the dustbowl.

Athena moves around to the side of the jet, and opens up a large compartment. Inside, I see two dirt bikes, old and rusted.

"You ridden one of these before?" asks Athena as she rolls them out onto the sand.

"I have," says Ajax. "We have one back home. Theo's played on it before too."

"Good. Right, there's plenty of fuel in them to get you to the Wars. Head due West for twenty miles or so, and you'll find them, they'll be hard to miss out there."

She digs into the compartment and pulls out another bag. Opening it up, she draws out two items. Both look similar: small black handles with grooves for gripping. She holds one out and presses a small button at its base twice. Immediately, two shining blades come bursting out, one from each end, extending into the shape of a double ended spear.

Ajax looks upon it, completely captivated by its sleek and deadly beauty.

"For you, Ajax," says Athena, passing it to him. "The grip is customised to your hand. Click the button once, and one blade will extend. Click it twice, and both will come out. Hold the button down to retract them. Go ahead, try it out."

Ajax holds the button down, and the two blades disappear like lightning. Then, he clicks the button once more, and a single spear shoots from the tip of the handle. Smiling with glee, he double clicks, and the other end appears.

"Thank you…" he whispers, admiring his new toy.

My eyes now turn to the other handle in Athena's hand, smaller and sleeker. Once more, she taps a button on its underside, and a lethal knife cuts its way out into the open air. With a double tap, the knife extends further, becoming more of a long dagger or short sword.

She hands me the weapon, and I test it out, the handle fitting perfectly between my tightly bound fingers.

"These are my gifts to you," she says. "Use them only if you have to. The metal is a special alloy, and trust me when I tell you, those blades can cut through anything." She steels her eyes one final time. "Now go, the arena awaits you. I will be watching…"

With that, she steps around the jet and back up the ramp, disappearing inside the plane as its engines begin to whir back to life. We watch as it rises, hovering high into the air, before shooting off towards the heavens, turning to nothing but a dot in the big, blue sky.

I climb onto my bike, and kick it into life as Ajax does the same. And together, we begin grinding across the dirt due West, alone in the wilderness for the first time.

Around us, the craggy desert remains lifeless as we kick up dust, the engines on our bikes chugging away loudly. We cruise along, side by side, moving through the wasteland at a decent pace as we pass by tall chunks of rock and navigate our way over crevices and canyons. Ahead, the horizon stretches away, an undulating wave of heat shimmering above its surface.

I'm protected by a cloak provided by Athena. It's sickly grey and something I'd expect to make me feel hotter, but in reality it helps to block out the sun. Its hood sits on my head, a handy facemask attached that blocks the dust from swarming up my nose and into my mouth. I wear goggles, too, to protect my eyes from the dirt and harsh rays of light cast down from the sun.

Ajax shares the same look as me, our outfits having the double impact of protecting us from the elements and helping to ensure we blend in out here in these lands. And soon enough, as the craggy rock formations grow larger, and the canyons deeper, the sight of life begins to form around us.

Bridges are built over the canyons now, providing easy passage across them without us having to take a detour. I look down into the deep cuts in the earth and see settlements built in shadow, people living their lives down beneath the surface of the earth. In places I see that proper communities exist, farming the deep earth and subsiding out here without interference from the more built up areas to the East. I always knew people lived on the Deadlands, but never like this.

The settlements come in patches, with plenty of dead space in between. We continue West, using the sun to ensure we keep to the right path, searching the horizon for some sign of our quarry. Soon, shapes form within the heat haze, a large rocky outcrop directly ahead. Around it, small little mounds dot the earth, difficult to decipher through my goggles.

As we get closer, however, the scene ahead grows in clarity. The little mounds take firmer shape, and I see that many of them are tents of varying sizes; some small and capable of fitting no more than a couple of people, others much larger and akin to the size of a small house. Beyond the sea of tents, more sturdy structures lie, fancy vehicles capable of transforming into luxurious accommodation. I suspect, looking upon the sight, that these are the spectators of the Wars, setting up base here for their duration.

My eyes are now taken by the large rocky structure ahead, which appeared not dissimilar to the many others we've seen from a distance. Now, however, as we draw nearer, I see that it's been carved and crafted and modified for a specific purpose. There are stairways cut into its side, leading up and within. I spy, through a small gap, levels of seating on the inside, the giant rock sculpted into some sort of arena.

We stop in the dirt, our bikes chugging lightly, and stare out at the scene. I pull the mask and goggles from my face, and Ajax does the same. And together, we marvel at the stadium, ruggedly cut from the rock.

"I guess that's where we'll be fighting," says Ajax. "I recognise it now from my visions…"

I nod, thinking the same. "It looks...bigger, though."

"That's good. More space to operate. Come on, let's take a closer look."

We kick our bikes back into gear, and continue forwards until we reach a rather primitive, wire mesh fence that surrounds the entire area. There's a gate leading in, guarded by men dressed as we are and carrying arms.

Just before we reach them, I whisper harshly to Ajax: "Remember, fake names..."

He nods as we stop at the entrance, the guards stepping forward menacingly.

"What's your purpose here?" one asks.

"To compete," I say.

The guard looks at us and raises his eyebrows. We may have aged over the last few weeks, but we're still only sixteen.

"You sure that's wise?" he asks. "You're just kids..."

"We're sure," I say coldly.

"Fine," he says, shrugging and stepping back, "it's your funeral. Go down the main track. There's a tent for admissions. Good luck."

We continue in, driving past the fence and inside the official site. Various areas appear now, the tents and more fancy accommodations cordoned off in the distance. I spot other spaces used for training and preparation for the competitors. Other tents are set up for official business such as signing up or renting space in which to stay. Then there are food and drink tents, and tents selling clothes and other items. The entire place is thriving, many traders clearly using the event as an opportunity to sell their wares.

Our destination, however, is the admissions tent. We park our bikes and go inside. There, we see others waiting to sign up, mostly grizzled men but the occasional woman as well. It's hard to know how many of them have Watcher powers. As Athena told us, people still sign up if they're good fighters and think they might make it through a couple of rounds to make a bit of money. Others, perhaps, are just desperate. Some may just be deluded.

Immediately, however, I begin scanning the people ahead, searching for signs of who might be a Watcher. After spending so much time around people like Link and Athena, and having now trained extensively ourselves, it's easier for Ajax and I to spot those who might be a serious threat. Currently, those signing up right now don't put any fear into me at all.

When we reach the front, we're asked to give our names, ages, and nothing more. I tell him my name is Nathan Sullivan and he looks up at me with frown, shaking his head. For a second before he speaks, I think I've been rumbled.

"No, no, no, that won't do at all. You haven't been here before, have you son?"

"Erm…"

"Look, just think of a more exciting warrior name. That's how you'll get introduced to the crowd. Do you really want the announcer calling you Nathan Sullivan? No, no, too boring. No one cares what your real name is…give me something else."

I 'um' and 'ah' for a second, looking over at Ajax who just shrugs. Most likely, he's trying to figure out something for himself.

"Oh for goodness sake, I don't have time for this," says the clerk. He looks at me briefly, and sees the bear claw necklace hanging around my neck. "Did you kill that bear yourself?" he asks me.

"Erm, well, it was my friend…"

"Oh, no matter." He begins writing onto his sheet. "Bear's Bane, that's what you'll be called."

*Bear's Bane*, I think…*I kinda like that.*

"And you say you're only sixteen years old?" he asks, looking at me again. I nod. "Well, you look older than that, but it'll make for a good intro. Fine. Next."

I step to the side and Ajax comes in. The man rolls his eyes, clearly knowing we're together.

"I assume you have a boring name as well." He conducts a brief inspection of Ajax, and then nods. "You can be Scarface," he says writing on the sheet. "Sixteen years old. Next."

"Hey! Scarface?!" says Ajax.

"Got a better idea?" asks the man. He gives Ajax

only a couple of seconds to respond before calling 'next' once more and shooing us away.

I see Ajax glare at him as we leave the tent and step back out into the sunshine.

"I wish he was in the damn tournament. I'd love to give him a beating," he grunts, squinting in the sun.

"You know, I think it's kinda cool...Scarface. It sounds pretty awesome to me. I wouldn't wanna fight you!"

"Yeah, well hopefully you won't have to, Bear's Bane," he says. "We just gotta wait and see how the draw plays out..."

As we stand there, a wrinkled old woman comes up to us. We look down at her, hidden from the sun in our shadow as she speaks.

"You two, follow me. I'll set you up in your accommodation."

"What about our bikes?"

"They'll be taken care of and stored with the rest. Come on."

We leave our bikes and follow her through the dirt. However, instead of moving off to the sea of tents, she leads us straight for the rocky arena. When we reach its base, I see a guarded tunnel leading down into the depths beneath it. Ajax and I share a look before we take the plunge, heading back down into a now familiar darkness.

We head down a passage and into a large central area, a fair bit bigger than the training cave. From it, many passages lead off, some lined with alcoves and rooms cut from the rock to house the competitors. Others, however, go sharply up, leading into the arena itself.

The chamber is lit by a mixture of natural light flowing down from the  passages, and fixings on the wall and ceiling. We move down a passage marked 'E', the fifth to the left of the main passage leading outside, and reach our assigned room. The woman opens the wooden door and lets us step inside the dank and claustrophobic space.

"This is yours. I hope you don't mind sharing…we're oversubscribed this year."

"No…I guess," I mumble, looking around.

"This place is just for sleeping," the woman says. "It may look like a prison down here, but it's not. Come and go as you please."

She hands us a key, before hurrying off again, ready to lead another competitor down into this dark and humid pit.

I place my bag down on the simple bed and take a cursory look around the room.

*It may not be a prison…but it sure feels like one.*

# 20
## Knight's Terror

We don't spend much time in that room, not wanting to linger any more than we need to. Dropping our bags, we step out and lock the door, before moving back down the passage to the main chamber. We go towards one of the passages winding upwards, and climb the steps until we come around a corner, and see a large barred door ahead. Beyond, light shines down through the slats, cutting into the darkness of the passage.

We move towards the door and find that it's unlocked. Pushing forward, it creaks open with a loud, piercing shriek, its rusted joins groaning. From the dim passage, we take our first steps out onto the sand of the arena, walking with wide eyes as we gaze upon its interior.

Around its perimeter, a high wall blocks off any chance of escape, the only way out though the barred doors stationed at points within in. There are four of them, including the one we've just come through, equally spaced out along the wall. Above the wall are layers of seating cut into the rock, dozens of them leading up into the upper reaches of the rugged outcrop. And among them, in places of prominence, separate areas have been developed for the higher paying spectators, large balconies fitted with comfortable chairs and marked with red drapes.

As we wander out, imagining what it will be like when filled with people, I see signs of past carnage written into the sand and rock walls. Dried bloodstains appear, here and there, with slices and cuts from swords and spears slashing across the stone. Everywhere, innumerable bullet holes mark its surface, relics of old battles waged here over the years.

Standing there, looking upon it, I feel my heart starting to gallop. But it's not fear that causes the surge; it's excitement and anticipation. Soon enough, I'll be out here, showing the world what I can do.

Suddenly, a voice comes from behind us.

"You there…"

We turn and see another official standing at the barred gate. He holds an electronic tablet in his hand, eyes hovering over the screen.

"How did you get out here?" he asks.

"The door was open," calls Ajax.

"Well, it shouldn't be. What are your competitor names?"

I offer Ajax a wry smile as I call out 'Bear's Bane'. He merely shakes his head and says 'Scarface.'

The man appears to tick us off his list.

"Right, come this way please. A briefing is taking

place for all competitors in the main chamber. It's about to start any minute now…"

I look at Ajax.

"Time to scout out the competition," I say with a grin.

We jog over to the man, who lets us pass through the gate before locking it tight. Then he steps ahead of us and leads us down the winding steps and back into the main chamber. As we emerge from the dim tunnel, I see that a sea of people has gathered. It's more than I'd have expected.

At the front, a man hovers around, watching as the final entrants come from various passages, led there by other officials carrying tablets. Once he gets the nod that everyone is where they should be, he begins to speak.

"Good morning, everyone," he says, his voice precise and crisp, "and welcome to the Watcher Wars."

I look closely upon the crowd as he speaks. Some eyes firm up at his words, cold and callous; they're the eyes of people with Watcher powers. Others, however, turn more timid amid the assembly, perhaps regretting their decision to sign up. Ajax and I hold the former, scanning the throng and sussing out our competition with a cool detachment.

Among them, several people stand out. Right in the centre, a true giant appears, towering above the rest. People give him space, looking up at him in wonder, eyes cloaked in fear as they pray they don't get drawn against him. Other men are gigantic too, if not quite so much as him, faces and arms crisscrossed with scars, muscles bulging from places I didn't even know they existed.

Ajax nudges me, looking at the same men. "If I'm Scarface, what the hell are they?!" he says, ogling their many old wounds.

Yet they're not the competitors who concern me. It's those with the cold, dark eyes that I'm more worried about. The ones who stand there, unaffected by nerves, jaws tightly knitted shut. They're the ones who have Watcher powers, the limits of which I can't possibly know.

As I look, I see two people standing side by side towards the back. They're not tall, and dressed in long cloaks that cover their bodies. What draws my eye, however, are the masks they're wearing, black fabric covering their faces, leaving gaps for only their eyes to see through. They watch on impassively, undaunted by the gathering. And it's them who most intrigue me.

The man at the front continues to speak, telling us the tournament rules.

"The games will start tomorrow," he calls. "The first round will be hand to hand combat, knockout rules, four competitors at once. Only the winner will go through. No protective garments are allowed. The draw will be placed here, in this chamber, for all of you to see this evening. After the first round is completed, we will announce our plans for the second." He smiles at the nervous faces. "We prefer to keep you in the dark. It's more fun that way."

A few people laugh, one woman cackling loudly. My eyes are drawn to hers, manic and brightly lit, even down here in this moody cave. She looks like she's seen one too many summers, her skin like leather.

"Now," continues the man, "I'd like to briefly introduce our defending champion, just so you know what you're up against. *Knight's Terror*, please step forward."

My breath gets caught in my lungs as a man emerges from the throng, walking confidently out to the front. He's tall and lithe and has lank, dark hair, his expression empty and skin pallid. Grey eyes point out from dark sockets as he turns and faces us all, his thin lips flat and delivering no smile.

It's obvious, just by looking at him, that he's a powerful Watcher. Others around me seem to cower at the sight of him, sinking back a little. Even the face of the giant in the middle of the room shows some concern. I turn to Ajax, who stares at him without emotion.

"Knight's Terror…" I whisper. "Do you think that's something to do with Augustus Knight?"

"Could be," he says. "Might have been one of his Watchers." His voice turns to a growl and lowers. "Maybe he's one of the assassins."

I turn back to look at the man and begin wondering the same thing. If he was affiliated with Knight, loyal to him all those years ago, maybe he's at the centre of all of this. He looks about the right age, maybe in his mid to late 40's, his face written with a mixture of wrinkles and scars, his hairline receding a little at the top.

He scans the crowd slowly, eyes drifting from one contender to the next. He stops on several people for a few seconds, inspecting them for longer. I know why: he can see exactly who the Watchers are, who his main competition might be. When his eyes find me, they do the same, scanning me for a moment before moving off again.

Nothing in his expression suggests that he's worried by what he sees.

The announcer's voice sounds again. "Knight's Terror is a man of few words," he says. "But words count for nothing out there. I suggest you all rest up as much as you can this evening. Tomorrow, the Wars will begin."

With those words, he turns and begins moving away up the main exit tunnel, the various officials following in behind him. Once he's left, the crowd slowly disperse, some moving back down passages to their rooms, others leaving the base of the arena altogether and going outside. As the bodies file away in various directions, I find myself staring directly at the reigning champion, and him right back at me.

And for the first time, in his eyes, I see a measure of anger rising to the surface.

Then, suddenly, he turns away and disappears down a dark passage, moving off into the shadows.

Ajax and I don't linger there in the main subterranean chamber. We're quick to move back outside into the burning heat, keen to explore the place and get a better feel for the area. We begin wandering through the little town that's built up around the arena, strolling past the thriving market area where dozens of tents and stalls have been set up selling food, clothes, jewellery, and all manner of other weird and wonderful things.

I spy a familiar looking weapons stand, and my eyes immediately lift to the proprietor. I nudge Ajax. "Hey, look who it is," I say.

He finds the man: "Huh…isn't that the guy from back home?"

"Looks like it," I say.

As we speak, I see his eyes flash on us. I see a glimmer of recognition in them, which forces me to turn away.

"Come on, AJ, let's get out of here…"

The man's eyes follow us as we go, perhaps trying to work out where he knows us from. I'd rather he didn't get to the bottom of that riddle, keen as we are to remain incognito.

We continue on past the market, where regular people browse the stalls and stands and go in and out of tents. Beyond, the town of tents and other more solid structures has built up, many owned by desert people who seem to be accustomed to this way of life. Others, however, appear to be from the regions, dressed in the sorts of outfits I'd see across

Lignum, while there are those that are more finely dressed, the more rich and prosperous who reside in the richer parts of the nation. Some, it seems, may even be from the sea cites and Eden, sitting in the shade of their temporary homes, sipping on cool drinks as they look over the throng.

Soon, we reach a larger area where some of the competitors appear to be training. Canopies spread out over a patch of dirt, blocking out the sun. Surrounding it is another fence, through which people watch these brutish men and women at work. Kids stare with wide eyes as large men do battle, fighting with their fists or practicing with swords and shields.

We stop, for a while, and look in closely. In the main, the fighters appear amateurish to our eyes, but these aren't likely to be the main competition. I suspect that any true Watchers will be more interested in keeping their abilities under wraps until the curtains are drawn open, and the games begin.

No eyes take much interest in us, of course, and that's just the way we want it. Outwardly, we're just two kids from the Deadlands, strolling around the arena, set free from our parents' sight for the afternoon. No one can possibly know that, tomorrow, we'll be out there on the sand, drawing blood.

As the afternoon begins to drift into evening, and the sun starts to descend, the world grows a little cooler. We find a place where we can sit in peace, drinking water from a local, communal well, and eating some of the food we brought with us for the trip, and watch the sun set on the golden sands. Behind, the atmosphere in the popup town turns festive and upbeat, music drifting to our ears as the people drink and celebrate the start of the games.

At one point, a loud bang sounds and we turn together to see fireworks lighting up in the darkening skies. It's the first time either of us have seen such a display, colours of red and purple, orange and yellow joining the glowing moon in the heavens. I'm reminded of the dazzling light show I saw during the genetics test, the place where all this started, where I saw myself fighting in the arena for the first time.

I turn and face it once more, a giant silhouette in the night, and imagine what it's going to be like in there when morning dawns; wonder who I'll be facing on the sand.

But really, it doesn't matter. No one is going to stand in my way.

# 21
## The Wars Begin

The ceiling shakes wildly. Dust falls from above. The entire chamber rumbles as thousands of voices cheer at once, calling together as heavy blows are struck.

I stand in the central chamber beneath the stadium with Ajax. Every time the crowd roars louder, you know that someone has fallen, or at least taken a brutal hit. Around us, other competitors pace nervously, dressed in their battle outfits. None, however, wear any armour. No gloves or padding or headgear have been provided. One good hit to the head and it's game over.

As the crowd roar once more, I glance over the main board and think again of my opponents – Iron Chest and Silver Mane and Redfang. All sound like brutal warriors, but then again it's so hard to tell. They could easily have been made up by the clerk in the admissions tent, just a bunch of regular Joes with no Watcher abilities at all.

I look around at the competitors as they pace, wondering who they might be. Among them are several women, all thrown in to fight among the men. Here, there are no dividing lines for gender or age. All who enter the tournament will be put into the same draw.

Some of the other competitors have already fought, several of them lying in corners, still a little dazed and confused. I've seen others carried down on stretchers, faces bloodied and bones broken. They won't get any rewards for losing in the first round; only those that win initial bouts will go away with anything.

Among the victors, however, are the two masked men I saw yesterday at the briefing. They fought in consecutive bouts, returning unscathed and dressed in their cloaks and masks. The way they carry themselves makes it obvious they have Watcher powers, a natural confidence spilling out of them. They sit together to one side, speaking casually and quietly between one another, their day done.

There's one combatant, however, who I haven't seen yet, someone I've been keeping my eyes peeled for all morning: Knight's Terror. As of yet, he hasn't appeared.

Another rumble echoes down the passages and shakes the ceiling above us, followed by a more extended round of applause. Moments later, I see the last four fighters coming back down into the chamber, brought in via the four different passages. One of them is being helped along by two men under his shoulders. Two others are on stretchers, unconscious. I look to the final passage and see the reason: the giant comes plodding down, blood on his knuckles. Of all the bouts, that was the quickest so far.

I turn now to Ajax, whose eyes have turned to steel. They stare forward, completely focused. Then, from the side of the room, one of the officials calls out the next four fighters. Among them is the name 'Scarface'.

I take Ajax's hand, and grip it tight. "Good luck, AJ," I say. His intense brown eyes stare back, and I know he's ready. He nods and turns, and I watch as he disappears up the passage.

Now it's my turn to pace nervously as the announcer calls out the new fighters up above. Each introduction is greeted with cheers, the final one louder than the others. Clearly, it's someone known to the crowd, perhaps a fighter from previous tournaments. If so, he's probably got some Watcher abilities…

I listen as the announcer calls for the beginning of the fight. For a while, there's a lull, a period of quiet. Then, suddenly, a roar bursts out, and I know that someone has hit the dirt, unlikely to rise again. Pacing from side to side, I feel my body tense each time there's a new hit. Each time the ceiling rumbles, I wonder whether it's Ajax who's been sent to the sand.

It's not long before I realise my nerves and doubts were completely unfounded. Possibly even quicker than the previous fight, the bout comes to an end, and the fighters emerge from the passages. Ajax strolls in casually, hardly a drop of sweat beading on his brow, a little smile cast across his face.

I pace over towards him, and see that he's suffered

no injuries at all.

"How'd it go?" I ask hurriedly.

He shrugs and glances at the three defeated fighters, now being checked over by doctors at various points in the chamber. "Piece of cake," he says. "One of them could see into the Void a bit, but the others were just normal people."

"Right…one did get a bigger cheer."

"Yeah, maybe he's had some success before. But he was quite old, and clearly things have moved forward. I took it easy on them, though. Didn't want to give too much away."

"Good move," I say. "No point in doing any more than we need to, right?"

He nods as the next group of combatants are called upon.

The day wears on, the herd thinning. Each time four fighters go up, and one comes down, we look closely at the victor. Many of them return as Ajax did, walking in having barely broken a sweat. Occasionally, a fight lasts a little longer, the competition more even, and the winner comes down looking like he's taken a fair few hits.

But they're few and far between, and I know that after today, this competition is only going to get harder.

As yet another fight concludes, there's a murmur among the occupants of the chamber. I look up to see all sets of eyes rising to one of the main passages leading outside. Glowing with natural light, a silhouette looms in the opening, growing clearer at it nears. A silence descends as the defending champion appears in the chamber for the first time. Clearly, he's staying elsewhere, away from this stinking pit.

As he arrives, the names of the competitors are called. Dressed in black from head to toe, he saunters towards his passage, all eyes following him as he goes. I spare a glance for the three men set to face him, their eyes all set with fear. He must have been the last name they wanted to see in their bout when the draw came out.

As the four men disappear up their passages, Ajax whispers to me: "This isn't going to last long."

Sure enough, all four men return in a flash, the crowd going wild up above. They chant the name of their champion over and over as he reappears in the chamber, walking back through towards the main exit like a metronome. He spares a glance at Ajax and I as he goes, that searing anger once more burning away his cold and calm expression.

His fallen foes all appear on stretchers, each of them out cold. One, however, appears in a serious way, the medical staff pumping at his chest and giving him mouth to mouth. A few of the other competitors crowd around, watching as the man's heart slowly gives out.

It doesn't take long for the doctors to call it. They stand, leaving the body of the man in the dirt, his face badly battered and neck horribly twisted. Slowly but surely, the rest of the crowd disperse, returning to the shadows around the chamber.

It's a stark reminder that, even in these early rounds, death is never too far away.

I have no time to dwell on it, however. As the body of the man is dragged away, I hear my name being called. Ajax grabs my shoulder, and fixes my eyes as I did with him.

"Focus," he says. "It's time, Theo. Now go get 'em," he growls.

I nod firmly, stand, and move to the passage entrance. Ahead of me, the twisting steps await, a faded light glowing towards the top. Up I go, and around the corner, looking up at the barred door ahead. Two guards stand beside it, waiting for the trigger to let me through.

I move closer, hovering in place, and feel my heart starting to thud. Beyond, the sun is shining bright in the stadium, the stands now filled to the brim with men and women and children, all cheering and baying for blood. In the main gallery, directly ahead of me on the far side, I see the dignitaries sitting in their comfortable chairs, eating fruits and meats from tables, drinking wine and chatting among themselves. Ahead of them, a man stands, raising his arms aloft. It's the same man who gave us our brief the previous day.

"And now, it's time to introduce four more fearsome warriors," he roars, his croaking voice spreading through the air. "First up, Iron Chest!"

The crowd cheer as the barred door opposite mine

opens, and a man walks out. He looks brutal, one of the larger men I saw yesterday, body filled with muscle and covered in gruesome scars and colourful tattoos. He beats his chest as he arrives, his roars echoing around the arena.

The announcer then moves onto the next fighter. "Please welcome, Silver Mane!"

From the left now, another man appears. Older, smaller, but calmer than the last, his head flows with a long mane of silvery white hair. His name is appropriate.

Next, Redfang is called out, and I look to the right. This one's younger, quicker, darting forward and doing a few acrobatic flips. He bares his teeth to the crowd, and even from here I can see that they've been filed into fangs.

"And…finally." The announcer's voice draws my eyes back up to him. "Introducing to you, only 16 years old…Bear's Bane!"

The two guards now step forward and open the gate, its creaking joints barely audible over the roars. From down below, the cheers were loud. Up here, they're truly deafening, splitting my eardrums and causing my eyes to water.

I stand and look up, and see all eyes on me. No faces stick out amid the throng, all of them blurring into one before my eyes. I turn my gaze back to my competitors, who stare from one to the next, sizing their foes up. And then, with a final, croaky roar, the announcer shouts: "BEGIN!"

The reaction of Redfang is immediate. Facing Silver Mane, he goes straight for the older man, covering the sand like lightning. He scampers like a crazed animal, barring those sharp teeth, raising his manicured claws to slice at his enemy as he approaches.

For a few seconds, I just watch, before realising that the same is happening to me. I turn forward, hardly able to hear myself think, as Iron Chest comes pouring towards me, roaring like a beast.

I regain my focus just in time as he comes, two striking fists slashing across me. I duck under them before they come, and send my own balled fist right into his stomach. It's so hard it feels like iron, and I quickly realise where he got his name.

He grunts, but nothing more, and turns his blazing eyes back on me. Brutish arms come at me again, swinging wildly like a bear, but I see them all coming. I flow in and out as he gets increasingly annoyed, his swiping attacks becoming quickly ragged.

Then, I turn the tables on him, and glide behind him, before whipping my fist right across the side of his head. The impact is greeted with a roar. The roar sends my pulse soaring higher, my veins widening with adrenaline. At that moment, I know I belong.

I begin smiling to myself as I fight the brute, sniping here and there, avoiding his attacks without fail. After spending so much time battling Ajax, and Athena in particular, I feel like I'm fighting a child. To me, the man's fists are coming at me through treacle, so slow and easy to spot.

As I toy with him, however, I don't see the threat coming from behind. So loud is the crowd, so narrow my focus, that the fist hits the back of my head without warning. I stagger forwards a bit, my vision blurring momentarily as I feel a heavy weight on my back, arms and legs wrapping around my body.

Then, a sharp pain flashes on my shoulder and the roar of the crowd grows louder. I dart my eyes to the side to see Redfang, body gripping my back, teeth embedded into my flesh. Warm blood starts trickling as I fall backwards, trying to dislodge him. He hits the ground hard, but clings on like a limpet, his strong, sinewy arms wrapping me up tight.

I writhe on the floor for a second before I sense something coming. Looming from above, the white shape of an enormous fist comes. I focus, searching the Void, the fist about to strike for real. And then, in a sudden movement, I roll myself a little to the left, pulling my shoulder and Redfang's head into the path of the oncoming fist.

A second later, I hear a heavy crack, and Redfang's body goes limp, his arms and legs dropping to the dirt. I quickly roll away to find Iron Chest retracting his paw, covered now in blood, as Redfang's skull lies decimated in the dirt.

The crowd hush momentarily at the gruesome sight, before roaring even louder. I turn, now wary of my surroundings, to see that Silver Mane has already been dispatched, his throat torn apart by

Redfang's razor sharp teeth.

Now it's just Iron Chest and me once more. His eyes look at Redfang's body for a moment, wide and stark, before turning back to me and blazing in anger. A ferocious, animal roar bellows from his meaty chest, and he comes flying towards me, wild with rage.

I stand my ground and take a breath. "Time to finish this," I say to myself.

He reaches me, and with my focus back, I have no trouble sliding around his attacks. Left and right I go, ducking and weaving, before I ball my own fist, summon all my strength, and launch it straight up into his chin.

I feel it crunch and break, watch his eyes roll into the back of his head, and stand tall as his body slumps to the sand with a heavy thud.

A brief lull drops, and in the silence, a single man, high up in the rocky seats, calls out: "BEAR'S BANE!"

And with that, the crowd goes wild.

## 22
## A Legend is Born

That night, after getting some attention on my shoulder, Ajax and I move back out into the open air outside of the arena. We don our cloaks, wishing to remain anonymous if possible, and find a quiet spot where we can eat and relax and discuss the day's events.

For a while, I sit there on the desert sands in the shadow of the arena, feeling a little disgruntled. When Ajax asks me what's up, I simply tell him my performance wasn't up to it.

"I should have seen it coming when Redfang punched me," I say. "If that was someone else, I would have lost out there today. Or worse…I could have been killed."

"Give yourself a break, Theo. It's so damn loud out there it's easy to lose your focus for a second. Next time you'll know what to expect. You'll see it all coming, don't worry."

His logic helps to soothe me a little, and he's right about the noise. It's hard to prepare for something like that, especially given how quiet our training was. We only ever fought each other, and Athena, in silence. Doing battle under the blaring sun, with thousand of cheering voices battering your ears, is a whole different prospect.

*Next time, I'll get it right.*

Still, my fight, in particular, appears to have caused the biggest stir. When we're done eating, we move off into the crowds again as the party vibe begins to pick up. Our faces hidden in shadow, we listen as people talk animatedly about their favourite battles. On more than one occasion, I hear my given name being spoken.

I can understand why. Not only was my fight one of the last, and so fresher in people's minds, it was also the most brutal. Out of the four of us, two people were killed: Silver Mane with his torn jugular, Redfang with his crushed skull. Such savagery is rarely seen in the early rounds; death usually only coming when things heat up and weapons are introduced.

As I listen, I begin to feel my displeasure fading. The more I hear my warrior name, the more the smile rises on my face. Finally, I'm being talked about for my own merits, for something I've done. Finally, I'm beginning to step out of my parents' shadow.

As we join the celebration, I find people peering at me under my hood. Eyes flash with recognition, and the people begin whispering between each other.

"Bear's Bane…is that Bear's Bane?" I hear them ask.

I turn my gaze quickly and dip my head down,

casting it back into shadow. But all that does is cause a greater stir as people begin to surround me. I hear them saying my name more and more, their voices rising.

"Bear's Bane!" someone shouts out, loud enough to be heard over the music and endless sound of chatter. "It's Bear's Bane!"

Suddenly, the people are swarming closer, looking under my hood for confirmation. Next to me, I see Ajax's eyes glare, telling me that it's time to go. We begin fighting our way out, trying to escape the attention. But part of me wants to stay, to soak up this new adulation.

Something takes me, a foolish impulse, and I tilt my head back. And as I do, my hood falls away, and my face is revealed for all to see. The crowd crow louder at the reveal, others now beginning to notice from beyond the throng. They move in, asking questions, dozens of voices buzzing around my ears.

"Are you really only 16?"

"What's your real name?

"Where are you from?"

The questions come thick and fast, and Ajax is forced to grab my arm and wrest me away from them. He begins pulling me through the crowd, still cloaked and hidden, not wanting any attention for himself. Really, he was far more impressive out there today. It should be him that they're interested in.

Perhaps they would be if he revealed himself. But

he doesn't, dragging me from the swarm and over to a quieter part of the temporary town. We manage to find our way into a new crowd, my hood once more draped over my head, disappearing once again amongst the people.

"Wow, that was intense," I say.

Ajax's dark eyes catch the moonlight, hidden under his cloak. "You enjoyed it," he says. "I can tell." There's a slight tone of accusation in his words that I don't like.

"Yeah, I did like it…wouldn't you? It's nice to get some recognition for a change."

"But for Bear's Bane…not Theo Kane. Remember what we're really here for," he says.

I grit my teeth but don't respond. Deep down, I know he's right. We're here to do a job, and keeping a low profile is a big part of that.

We appear to be in a slightly more upmarket portion of the camp now. Around us, the people are more finely dressed and quieter, the crowd thinner. They talk more casually, sipping on fine wines as they sit at little tables. The tents are larger and the food more luxurious, and just beyond lie the stately and lavish mobile accommodations brought here by the more affluent supporters of the event.

Hidden once more in shadow, I scan my eyes forward and see one particular structure stick out. It's larger than the rest, a mobile vehicle that's been folded out and expanded into a mini estate, protected by armed guards at various point. I see several rooms and compartments inside, and on the front a little veranda has been extended, covered in a marquee that flaps lightly in the evening breeze.

Beneath the canopy is a table, set up with various foods and goblets, plates and cutlery. It looks as though whoever owns this place is hosting a little get together. Inside, through the faded windows, I see the shapes of bodies moving. Moments later, the front door opens, and several men walk out into the night.

There are three, all finely dressed, colourful robes hanging around their bodies. One wears a particularly extravagant one, dark maroon and with various golden embellishments. His hair is dark, but greying at the sides, his face tanned and wrinkled and teeth a dazzling white. He shakes the hands of the two men briskly before they turn and depart, moving off to their own temporary homes.

Still watching from the shadows, now I see two other men walking out through the door. Next to me, Ajax's attention is drawn to the same spot. When he sees the men, he whispers: "It can't be…"

Knight's Terror and Iron Chest step onto the veranda, joining the maroon robed man at the table. They speak for a moment, the looming figure of the man I defeated shrinking into his shell, his head drooping low. I see Knight's Terror staring at him through cold sockets, and notice that the large brute of a man has more injuries on his face than I inflicted.

Coolly, the well-dressed man talks to him, looking

up into his battered face. Iron Chest's gaze doesn't meet his once, his pose deferential and subservient. After a brief chat, he trudges off into the night, leaving the other two men alone.

As I continue to watch the two men from afar, a drunken voice sounds behind me.

"Hey…it's Bear's Bane," says the man.

Clearly, one of the masses has managed to infiltrate the more up market crowd. A murmur starts again as people begin looking at me, drawing the eyes of the men on the veranda.

"We better get out of here," says Ajax, once more grabbing my arm and leading us off. We hurry away, not wanting to outstay our welcome, and return to the depths of the arena and the small humid room we occupy. There, we discuss what we saw, a feeling of disquiet beginning to fill me.

"It looks like they were working together," I say. "As if Iron Chest was meant to take me out and failed."

"Could just be coincidence. I've heard that some of these fighters have sponsors. Maybe that guy in the cloak was sponsoring Iron Chest."

"And Knight's Terror? Why would he bother with Iron Chest if he had a guy like that in his corner."

Ajax shrugs. "I dunno. Can't hurt to have more than one…"

"Nah, there's something else going on here. You didn't see the fight. When Iron Chest accidentally killed Redfang, he looked, I don't know…upset.

Like they were friends. They were trying to take me out, I know it…"

"Well that's an unnerving thought," says Ajax. "You think they know who we are?"

"Probably. If Knight's Terror is one of the assassins, it makes sense that they'd try to kill us here. It's kinda more legit, doing it this way. I don't like this, AJ."

"Yeah, I don't like it much either. But, at least we're getting somewhere. Drake was right…there's something fishy going on here. And now…we've got our heads up. Keep focused. We'll see it coming."

That night it's hard to sleep, too many thoughts bouncing around my head. Down the passages, the sounds of pain and suffering reach my ears too, nightmares a common feature among the contestants here. I suspect that many of those with Watcher powers have visions as I do, seeing horrors in their sleep on a nightly basis.

At regular intervals, the sound of shrieking pierces the pitch darkness, echoing through the central chamber and up the many tunnels. I open my eyes in the blackness and wonder what that person has seen, how long they've suffered from this nightly affliction. And as I begin to drop off, my own visions come to me; images of carnage and bloodshed and death, all melded into one.

It's a long night, and I doubt I'll get any short ones down here, warm and suffocating as it is. When dawn comes, I go straight up and outside into the relative cool of the morning before the sun heats up. At the main communal well, I fill two bottles with water and return to Ajax before anyone can see me, passing him the refreshing liquid. In this heat, more than anywhere else, it's important that we keep on drinking to stay hydrated.

Then, without any respite after the previous day's events, it's right back to work. In the main chamber, the remaining contestants gather, now quartered after the previous day. It's kind of weird seeing the field reduced so starkly. Once more, the main announcer stands before us and tells us what to expect.

"Round two will start in a couple of hours," he tells us. "The draw is being placed on the board now."

We turn to see a couple of officials pinning a new list of names up on the rock wall.

"Today, you will be engaging in hand to hand combat once again. However, this time it's with a twist," continues the announcer, pointing upwards to the ceiling. "You see, up there, the arena is being altered, split in two by a wall with a gate in the middle. Two of you will enter at once, one on each side. Within your half, you'll be facing four men, criminals gathered from across the Deadlands. Your goal is to defeat all four of them. Once you've done that, the central gate will open, and you'll be allowed entry into your opponent's half of the arena. After that, the mission is simple: defeat your opponent."

He wanders over to the board as some of the contestants whisper among themselves, eyes frowning. This particular format, it seems, is alien to most. I look over at the two masked fighters, sitting quietly in a corner, seemingly unperturbed. Then, my eyes turn to some of the others, including the giant, whose expression remains blank. Once again, however, the defending champion is nowhere to be seen.

Over at the board, the announcer continues speaking.

"The faster you can defeat your four opponents, the quicker you'll be able to take on the real threat," he says. "And remember, if he or she is still doing battle with their assigned criminals, well…all the better for you. This is a challenge of speed and the ability to take down multiple enemies quickly. And first up," he says, his eyes scanning the list, "we have Battleborn…and Bear's Bane."

His eyes swing to me, then to a gritty eyed man standing quietly nearby. "Good luck to the both of you. And to you all…may the best man, or woman, win."

# 23

## In Too Deep

Ahead of me, the arena awaits, this time split in two. From one side to the other extends a clear screen wall, with a door in the middle. Beyond that, I can just about make out the shape of my opponent, Battleborn, waiting patiently behind the barred door.

Up in the stands, the announcer steps forward and hushes the crowd. Behind him, I spot the maroon-cloaked man, sitting casually as he looks down upon the sand. The announcer's voice reaches out, cutting through the quiet, calling for Battleborn to step into the arena. Ahead, the barred door opens, and my adversary steps out.

Next, it's my turn to be announced. I hear an excitement in the crowd as they await my name. And when it comes, they erupt into a communal song of cheering, the very earth beneath me shaking hard as I step forward.

I feel a thrill fill me, and my arms rise up to the heavens. The little movement sends the gathered masses chanting louder, my name beginning to spread from one end of the stadium to the other. Still fuelled with lingering wine and spirits, the atmosphere is even more febrile than the previous day. This time, however, I'm prepared for it.

Finally, as I wander into the centre of my half and look at my opponent, the announcer makes his final call, hushing the crowd with his booming voice. "Now, release the prisoners! Let them fight for their chance of freedom!"

Suddenly, the two doors to my left and right, cut in half by the wall, open up wide. Out from each pour four men, two coming at me, two at my primary opponent from either side. I turn from one side to the next and quickly size them up before they reach me. All are large, similar in scale to me, with cast iron jaws and enraged eyes. As the announcer told us a little earlier, if any one of them defeats us, they will be set free.

It's all the motivation they need to ensure they put up a good fight.

I prime myself for action as the noise levels in the stadium reach fever pitch. I take a deep breath, relax my body, and focus hard as the first two men reach me, coming from either side. Around me, everything begins to blur, and from the murky darkness, I see the wispy attacks of their fists begin to glow.

I waste no time in fighting back this time. Ducking beneath their blows, I twist to the right and flatten the first man, rocking his head back with a mighty blow to the nose. It explodes with a burst of blood, splashing onto my cheek as I move straight onto the second criminal, rushing in behind him.

The ferocity of my attack sends him sliding to a stop in the sand. He backs off as the other two loom behind me. Today, though, I know it's coming, and am able to drop to the floor and trip the first guy up mid-flight. He collapses to the sand and I'm onto him quick, dropping a knee into his solar plexus that puts him right out of action.

Now it's just two, and they're not too sure how to act. I spare a glance up and see that my opponent is working at the same rate as me, two men already sunken at his feet. The glance of my eyes is enough for my final two attackers to act, thinking they see an opportunity. They're wrong. As they plummet into me together, I quickly send them both back just as fast.

And within a minute of their attack, all four are now out of commission.

I look up now, and see that the door in the middle of the partition wall is swinging open. The crowd burst out in a feverish roar as I storm forward, Battleborn just about finishing his own job as I reach his side of the wall.

With his final enemy downed, he turns and looks at me, sweating and panting, fists dripping blood.

"Just you and me now, Bear's Bane," he says with a wry smile. I return the look as we start to circle each other, just as I have with Ajax so many times.

For a few moments, we try to suss each other out, sniping in occasionally to see if we can get through the other's defences. Each time he comes, I see it a mile off, my body now truly primed for action. A delirious excitement surges through me as I see deep into the Void, feeling everything around me. There's not an attack he can make that I won't see.

There's nothing this man can do to me.

I wait for him to make a mistake, to overreach. Soon, the crowd are getting restless, impatiently calling for action. It's Battleborn who is first to crack under their relentless calls, the pressure getting to him. In he comes, darting too close. It's the final mistake he'll make in this tournament.

With a quick one-two punch, both my fists slice across his jaw, and he finds himself hitting the dirt hard. He lays there, body limp, face planted into the sand, and doesn't move. I keep my eyes on him for a second, watching him twitch, before the announcer stands and roars once more.

"Bear's Bane is the winner!"

I shut my eyes, and raise my arms, and soak in the cheers as my name is called once more. And suddenly, a strange thought passes through my head: *I wish my parents were here to see this.*

A minute later, I'm heading back down into the bowels of the stadium, passing Ajax on his way up to fight. We grip hands as we pass and nod at each other with gritty eyes. I know that he'll be joining me back down in the main chamber pretty soon.

As I get myself cleaned up, washing my body of sand and dirt and blood, and wiping the sweat from my face, I listen to the crowd roaring once more. Soon after, Ajax is coming back down, victorious again but not without cost.

"He got me," he tells me, his nose bloodied and bottom lip cut. "The guy was quick."

"But not quick enough," I add.

"Yeah…but they'll get quicker. We're still only in round two."

I can tell he's annoyed with his performance, as I was last night. If he can get caught now, who knows what will happen when we face sterner tests? So far, neither of us has faced anyone with much talent or training. And looking around the chamber right now, there are plenty who appear to have both.

The rest of the fighters continue to be called, two marching up the passages, only one marching back down. We sit to one side and watch, taking bets on who'll be the victor as each pair step up.

Some, of course, we agree on, the giant being one. When he ducks into the passage, we just look at each and nod. Whether he can see into the Void or not is almost irrelevant. If he gets hold of you, it's game over, and any time you move in to strike, you run that risk.

Others, however, we debate more fiercely. The two masked fighters don't seem to have had the same effect on Ajax.

"They're too small," he says. "Look at them. When they come up against a proper Watcher, it's curtains for sure."

I take the bet, and watch both of them reappear down the tunnel having won their bouts.

"They must have gotten lucky," Ajax says, unwilling to admit defeat. "Clearly they haven't seen any real competition yet."

"Sore loser," I say, laughing, as we move on to debate the next pair.

It's not until mid afternoon that our next unanimous agreement comes. Once again, as before, Knight's Terror stamps his way into the room mere moments before he's set to fight. Whether it's the reigning champ's prerogative to steer clear of the chamber, or whether he's simply too arrogant to rub shoulders with us, I don't know. Whatever the case, we quickly agree that no one is going to lay a finger on him today.

As he marches straight in and up his passage, I feel an urge to follow.

"I wanna see him fight…see what he can do. Come on."

I stand to my feet and begin moving up the same passage he disappeared into. Ajax tries to call me back but his words have no effect. In the end, he just follows me up the stairs and around the corner. We stop at the top just as Knight's Terror is called into the arena, and the two guards open the door.

Once they've shut it again, we pace up towards them.

"Hey…you can't be here," one says.

We ignore him and rush up to the bars. It's obvious they recognise us, because they don't push it.

Staring through the metal slats, the announcer's voice booms and the eight criminals come pouring out from the left and right. I wonder if they know who they're facing, what they're getting themselves into. I doubt any of them will have much hope of winning their freedom against him.

Still, the four on his side of the arena pour forwards with gusto, seemingly having decided to work together to try to take him out. Drawing near, they surround him, four large men enclosing the more lightly framed champion.

The man in the middle doesn't flinch, however. He merely stands up straight and tall, adorned in black, his appearance striking against the yellow sand. With his hands hanging casually to his sides, he appears a vision of calm, eyes almost closed as he waits and watches, searching the Void for the inevitable attack.

For a moment, the four men freeze in place, none of them acting. And then, as if on cue, they suddenly come forwards as one, advancing on the champion as the crowd watch with bated breath.

What happens next, however, is enough to take the breath right out of me. In one impossibly quick motion, Knight's Terror flashes like a dart of lightning, his limbs all striking out at once. All four of his opponents are hit simultaneously, each of them rocking on their legs before collapsing to the ground.

I stare in awe as the door in the partition wall swings open, and the reigning champion strolls through to the other side. There, his opponent continues to battle his four attackers, struggling to fend them off as they dart in at him from all angles.

They're all so busy that they don't see the new entrant approach, his eyes on his final victim.

With every eye in the crowd staring at the man, however, he chooses to extend his stay on the sand, if only by a few moments. Casually walking from one criminal to the next, he lays them all out flat. When one attempts to strike him, he takes it personally. A moment later, the man's body is lying motionless in the dirt, his neck twisted back in reverse.

Now, it's just him and his primary foe, cowering at his knees. Even from here, I can hear him calling for mercy as Knight's Terror stands above him, enjoying the calls of the crowd, relishing the fear of the poor soul at his feet.

Then, I see him looking up to the maroon cloaked man in the gallery, who smiles down at him with a measure of pride. And with the tiniest of nods, his charge ends the man's whimpering, his sobs turning to silence.

Standing at the bars, I turn to Ajax, a deep frown now cast down over his eyes. He's shaking his head slowly as he gazes out, his breathing a little sharp. Then, still staring forward, he speaks.

"We might as well go home, Theo," he whispers. "There's no one here who can beat that man…"

And when I turn back to the arena, I see that Knight's Terror is looking at us, pacing back towards the bars. And this time, that anger in his eyes starts shining, and a smile erupts across his hateful visage.

It's a smile that says one thing: "You're mine."

# 24
## Twin Threats

The chamber is beginning to grow empty.

Each day that passes cuts our numbers down further. Some leave the tournament with nothing but a sore head or minor injuries, chins low in defeat but grateful to live to fight another day. Others aren't so lucky, their bodies dragged from the sands, blood gushing from wounds inflicted by weapons and beasts and traps.

The challenges are getting harder now, more combatants falling to death as the rounds advance. No longer do we engage in hand to hand combat, fists not enough to entertain the crowd. Now we face new threats, wild threats, threats that few would survive.

On day 5, I find myself in the arena alone, not knowing what's coming. The announcer didn't give us a brief. He merely told us that the challenge would be the hardest yet, and we'd be fighting by ourselves.

As I stand there, I focus and search the Void, and in my mind's eye see the sight of beasts pouring forward from the gates. In my right hand, I hold a sword, heavy and sharp and shining silver. In my left, a shield is fixed, circular and lightweight and similar to the sorts I trained with in Petram.

I open my eyes bright and look to see different animals coming at me from the four doors. Quick on its feet, a mountain lion springs forward fastest, ready to pounce. From another door a ravenous wolf snarls, larger than any I've encountered back home. I turn my eyes left and see a giant wild boar snorting as it steps onto the sand, huge tusks fitted with razor sharp embellishments. And, from the final door, I watch as a towering bear walks out, roaring loud and beating the earth with its paws.

I allow myself the smallest of smiles as the crowd cheer louder at the final entrant. 'Bear's Bane' they chant, over and over. I look at the beast that gave me my name, and feel the necklace dangling around my neck.

*My specialty*, I think to myself.

The beasts don't act like men. They don't form a strategy and work together. One by one, they charge at me, taking it in turns to turn me into a meal. They have no chance of such a thing. My body is primed, my focus pure and deep. And one by one, I fend them off, sliding from side to side in the sand and slicing them apart with my sword.

As they come, traps open in the ground, springing from the earth and sending darts and sharp projectiles right at me. I see them coming too, dodging left and right, battling the beasts as I go. Other traps send spikes surging up from the sand, something only a Watcher would see coming. It's a true test of my strength, and something that no regular person could possibly contend with.

I avoid all threats without fail, sometimes utilising the traps to take down the beasts. When I see arrows coming at me, I step to the side and let them strike the boar or lion. When I sense the spikes surging upwards, I lure the wolf into the trap and watch as its underside is pierced by the blades.

Soon, three beasts are dead and only one remains. It seems quite fitting that it's the bear, something not lost on the crowd. The traps go quiet now, leaving just my final adversary and me. Looming forward, I don't let the towering beast suffer. With a quick slice of my sword, I end its misery, it's body already dripping blood from many wounds.

Then I stand, surrounded by carnage, and listen to the roar of the crowd.

That day, several people die, caught by an arrow or surging spike or slashing claws and biting fangs. Those that do survive often return with wounds and injuries, some of the more powerful foes needing medical attention. To my relief, Ajax returns with no ill harm done to him. To no one's surprise, Knight's Terror ends his bout in record time, cruising back through the central chamber without so much as a splash of blood on him.

The following day, the announcer arrives back in the chamber to tell us that we're to be fighting one another once more. This time, it will be a three-way battle, with only one coming out the winner. And this time, we'll be using any weapons that take our fancy.

"Winner is by death or knockout," the announcer says. "Three will go into the arena, and only one will be left standing. Make no mistake, all of your lives are very much on the line…"

I look around at the gathered fighters, and note that we're now down to twenty four. What started as several hundred has been gradually carved up, leaving only those with Watcher abilities to fight it out for the victory. It's a stark reminder of just how many people do have the genetic mutation.

As he speaks, the new draw is once more pinned to the rock wall. The remaining combatants begin moving towards it to find out who they'll be facing. I watch as the giant lumbers forward, brushing other people aside. He stoops down to look at the list, and then his eyes turn to two of the assembly. One of them is Ajax.

"Great," mumbles my friend. "That's just great…"

"Don't worry about it," I say. "I reckon you've got lucky."

"Lucky?! How'd you figure that out?"

"Well, I doubt he can see too far into the Void, and this isn't hand to hand combat. You don't have to worry about getting too close or trying to knock him out. Just cut him down with a sword or whatever else you can get hold of."

He nods, seemingly agreeing with my logic. Truly, I don't consider the giant to be the biggest threat at this stage. His race, I feel, has been run.

"Right, let's see who you've got," says Ajax.

We push ourselves forward through the fighters and take a closer look. To my right, Ajax spots my opponents first and utters: "It's *you* who got lucky.

When I see who I'll be fighting, I'm not quite so sure. *Faceless* and *The Shadow*. Otherwise known to me as the two masked fighters.

We retreat to a quiet part of the chamber, taking a few moments to let it all sink in. I begin shaking my head as I think of my opponents. Ajax has never considered them too strong, but clearly he just doesn't get it.

"You'll be fine," he says. "Don't worry…"

"Think about it, AJ. There's two of them, they're gonna try to take me down together. I'm handicapped."

The truth dawns on him.

"Ah…yeah, I see," he stutters. Then he paints a smile on his face that's meant to be comforting. It's a look that doesn't fit him well. "Still, you got this, Theo. You've been sailing through so far, no reason why that's gonna change…"

I don't take the conversation further. Frankly, we've both got our own bouts to worry about, and it's not fair to dwell on mine when he's got a serious match up of his own.

Ajax's fight comes first, and for the first time I go up and watch him from behind the barred doors. He stands with the giant, officially announced to the crowd as 'Colossus', a quite fitting name, as well as another of the steely eyed combatants I remember from the very first briefing called Wolfheart.

Around the arena, fitted to the walls, I see weapons at regular intervals: swords and spears and knives and shields. All blades, no guns; designed perhaps to create the most bloodshed. Over the last few days it's become clear that the sight of spilled crimson is what the crowd most want, their bloodlust turning insatiable. Today, they'll get their fill.

Ajax is a vision of calm as I watch him stand there, the fight about to start. I can see his eyes looking at a spear affixed to the wall, always his weapon of choice. When the announcer bellows out for the beginning of the bout, he charges straight at it, speeding across the sand. Within seconds, he's got the weapon between his lethal grip, the others having gathered up swords and shields for protection.

I find it hard to watch, standing there at the bars. When I go out there, I know I'm in control, my fate in my own hands. Watching my friend, however, I'm more nervous than I've ever been, his life very much at stake.

The first of the three to fall is Wolfheart, falling foul of Colossus' mighty sword. I note that the giant is more fleet of foot than I'd expect, and clearly capable of seeing somewhat into the Void. Wolfheart, it seems, made the same fatal assumption, charging in expecting to duck through Colossus' attacks and cut him up from up close.

Instead, it's the man mountain who slides to one side, bringing his enormous sword right down on Wolfheart from on high. The blade meets his shoulder at an angle, cleaving right through him as his body splits in two. The crowd gasp and cover their eyes at the horrific sight, blood quickly flowing out onto the sand.

My eyes quickly rise to Ajax, standing a little way back. He doesn't appear to have been shaken by it at all, his eyes still calm and intense. Now all eyes turn to him, the giant's included, standing up tall as his mighty blade drips with blood. They stare at each other for a moment, before Ajax begins coolly walking forward.

In his left hand, I see the spear, slowly rising up to firing position. In his right, he's fetched a long dagger, secretly hidden slightly behind his back. I know what he's doing…he's going to use the spear as a diversion.

When he's near enough, only ten or so metres out, his left arm whips through like a striking snake, sending the spear towards Colossus at a frightening speed. The giant's abilities are good enough to see it coming, ducking under it as it flows over his monstrous head.

As he does, however, he takes his eyes off Ajax, who rushes forwards as quick as lightning. By the time the giant's eyes have risen back up, Ajax is there, dagger now ready to slice. Colossus sees it too late, and the blade cuts right across his belly, opening him up.

Colossus drops one hand down to prevent his insides from spilling out, his eyes stark and filled with fear for the first time. And, for the first time, Ajax has shown his full worth to the crowd. They stare, slack jawed, as the young man takes down the beast before their eyes.

And when a second slice of Ajax's dagger cuts through the giant's throat, they begin to roar the name of Scarface, finally giving Ajax the attention he deserves.

He doesn't linger long after his victory, though. In the gallery, I see the maroon cloaked man glaring down at him through slits in his eyes, notably unhappy to have seen him win as Ajax walks off. He comes right towards the door I wait behind, and passes out of the hot sun and into the shadows. There's a cold look on his face as he enters and I congratulate him.

He doesn't raise a smile, his face spattered with blood, and I know exactly why: he's just killed a man for the first time. And even though it had to be done, it's not something he's ever likely to forget.

As I return to the depths with him, however, I know it's time to turn my thoughts to my own fight. As I sit and wait for my name to be called, I look over at the far end of the chamber and see the two masked fighters, Faceless and The Shadow, looking at me. As always, they whisper quietly among themselves, figuring out their plan of attack. It'll be a simple one: disable me by knockout or death, and then battle each other for the honour of going through.

I wonder, though, if either actually want to advance any further. Today it's possible to win by knockout. Tomorrow? Perhaps not. Soon enough, it might just be death or nothing, and with the shadow of Knight's Terror an ever-present threat, losing by knockout at this stage might not be the worst thing.

As I sit and watch them, time whistles by, and soon we're all being called up to enter our passages. They part ways with a final word as Ajax offers me a last minute pep talk. And then, it's back up the tunnel, back into the arena, and back out under the blazing sun.

The crowd roar once again as I enter, my eyes immediately searching for an appropriate weapon nearby. I scan my two opponents and notice that they don't seem to be doing the same. Instead, they're both merely staring at me. I glance again to a set of swords to the right, then back at Faceless. I see him shaking his head slightly, giving me a sign.

*Is he telling me not to get a weapon? Is he telling me that he wants to fight hand to hand?*

When the announcer calls for the fight to begin, I get my answer. Neither Faceless nor The Shadow move for the weapons. They both come towards me instead, raising their hands as if gesturing for me to do the same. For a second I consider going for a sword, but something in their eyes stops me, staring at me through slits in their masks.

I begin moving in towards them instead, all of us making a silent pact to battle to knockout, and not to death.

As we loom closer together in the centre of the arena, I sense the attacks coming. Together as one they spring their trap, one coming from the front, the other slinking behind me and attacking from the rear. They're fast, their fists slashing white across me as the noise of the crowd goes dull in my ears, and I search the Void for their strikes.

It's the closest I've been to both of them, and I realise now how small they are compared to me. I tower above them as they snipe, one going low, the other high, kicking and punching and trying to connect. Mostly, I find myself on defence, but occasionally have the chance to lash out and fire back. When I do, I notice that they see me coming, but not quite as early as I do with them. My fists get near, grazing their cheeks, touching at the fabric of their black masks.

It gives me confidence as the fight goes on. Around me, I begin to hear the crowd rising higher, louder, displeasure echoing around the stadium. They came here today for blood, to see us clash with weapons and armour. These hand to hand bouts are no longer interesting enough. Nothing will satiate them but the sight of blood and cleaved limbs.

But I don't care what they think. If Faceless and The Shadow refuse to use weapons, I'll do the same. Soon, boos are sounding, and trash is being tossed at us. The noise grows more deafening by the second, the atmosphere turning more violent.

And in those moments, I see my chance.

Distracted by the crowd, my opponents begin to

lose focus. I step in and let loose a blistering flurry of attacks, finally connecting and getting through the gate with a heavy hit to Faceless' stomach. And as I do, I hear a grunt, the wind blown from their lungs.

I stop for a second, stunned, and look down at the small frame before me. And suddenly, it makes sense.

The grunt was feminine, high pitched.

*These two aren't men at all.*

I take my chance, and slide right in behind Faceless, my fingers rushing up and pulling away their mask. Shoulder length hair, rich and brown, flows down, eyes of sparkling hazel shine out. I take a step back as the crowd suddenly hushes, a silence descending as I look into the face of a girl, no older than I am.

Her face is small and features pretty, yet her expression harsh and intense. To her side, The Shadow steps, pulling of their own mask and revealing identical features. I shake my head in disbelief.

*Twins…*

The two girls look at me together now, all three of us in a standoff. In the crowd you could hear a pin drop as I hold my hands firmly to my sides. Seeing them now, I know I can't fight them.

My tournament is over.

A few long moments pass without action before, suddenly, the announcer stands and calls loudly:

"You must fight. There must be a winner."

The girls look at each and back at me. I pull my hands behind my back, and nod at them.

"Knock me out," I say. "I won't fight you."

They look confused as to what to do, the crowd now beginning to come back into it. The announcer calls for us to engage again, that we'll all be disqualified if we don't fight.

Once again, the girls share a look, and I see them whispering quietly to each other as they have so many times in the chamber beneath our feet. Then, Faceless turns to me.

"Neither of us can win this tournament," she says, her voice sweet but strong. "But maybe you can…"

Then, just as the announcer calls out again, I see the two girls stand and face each other, raising their fists. Smiles rise on both their faces as they nod and countdown from three to one.

And on one, they both launch their fists at the other's face, knocking each other out. They fall to the sand, eyes going blank, as the crowd watch in stunned silence.

Leaving me alone once more, victorious.

# 25
## Baron Reinhold

That evening, when the world grows quiet in the main chamber, Ajax and I sneak down the passage marked 'H'.

There's no one around, the night late, most of the rooms now lying empty. Only eight remain in the tournament, set to fight again when the sun rises. Today, sixteen contestants were knocked out, over half of them losing their lives in the process.

There are two, however, who didn't. And it's them who we want to talk to.

"Are you sure this is the right one?" I whisper to Ajax as we stop at a wooden door towards the end of the passage.

He nods, but doesn't look certain. "I think so. I followed them, like you said. They definitely were on the right…it's either this one or the next."

We both take a silent breath, and I lightly knock on the door. There's no answer. We wait a second, before trying again. Once more, we hear no sound within.

"Must be the next one," he says.

We step away, moving off a few metres. Then,

behind us, a creaking noise sounds and we turn to see the young face of a girl staring at us. In the darkness, her eyes shine out hazel, yet suspicious.

"What do you want?" she asks.

"To talk," I reply quickly.

She looks down the other end of the passage to see that the coast is clear. Then she nods and steps back inside the room, leaving the door slightly ajar.

We move towards it and creep inside, shutting it quietly behind us. The room is exactly the same as ours, two small beds set up against rocky walls. The girl who let us in goes and sits next to her sister, two identical faces watching us as we enter.

"Can we sit?" I ask.

They nod, and we take a seat opposite them.

They continue to peer at us in the silence, waiting for one of us to speak. It's me who takes the lead.

"I wanted to check if you two were OK," I say. "And…um…we were wondering why you did what you did?"

The girls look at each other, like mirror images, and smile. In the dark, their faces are lights, their intense scowls softening briefly before hardening once more. The girl who let us in is once again the one to talk.

"I said it in the arena," she says. "We were never going to win. We're not here for that…"

Ajax frowns. "Then what are you here for?" he asks.

Her eyes turn to his, but she doesn't answer.

"No one is going to beat Knight's Terror…not even you. You're not strong enough yet," she says.

"How do you know how strong we are?" I ask. "You don't know us."

"Because it's obvious. You're too young. You haven't lived hard lives."

I frown and ask again, getting a little defensive. "What do you know of our lives?"

"We know," says the girl. "We know you're both from Lignum. We know who your parents are. We know your real names are Theo and Ajax. There's a lot we know about you…"

I feel my heart start to race. Her words are strangely unnerving. I turn to Ajax again, but his face is calm.

"How do you know?" he asks.

"Our father…he told us. He knew both your parents well."

"Your father…" I say.

The girl's eyes drop a little, sinking to the rock floor. The faint sign of a welling tear appears but is quickly blinked away. Then, for the first time, the other girl speaks, sitting forward next to her sister.

"Our father is dead," she says. "He was killed not so long ago. His name…his name was Troy."

Now Ajax's face does change. His eyes narrow in the darkness, the silence turning absolute. Then, his voice comes out in a whisper.

"The Master of Petram…"

The girls nod, eyes firming up again.

"We're here to try to find out who killed him," says the second girl. "We didn't come here to win, just to fight…"

My voice comes back to me, surging out a little too loud.

"That's why we're here too," I say quickly. "My grandfather is the President now. He asked us to keep our eyes peeled, to find clues about the assassins."

"Well it looks like we're on the same team then, doesn't it," says the first girl. She reaches out her hand, small and feminine yet worn out and lightly scarred. "My name's Velia, and this is my sister, Vesuvia…"

I take her hand and see her eyes brighten, losing their cloak of distrust. Next to me, Ajax does the same, reaching forward and taking Vesuvia's hand. I see her smile at him, and he turns away, his cheeks visibly blushing even in the darkness.

For the next hour, we enter into quiet discussion, our missions suddenly aligning. We tell briefly of what's been going on since the spate of assassinations and attacks, giving them more background than they knew. They tell us of their lives on the Deadlands, and how the murder of their father set them on this path.

I find it surprising when they tell me they don't

live in Petram.

"We didn't know our father too well," Velia says. "He wasn't with our mother long, but was always good to us. Whenever he came to the West, he'd spend time with us. He wasn't around much, but we loved him all the same."

"So, you live further West than even here?" I ask

"A long way from here, yes. But we know these lands well. We've lived in the desert forever."

"And…did your father train you? Is that how you can see into the Void?"

Velia nods. "He did a bit, when he was around. He invited us to come to Petram to train, but we couldn't leave our mother."

"Petram," says Ajax. "You mean…to train with Athena?"

They nod. "She trained you, didn't she?" says Velia.

"You're perceptive," I say. "We've been training for weeks now."

"It still won't be enough. Not against Knight's Terror. We've known about him for years. Everyone around here knows about him."

"Because of the Watcher Wars?"

"Those…and more," says Vesuvia. "He's been working for Baron Reinhold ever since the end of the war, doing all his dirty work. They rule these lands with an iron fist."

"Baron Reinhold," I whisper, thinking of the man in the maroon cloak. "We saw Knight's Terror with one of the men from the gallery the other night. They looked close, like they knew each other well…"

"Oh, that'll be Baron Reinhold," says Velia. "He's the most feared man across the Deadlands, and the richest too. He pretty much runs all the major crime in the region, running drugs and things like that. Knight's Terror is his attack dog, and he does everything his master asks of him."

"You seem to know a lot about them," says Ajax.

Vesuvia fixes him with a stare. "Like we say, we've lived here all our lives. We know what goes down around here. You wouldn't get it, you're outsiders. Life isn't as easy as over on the regions."

"Well, you do realise that Knight's Wall has been taken down now, right? You can move over there if you want…"

"Yeah, like it's that easy. We were born here, and we'll die here. That's how it is for these people."

Ajax shakes his head, but doesn't say anything. Now isn't the time for such a debate.

"So what, Knight's Terror just comes here for fun or something? I mean, he doesn't seem like he needs the prize money," I say.

"It's not about that," says Velia. "He does it because it makes him even more feared, and that's good for the Baron's business. And, well, the Baron lays bets on him too. I guess, with how dominant he's been, it's pretty much like match fixing."

"One of his many illegal activities," adds Vesuvia. "But he's done so much more. We've been training since we were kids because of what he does to our people. All we want to do is take him down…"

"But…I don't understand," says Ajax. "If your dad was Master of Petram, why didn't he just, I don't know, arrest the guy?"

Vesuvia laughs. "Like it's that easy. Petram's authority doesn't stretch out here…no one's does. This isn't like Eden ruling the regions. That's not how it works. On the Deadlands, it's a free world, always has been. We weren't alive before the war, but we know that it's only gotten worse. What your parents and our father fought for…they thought they were doing good, but not everywhere. Not here."

"Why?" I say quickly. "Why is it worse now?"

"Because there's no common goal now," says Velia. "Before the war, people were united against Eden. Now, what are they fighting for? Nothing, only themselves. People like Baron Reinhold came down here and took over, bringing deadly Watchers with them. A lot of people on Eden didn't exactly profit from Augustus Knight's death, and some have come here and taken charge."

"So you're saying Baron Reinhold was from Eden before?"

"Yeah…he was one of the richest men in the city, and good friends with the Chancellor. Knight's Terror was just a normal Watcher back then, assigned to protect the Baron. When Knight died, he came here…and he brought his bodyguard with him."

"So I guess that's where the reigning champion got his name then. We suspected he was a Watcher over on Eden before…" says Ajax.

"Well, you got that right," chimes in Vesuvia. "We came here because we wanted to see him up close. We never expected to go too far, only to blend in. But now that we're out, the real work begins."

"The real work," I say. "You mean finding out who killed your father?"

They nod together.

"And you think that Baron Reinhold is behind it?"

They continue to nod.

"There are lots of powerful people who lost out when Knight was killed," says Velia. "And we know who they all blame. Your parents were attacked. President Stein and General Richter were killed…and our father too. That's no coincidence. Something's going on here, and we know that the Baron is right in the thick of it."

A sudden noise clatters down the passages outside, breaking the quiet. We stop for a moment and listen as the echoes fade away, before silently continuing.

Velia leans in closer, her voice turning to a barely audible whisper.

"Tomorrow, you'll be fighting again," she says.

"And when you do, the whole world will be distracted. That's our chance…"

"Your chance to do what?" asks Ajax.

"To find proof," whispers Velia, "that the Baron masterminded everything…"

## 26
## A Connection Made

The searing heat of the sun burns down on my neck, high in the sky as the day hits its peak. I glance up and see a slight reflection above me, shining on a thin barrier hanging above the perimeter wall of the arena. It's see-through, but bulletproof, designed to stop any errant bullets from wandering into the crowd.

Today is the penultimate day of the Watcher Wars, and for the first time I see the sight of guns spread before my eyes. Like the previous day, they're affixed to the perimeter wall, an abundant display of options available.

I look forward and see my opponent standing before me, eyes as cold as ice. His face is dark, his head cleanly shaven, tattoos and strange markings littering his skin. Sinewy muscles ripple along his arms and chest, his bare upper body exposed to the elements.

To my left, the sound of the announcer's voice rings out, now so familiar. "This is the penultimate bout of the day," he calls, "between Bear's Bane, and Deathstrike. So far, Knight's Terror and Scarface have been victorious, and have progressed to the final round. Let's see who'll join them!"

The crowd go wild as I stand there, unfazed. Deathstrike, too, appears to be completely detached from the tumult, a quality that Watchers are able to develop. I know, right now, that nothing will affect him. Until I'm dead on the sand, he won't lose his focus.

Today, it's a fight to the death. Already, I've seen Ajax make his second kill, battling through a tough round that saw him come so close to defeat. In the end, he outlasted his opponent, putting a bullet into his heart. Knight's Terror, on the other hand, had no such worries. He tore straight through his opposition, ending it quick before marching back away out of the arena.

And now it's me, sleep deprived and hungry, my mind threatening to waver and drift off elsewhere. After the revelations of the previous night, I've found it hard to concentrate so far today, hard to get pumped up for battle as I usually might.

But now, out here under the screaming crowd, I have no choice but to do what must be done. Today, I'm going to have to make my first kill.

As the announcer calls for the bout to start, and Deathstrike charges straight for an automatic rifle on the nearest wall, my mind turns to my training. I think of the hours spent down there in the training cave under Athena's guidance, sending bullets right at her. She drummed it into us, again and again, that we'd need to get used to firing at another person. That, if it came to it, we'd need to be willing to kill.

Now, my training is going to be put to the test.

And I'm going to find out if I have what it takes…

I'm a little slow off the mark, my mind wandering. As Deathstrike reaches the wall and turns the gun on me, I take a few deep breaths and narrow my mind, focusing on the gun ahead of me. As I do, the stadium fills with white lines, spraying from one side to the other as Deathstrike empties an entire clip right at me.

He's far enough away, right on the other side of the stadium, for me to get away with my slow start. Just in the nick of time, I duck and dodge, several bullets filling in quick and following their white precursors into the rock wall. Bits of stone chip and crack, the bullets fizzing as they chase me around, desperately seeking my flesh and bone.

I duck low, darting to one side to fetch my own weapon, and feel a sharp sting in my left calf. I turn down to see that a bullet has grazed the muscle, cutting through several millimetres deep. It's enough of a wake up call, sending my blood rushing with adrenaline. Around me, things blur further, the crowd's cheers dampening, their faces becoming a mess of colour.

I fetch my own automatic weapon, and swing it up at Deathstrike, finally returning fire. He seems to have no trouble dodging from this range, the two of us quickly entering into a brief stalemate.

Moving left, he drops his gun, and scoops up another. In one move he turns, and as he does the large glow of a white cloud spreads around me at my feet. I roll along the sand to the right, escaping the cloud just as an incendiary projectile comes storming towards me. It enters the white mist and disappears, moments later exploding into a fiery red and orange fog.

I saw it just in time, its burning tendrils unable to catch me, reaching out to lick at my skin. I look up and then see another cloud burst ahead, just before me, and another in front, enclosing me in a deadly vice. In seconds, the entire space will burst into flame, cremating my body right here before the crowd.

I have no choice but to trust I saw it early enough. I rush on, my legs thundering forward, dragging me through the mist and out to the other side. I'm there just in time, the flames starting to burn once more, chasing me down and setting fire to my back.

Quickly, I hit the deck, dropping my body into the sand, and roll over to douse the flames. As I look up, I see Deathstrike coming at me now, closing the gap, a scattergun in his hand. When he pulls the trigger, bullets burst out in all directions, filling a space several metres wide.

Again, I'm just quick enough, moving away and through the gaps, putting some extra distance between us. I'm on the defence, a constant flow of bullets filling the air, Athena's words once more rattling around in my head.

*"Now imagine those knives and spears coming ten times faster,"* she'd said to me. *"And imagine dozens of them coming at you at once. Then you'll have some idea as to what you'll be facing at the*

*Watcher Wars…"*

Her words were prophetic. She knew what we'd be up against if we made it this far. Any Watcher with even minor training can dodge a spear or knife. Dodging dozens, even hundreds of bullets at once is an almost impossible feat.

And that's what I'm contending with now. Shot after shot comes at me, forcing me to stay constantly on the move. I know what Deathstrike is doing. Even if none of these bullets hit, he's wearing me out, making me move and sweat and pant under the hot sun. Soon enough, fatigue will kick in…and when that happens, it's game over.

*I have to turn this around.*

I continue to move away from him, heading towards the nearest set of weapons. Each time, however, he paints the air white with more bullets, spray after spray cutting me off. Then, I get a stroke of luck – his ammo runs out, forcing him to drop the scattergun and pull a handgun from his belt, surging towards the wall to fetch a better weapon as he fires.

After the other weapons, the pistol is a Godsend. With only the odd bullet coming at me, easy to dodge, I'm able to rush to the wall and reach it as he does. On either side of the arena, we fetch more firearms, turn, and begin blasting each other once more.

With honours even now, I feel a fresh surge of hope fill me. *I can win this. I can win…*

Firing relentlessly with a machinegun in one hand,

I pick up another slightly more modern automatic weapon in the other. My finger hits the trigger, and both guns bellow loudly, cutting up the far wall. Deathstrike, having already used the best weapons at that cache, doesn't have as much firepower to defend with.

Inundated with flying bullets, the tables are turned, my adversary having to duck and weave and constantly focus on what's coming. Firing back only sporadically, I begin marching towards him, both guns still rattling away, closing the gap and reducing his time to react.

Soon, however, the older machine gun comes to the end of its clip. I drop it to the floor and hold the newer model in both my hands, it's ammo capacity much greater. I glance down, and that's when I see it: the gun has another attachment.

Quickly flicking a switch, I fire once again, and this time an explosive round shoots out from the tip of a larger barrel. It hits the back wall of the arena, shaking its foundation, fire blazing up and stopping at the bulletproof barrier above.

Smoke starts to spread, and out of it I see Deathstrike, coughing hard and rubbing his eyes. He shoots wildly, his focus lost, as I continue to step forward. He has just enough sense to dodge a few more rounds as I advance, marching confidently now through the sand. But I know now, looking at his red eyes and spluttering mouth, that he's done for.

He comes charging at me wildly, only metres

away now. He turns left and right and swings his fist, but it's inaccurate and manic, a desperation setting in. I swing the butt of the machine gun up as he passes and connect with the side of his head. Hearing a loud crack, he drops straight down to the earth, knocked out cold.

Now, slowly, the sounds of the crowd come back to my ears, rising constantly in my head. My name is once more called and chanted, the people throwing their arms into the air to salute. I look up at them and smile wide, dropping the gun and raising my hands in victory.

And then, over the din, the announcer's voice booms out.

"This fight is not over yet!" he calls. "The battle is to the death…to win, someone has to die."

The crowd quieten again, realising their cheers were premature. They all stare at me, eager to see the finishing blow. Slowly, I walk to the wall and take a pistol in my hand. Holding it to my side, I return to Deathstrike, lying prostrate and helpless at my feet. His tattooed face looks up, eyes shut, blood trickling from one of his ears.

The stadium goes deathly quiet, people breathless with anticipation as I raise the gun and point it at Deathstrike's head. I stare down the barrel, my finger hovering on the trigger, ready to execute this defenceless man. A man I have no hate for, no reason to kill but to satisfy these people.

For several long, drawn out seconds, I stand there taking aim. And gradually, a rumble begins to flow through the crowd, the sound of hundreds of people whispering quietly, their voices building as one.

Once more, the announcer calls out.

"Bear's Bane must finish the job. Deathstrike must be killed…"

I slowly look up into the audience, see their eager faces waiting for the killing stroke, to see the bullet tear into this man's head. But not all are like that. Some show different eyes; compassion for the defeated man.

"Don't do it," I hear. "Let him live…"

Others join in, and soon there's a dissonance among the throng, some baying for blood, others wishing me to show mercy. I scan my eyes across, and in a flashing moment, think I see the face of Athena, hidden amid the mob, her keen eyes staring out from under a cloak. I blink hard and look again, but she's no longer there.

Now, my eyes sweep over to the gallery, and the eyes of Baron Reinhold. He sits there calmly, dressed in his finery, half smiling at me as he watches on. And then, a fresh jolt of excitement swells among the gathered horde, and the eyes of every person in the stadium swing to the sands behind me.

I turn with them, and see the lithe figure of Knight's Terror coming up at my rear, smoothly gliding across the sand dressed in his usual black. The sight causes my body to prime itself for action as I swing around to face him. But his eyes aren't on me. They stare directly at my defeated opponent, lying in the dirt.

He's at my side quickly, and I see his left hand pull up from inside his cloak, bringing a sleek black pistol with it.

"No…" I say as he takes aim.

But there's no delay to his action. Without breaking stride he pulls the trigger and sends a bullet clean through Deathstrike's head.

Only now does he seem to acknowledge my presence. As half the crowd start to cheer, he turns to me with a sickly grin.

"That's how you do it," he grunts in a scratchy, bitter voice.

I feel my body burning at the look on his face, smug and self-satisfied. An arrogance exudes from him, and a hatred too, eyes caught between loathing and disdain.

And with that look, I can't help but act. With a sudden burst, I feel my fist pouring towards him, desperate to wipe that look from his eyes forever. But as my fist comes, his smirk merely deepens, no alarm on his face at all.

As the crowd gasp, he slides left and my fist goes right past him. I stumble forward, losing my footing, and feel the tight grip of his narrow fingers grasping at my throat.

And at his touch, I feel my mind flashing once more, images pouring forward. Everything around me blurs, the sands and crowd and rugged arena fading before my eyes. Instead, my mind becomes filled with broken images I've seen before: the old lab, the shadows in the tubes, the tables covered with utensils.

It's all clearer this time, closer than ever before. And then, more flashes come to me, new sights that I haven't yet seen: a large training room, a compound in the desert hills, armed guards on patrol.

I feel Knight's Terror loosen his grip on my throat, feel him tossing me back onto the sand. I hit the earth with a thud, and gradually everything clears before me again. I look up and see him looming over me, then glance up to Baron Reinhold, staring down from on high.

And suddenly, I know the truth.

The girls were right…and everything is connected. The Baron, Knight's Terror, the desert compound and the old, dilapidated lab.

Everything I saw under the scanner back on Eden has led me to this point.

And now…I know exactly where we need to go.

# 27
## The Secret Compound

Outside, the people gather in celebration, toasting their favourite fighters who have made it to the final. They laugh and drink and dance under the moonlight, excitedly debating what they'll see in the final bout, and who'll come out on top.

There are only three names they're talking about: Knight's Terror, Scarface, and Bear's Bane. No one else is left.

Earlier, the last bout saw the death of both combatants, leaving no one to progress to the final. The two warriors fought long and hard, fighting with guns and blades and even their fists. They cut each other up so badly, inflicting so much damage, that both were declared dead at the scene, lying next to each other in the sand.

And now, because of that, it's down to three. Three fighters who'll battle it out for the crown of Watcher Wars champion. At least, that's what the people thing. Because tomorrow, when the crowd gather for the grand finale, only one fighter will appear out under the blazing sun...

As the party rages outside, Ajax and I sit with Velia and Vesuvia in their room, talking in whispers.

"Did you find anything out?" asks Ajax.

The girls look frustrated. "We barely had a chance. There were guards everywhere and we couldn't get into the Baron's house…"

"It doesn't matter," I say sharply, cutting off Velia. "I know where we need to go, although I don't know exactly where it is."

"That's not helpful, Theo," says Velia. "What exactly are you talking about?"

"When Knight's Terror touched me out there, I saw something…something I've seen before in my visions. I didn't know where it was at first, but now I do…"

"What? What did you see?"

"There's a lab, hidden somewhere in a compound in the desert. It's gotta be Baron Reinhold's stronghold. He's been busy out there…and we need to know what he's been up to."

I scan the girls' eyes: Velia's hazel and bright; Vesuvia's a little darker, one with shades of blue. It's the only way of telling them apart.

"We know where it is," says Velia. "It's deep in the desert, up in the hills…and well protected."

"How far?" I ask quickly.

"A hundred miles, maybe more," she says.

I look to Ajax, then back at the girls, and lean in closer. They all follow me, the four of us joining into a tighter huddle.

"We need to leave…tonight," I say. "We can get there before dawn and find out what's going on without Knight's Terror around. He'll be here for the final. I'm happy for him to win by default."

"Me too," says Ajax. "I don't much like the idea of fighting him anyway."

The girls smile, and begin nodding.

"Do you know how to get there?" I ask them.

"Like we told you, we know this desert like the back of our hands. We can get you there."

I put my hand between us, and one by one they add theirs.

"Then we go tonight," I say. "When the party fades, we'll sneak away out of sight. Be ready…we'll come for you."

I stand and move to the door, Ajax following behind me. Outside, it's deathly silent down the passages and main chamber, all but a few of the fighters having gone. Only a handful remain, like the girls, wanting to watch the final bouts after being knocked out.

We sneak off back to our own room, the others down our passage completely unoccupied, and shut the door tight. And as the party continues outside, we begin to pack up our things and prepare to leave.

"I'll be happy to get out of this place," says Ajax, stuffing his bag with clothes. "I hate it down here…and the people up there. They're sick, finding all this bloodshed entertaining."

"I think it's just the custom out here," I say. "They grow up with it, and are used to it."

"But can you imagine seeing this sort of thing in Lignum. The people wouldn't stand for it."

I nod, agreeing with him, the mention of Lignum having a strange effect on me. I think of the trees and rivers and lakes, the sounds of birds and beasts in the woods. The greens and brown and cool night air in the winter, so different from this stark and desolate dustbowl.

"Do you miss it?" I ask. "Home, I mean?"

He stops packing and looks at me. I see his dark eyes swimming with memory of the place we grew up, and a small smile lift in the corners of his mouth.

"Sometimes," he says. "When I stop and think about it. I don't know, all we wanted was adventure…and now we've got it, it doesn't feel like I thought it would. This is bigger than us, Theo. Sometimes I just want to go home and live a simple life again."

I move over and lay my hand on his shoulder. "Me too, AJ," I say. "Maybe when this is over, we can do just that."

We return to our packing, which doesn't take long, before sitting and waiting for the opportune moment to make our escape. I fix my hunting knife to my belt along with the extendable blade Athena gave me. Over on the other bed, Ajax fiddles with his, clicking the button and extending the two ends of the spear, before retracting it. He repeats the sequence over and over as we wait, the sounds of the party outside the arena beginning to slowly die down.

Soon, only a few lingering voices remain, fading away one by one. We creep out into the chamber and up to the main tunnel entrance. Outside, the place is quiet, the people having returned to their tents and mobile accommodations for the night. Here and there, a few drunken stragglers sit in the dirt, swigging on whiskey and wine until their heads drop to the sand. We watch, scanning the space, before deciding that the time is now.

We go back down to our rooms to fetch our bags. Then, we quietly creep down passage 'H', knock on the girls' door, and wait for them to appear. Dressed in desert cloaks as we are, they step out with bags on their backs, eyes shining under their hoods.

"Ready?" I ask them.

"Always," says Velia with a smile.

I lead them on, back down the passage, through the main chamber, and up the tunnel towards the exit. Once more, we hover in the shadows and look out, checking if the coast is clear. I turn to the others.

"OK, looks good. We need to get our bikes, they're over in the storage pen. Follow me, and stay quiet."

Keeping low, we sneak from shadow to shadow,

moving right around the arena and away from the main sea of tents. A little way away, the main gate through the mesh fence remains guarded, a couple of men posted there overnight. Their eyes stare out, however, and not in, allowing us to sneak across the camp unseen.

Soon, we're at another fenced off area. Inside, a large number of cars and bikes and other forms of transport sit, parked across the sand. We begin moving around the fencing until we reach the area filled with bikes, scanning them for some sight of ours.

"We need to get in," I say, taking out my extendable blade.

The girls look at me with confusion as I hold up the sleek black gip. Then, I click the button on its underside once, and the razor sharp dagger comes surging out.

"Wow…where'd you get that!" asks Vesuvia, her two-coloured eyes bulging.

"Athena gave it to me. Ajax has a spear version."

She looks at Ajax. "Can I see it?"

He looks a little unsure at first, but passes the handle to her. "You've gotta tap the button…" he starts, but she's way ahead of him. The spear shoots out quickly, almost catching her sister who jumps back just in time.

"Careful! Jeez, Vesuvia…"

"Sorry," she says, eyeing the beautiful blade. "It's gorgeous."

"And lethal," says Ajax, taking it back. "Check this out." He clicks the button twice, and the other end of the spear extends. Then, holding it down, they disappear just as quick.

Vesuvia turns to her sister. "Maybe we should have gone to train with Athena if that's what you get," she says. It's pretty obvious that Vesuvia and Ajax share a mutual love of spears.

My voice cuts back in, bringing their focus back to the task at hand.

"Are you guys done?" I ask. "Come on, we need to find those bikes."

Using my dagger, I turn back to the wire mesh fence and begin slicing through it, creating an opening big enough for us, and a pair of bikes, to get through. It's the first time I've actually tested my weapon, and it doesn't disappoint.

"That thing is *sharp!*" whispers Velia. "That was like cutting warm butter."

Unlike her sister, she appears more taken with my blade.

I pull apart the fence, and through we go, entering the vehicle pen. Immediately, Ajax and I begin scouring the many bikes, searching for the ones Athena gave us. It's hard, many of them looking so alike, but before long we manage to find them.

Silently, we begin rolling them over the sand, the girls pulling apart the fence for us to get through. When we're out, we put the fence back in order as best we can before continuing through the camp and towards the outer perimeter. When we reach the main fence, we go through the same motion, cutting it apart before sneaking out of the site altogether.

I let out a breath as we look out over the endless desert, the night comparatively cool after the sweltering day. Above us, the moon glows bright, and black sky littered with stars. They shine down, illuminating our path ahead, the desert tundra rolling into the far distance, peppered with canyons and large rocky outcrops.

For a little while, we walk the bikes out, moving away from the site. The arena begins to get smaller, becoming nothing but a silhouette against the night sky as we stretch away from it, putting enough distance between us so the engines on our bikes won't be heard. When we're far enough away, hidden behind some rocks, we climb on and set our sights ahead.

Behind me, Velia sits, her arms gripping tight around my chest. I can feel her breath on my neck, warm in the cool air, sending sharp tingles down my back.

I turn my head back to her, and see those hazel eyes lighting in the dark.

"You sure you know the way?" I ask.

She smiles.

"Do you not trust me, Theo Kane?"

"After the time we've had, it's hard to trust anyone right now," I laugh.

She nods ahead, straight at the dark shadow of a

large mountain in the distance. "That way," she says. "Head for that mountain for starters."

I turn back and kick the bike into gear, its engine chugging lightly in the quiet night. Next to us, Ajax does the same, Vesuvia wrapped up behind him. And then, slowly, we begin grinding off into the desert.

Under cover of darkness, with the rest of the world sleeping, we sneak off across the sand, slowly at first, then faster as we speed away from the arena. Soon enough, we've put enough distance between us, and are able to push the engines a little harder. They grumble loudly into the night as our eyes grow accustomed to the darkness. Thankfully, the sky above is clear, no barrier of cloud blocking the glowing moon. It swamps the desert floor with a cool glow as we rush along, the flowing breeze causing our jackets to billow behind us.

Out here, it's hard to gauge distance, little perspective given in the darkness. It takes us a while to reach the mountain, looming larger as each minute passes. By the time it towers over us, casting its base in shadow, we're many miles from the arena and making good progress. I look back and see that it's no longer visible on the distant horizon, never to be seen again. At least that's what I hope.

At the mountain, we stop briefly as the girls confer and determine our route. Then, they climb back onto the bikes behind us and tell us which landmark to head for next.

Stage by stage, we cross the desert, the world

growing increasingly mountainous as we go. Around us, higher mounds of earth begin to form, small settlements appearing at their tips. Velia talks to me in my ear, shouting over the racket and teaching me about the lands she knows so well.

"People live up in those peaks," she says. "That's how it always is around here…the people live high or low. Either up in the mountains or down in the canyons; anywhere where they can escape the heat."

"And what about you?" I ask. "Where do you live?"

"Closer to the coast in the West. It's a little cooler that way near the sea. Maybe you'll see it sometime," she says after a short delay.

"If we get out of this alive, then it's a deal," I call.

Her hand comes forward, small and yet tough, her skin rough from many years in the sun. It's the hand of a worker. The hand of a fighter. I take it in mine, and she shakes.

"Deal," she whispers, her lips close to my ear.

Soon, we're stopping again and taking a short break. We pass around our water bottles as the girls search the horizon and look up into the night sky, using the stars for guidance.

"We're getting there," says Velia. "The Baron's compound isn't too far now."

As we continue our journey, I ask Velia how she knows exactly where the compound is.

"I would have thought it would be secret," I say.

"You know, hidden away somewhere?"

"It is to most, but with a father like Troy, I guess we found out a few things."

"But you haven't been there?"

"Not personally, no. But don't worry, we'll find it."

We drive for hours that night, cutting across the desert and gradually rising up into the low valleys. The mountains here aren't like those around Petram, not as grand or spectacular. They're smaller, and yet wider, stretching for miles in every direction, long swathes of space in between the peaks. As we climb, more vegetation appears, shadows of trees and thickets in the darkness. We move through them, getting ever closer, the moon's journey across the sky gathering pace.

Soon, it'll be dawn, and our escape from the arena will be discovered. We need to act fast, only a small window of opportunity available to us. Because when the Baron realises what we're up to, he'll come right after us with everything he's got.

Winding through the valleys, Velia leads us deep into the seclusion of the desert hills. We keep our eyes peeled, slowing as we draw near. Then, to my left, I see Ajax gesturing so something ahead. We slow down and stop for a moment.

"Tracks," he says sharply.

Written into the earth, tyre tracks lead off right, moving through a gap between two large boulders. Slowly, we follow them, quietening the engines on our bikes as we roll along the dirt. We reach the gap, and go round the corner, and ahead see a large open space, covered on all sides by tall hills and jagged rocks.

And in that space, the shapes of buildings appear, stretching left and right, a grand compound hidden away in the hills.

And as we stop and look, the faintest signs of dawn begin to appear, a red glow rising behind us.

"Let's hide the bikes, quick," I say. "We have no time to lose…"

## 28
## Shrine to Evil

As the tiniest glow of dawn begins to rise, we take in the compound ahead and quickly discuss a plan of action. Hidden amid some low shrubbery, we all search for movement, and immediately spot several guards on patrol.

At certain points, some are motionless, looking out ahead from the front gate. At others, armed men wander casually down certain routes, tasked with keeping an eye on a certain way in. There appear to be a half dozen in all, with who knows how many in the house or currently out of sight.

When we've had a good look, we crawl back and begin figuring out the best route in.

"OK, the way I see it we have two options," I say. "Either go in hard and fast or try to sneak past them and get in without anyone noticing."

"Hard and fast I say," says Ajax. "Take them out and then we can search in peace."

Vesuvia is shaking her head.

"OK, what's your idea?" asks Ajax a little sharply.

"Well, we don't know who these guards are. They might be Watchers. Sure, if they were just normal guards, maybe we could take them out. But if they're Watchers then we'll have a proper fight on our hands. I say take the stealth option."

I look at Velia. "Over to you…"

"I agree with Vesuvia. Let's go in quiet. We can take out anyone if we need to, and slip past the rest."

"Sorry AJ, but I agree with the twins. Let's play this one safe, but quick."

We take another minute or two to figure out the way in. By the looks of things, the space is littered with low areas of bush around the perimeter near the hills, allowing us to sneak around to the rear. That looks to be our only option.

Silently, we begin moving, stopping at any point if a guard glances over in our direction. The compound, however, is far enough away, and the night still dark enough, for us to make decent progress. Hidden under the shadow of the hills, the dawn is delayed, giving us an extra few precious minutes to make our move.

We sneak round to the left, going from bush to bush, hiding behind rocks and anything else we can find to give us cover. We see vehicles as we go, many of them parked together, fitted with turrets and gun placements. Other outbuildings appear to be stock rooms for weapons and ammo, the Baron rich enough to own a private army. Elsewhere, larger warehouses appear to be used for drug production, the lands here being flooded with various narcotics in recent years.

I quickly think back to the ravenous crowd in the arena, and the wild parties they held at night. It was probably more than alcohol that gave them such a lust for blood.

Through we go, sneaking now between the external buildings, dodging the sight of cameras as they watch over any parts unpatrolled by guards. We use our Watcher senses as we advance, one of us always able to know just where an unseen camera might be, or which direction a patrolling guard might be coming from. And inch by inch, we move in until the sight of the main estate appears, hidden behind a wall.

"It's in there somewhere," I say. "The lab."

"How do you know?" asks Velia.

"I saw it in my vision. It was inside the main house, hidden somewhere at the back. Come on."

Together, we rush across the short space, stopping up against the stone wall. Over the other side, we hear the sound of voices, guards passing by. We wait a moment until they're gone before the girls help boost Ajax and I up. Then we turn, lean down, and pull them over, the four of us dropping quietly to the other side.

Stooping low in the shadows, we continue to focus, searching for danger. Our eyes dart between one another. We know the coast is clear.

Ahead, the main house sits, spread out wide and low. Along its extremity, various windows allow easy passage inside. We move towards one right at the rear, tucked up against the tall hills, and I slip out my trusty extendable dagger.

"Let's hope it cuts glass as easy as wire," I say, slicing it across the surface of the window.

It glides through, hardly making a sound, as I chop a hole big enough to fit my arm through. As I'm about to reach in and open the lock, Ajax's arm pulls me back.

"There's an alarm…I can feel it," he says, eyes closed and face scrunched up.

With his eyes still tightly shut, he begins feeling along the wall near the window, searching for something. The girls and I share a look that suggests none of us know what he's up to. Then, suddenly, he pulls out his spear, pressing the button once to extend it, and thrusts it straight at the wall.

"What the…" I say.

He raises his hand to cut me off. "Try it now…open the lock," he says.

I move back to the window and tentatively reach in, opening up the lock. The window swings open, and no alarm sounds. When we climb into the room, I see why. There, cut right through by Ajax's spear, is an electronic sensor, completely disabled.

"Impressive," says Vesuvia. "How'd you know it was there?"

Ajax shrugs. "I felt it. It was nothing, really…"

Vesuvia laughs at his attempt at modesty. It's not something Ajax is very good at.

"OK, so now what?" asks Velia.

I look around the room. It's large and fitted with bookcases and filing cabinets and tables.

"Looks like a good place to start," I say. "Get searching."

We spread out, zeroing in on anything that jumps out at us. I find myself at a filing cabinet, sifting through documents and personnel files. The Baron seems to have information on everyone, from his guards to his drug cooks to his maids and servants. There's nothing of interest here, and the others have little more luck.

Outside, the light begins to grow brighter, the world waking. We decide to call it quits in that room and move to the next, walking down a short corridor right to the back of the house. We enter, and find a dead end, the door the only way in and out.

It's dim in the room, only the light from behind us giving any illumination. Velia finds a switch on the wall and flicks it, bringing a bright yellow glow to our new surroundings. And as the room lights up, so do our eyes.

"Wow," whispers Vesuvia, staring at the walls.

Everywhere, pictures fill the space, hanging on the walls and set up on tables. On them, we see the face of the Baron, but not as he is today. He's younger, the sides of his hair less grey, his face less wrinkled. His skin, too, isn't as tanned, his clothing less colourful. The reason becomes immediately apparent.

Because with him in each picture, I see the face of Augustus Knight, staring at us through cold grey eyes in deep, dark sockets. His face is plastered all over the room, those emotionless eyes watching us from all angles. Many of the pictures feature him and the Baron from his time on Eden before the war. Many others are purely dedicated to the High Chancellor himself.

"What is this place," whispers Velia.

I look at the face of evil on the wall, at a large portrait of the man who once ruled Eden, and shake my head. "It looks like some sort of shrine," I say.

"He worships him," says Ajax, looking around. "As if he's some sort of God."

"The devil more like," growls Vesuvia. "Evil people worship the devil."

We move around the room, staring at the dozens of images of the ex Chancellor, long since deceased. But it's not just pictures that we see. There are figures too, mini statues set up on tables and in corners, books dedicated to the man who caused such pain and suffering. Everywhere, the achievements of the man are documented, programs that ended up killing hundreds of thousands, maybe even millions, celebrated.

"This place makes me sick," says Ajax. "What's the Baron trying to do, emulate him or something?"

None of us have the answer. We continue to drift from place to place, forgetting suddenly that the light is growing outside. Then, over on the far wall opposite the door, I hear Velia speak, her voice drawing our eyes.

"There's a draught..." she whispers. "I can feel air coming through."

I rush over and the others follow. Her hands glide along the bricks, her eyes shut tight. I reach out, and my fingers follow hers, and the slightest caress of moving air touches at their tips.

"She's right! It's hollow behind this wall." I look up, my eyes searching for a switch. "There's gotta be a hidden door. Find the switch."

With no time to waste, we begin moving more hurriedly now, a sudden urgency driving us on. We spread out, feeling around for a switch or button or lever. I take a step back, and scan the wall and its surroundings as the others continue to rush. And as I stand there, I find my eyes drawn up towards a candleholder on the wall, set within a glass case and in the shape of a figurine.

I step towards it and inspect it closely, and see the cold face of Augustus Knight looking back at me once again. My hand reaches up, and I open the case, slipping my fingers around Knight's body. And when I pull down, the figure comes too, and I hear a loud click sound to my left.

Everyone stops, staring at the wall. A brief but heavy silence falls. Then, with a puff of dust and a low, grinding sound, the wall begins to slide to one side, revealing a dark tunnel beyond.

We all look at each other, one to the next, our eyes widening as the hidden passage is revealed.

And then, together, we all step into the darkness.

# 29

## The Seekers of Knight

We're running now, down into the gloom, our keen eyes watching ahead for any pitfalls. The tunnel is wide, though, and rectangular, not rocky like the passages at the arena or in Petram. We reach a set of stairs, and move down deeper, before continuing straight on, the walls fitted with little lights that glow and give shape to the space ahead.

Soon, we're coming to a set of double doors, large and metal. There's a lock in the middle, thick blocks seemingly opened by a key. Once more, my razor sharp blade proves its worth, cutting through the metal and allowing us entry. Ajax steps forwards, pushing the doors open, and ahead we see a circular room, small and empty, fitted only with three doors: one directly ahead, one to the left, and one to the right.

We step inside, leaving the double doors open.

"We should split up," says Velia. "We'll cover more ground."

A sense of foreboding reaches me, the place feeling so familiar now. Somewhere, perhaps through one of these doors, is the lab I've seen in my visions, the place we're here to find.

My eyes scout forward, at the door directly ahead. I begin moving straight towards it, as Ajax goes left, and the girls go right. We reach the handles simultaneously, and pull down. All of the doors open, revealing their secrets beyond.

I look forward into the darkness, and see what I saw in the arena, when my mind flashed at the touch of Knight's Terror. Ahead, a sprawling training room stretches, spreading left and right and far into the distance. It's dim, but I can make out the shapes of weapons stocked on the walls, dummies positioned here and there, other equipment used to develop fitness and endurance.

"It's a training room for Watchers," I whisper to myself.

It must be where Knight's Terror continued to hone his skills after he fled with the Baron from Eden, when they came out here to the Deadlands and started taking over. Everything here – the equipment and weaponry and the size and scale of the room – is far greater than what Ajax and I had in Petram.

I continue peering forwards, and see the shape of a door at the back wall. I make a move to go towards it, but am halted by the sound of the girls coming back out of the room on the right.

"What is it?" I ask.

"It's…accommodation. There are beds lined up against the walls, like a military barrack."

"Accommodation? But for who?"

We don't get a chance to figure out an answer. From the left room, we hear Ajax's voice calling. "You guys better come look at this," he shouts.

In a flash, we're darting over towards the room and rushing inside. My eyes take in the interior. Tables are set up here and there, with filing cabinets on the walls. It looks almost like a classroom, notes and books and records everywhere.

Ajax stands over by one table, his eyes staring down at various documents littered all over it.

"We wanted confirmation that the Baron was behind all this," he says. "Well, we got it…"

Over on the table, I see pictures of people and places: President Stein, General Richter, Troy and my parents, Ellie, Link, Markus, Athena…all of their faces appear before me. There are notes on them: where they live, their ages, information about their lives. I see schematics for Petram and Fort Warden and Eden, even maps of the woods around where I live.

"This is where they planned it all," says Ajax. "They have information on everyone…even us."

He looks up at me and hands me a file with my name on it. I take a quick look inside and see that they have extensive notes on me, page after page with details about my life.

"OK, we've hit the jackpot here," I say. "Fan out…we might find more planned attacks."

I know time is running out now. Over at the Watcher Wars, someone might well have figured out that we're gone. As soon as they do, the Baron's going to suspect that something's up, and we don't exactly want to be here when he gets back.

Files are searched quickly, all of us moving from table to table, cabinet to cabinet, to try to hunt down any clues of where the next attack might take place. Mostly, however, we find only the plans for the first wave, all neatly coordinated and masterminded from this room.

Then, I hear Velia calling me over from a cabinet in the far corner.

"This one's locked," she says. "Theo, help me out will you?"

I rush over and cut the lock with my knife, as Velia pulls open the doors. Unlike the others, this one's dusty, stale air pouring out. It's as if it hasn't been opened in years.

At the bottom, a metal box sits alone. I pick it up and place it on a nearby table, before opening up the lid. Inside, I see a single file, thick and discoloured, and across the front are stamped the words: "The Seekers of Knight."

I open the file, and on the first page, see yet another picture of Augustus Knight. It's the same portrait picture that hangs in the room up above us, his sleek grey eyes looking at me from beyond the grave.

"It's all about him," whispers Velia. "Even after 20 years, it's still about him…"

Across the room, Ajax and Vesuvia continue to

ransack and pillage, searching for information. As I look up at them, I feel Velia's hand on mine, shutting the file.

"We can look at that later," she says. "I think we should get out of here." There' an intensity in her eyes that puts me on edge. As if, maybe, she can feel someone coming…

"I shake my head. There's one more thing I need to see."

"What?"

"The lab. I know it's down here, and I know I go there…I've seen it in my visions. I have to know what it is."

"But where is it? There are only three doors down here."

I shake my head. "There are four. I saw one at the end of the other room. I'm going…"

I begin to move off as Velia shuts the file tight and tucks it under her arm.

"Where are you going?" asks Ajax as I rush past.

"The lab," I say. "I've gotta see this lab…"

I begin moving faster, going through the door, across the circular room, and straight into the large training hall. As I start jogging through, I hear the footsteps of the others behind me, all following me into the gloom. The place is cavernous and vast, our steps echoing as we go. Soon, out of the darkness on the back wall, the shape of the door appears.

I feel my heart racing as we approach, my hand

shaking as I reach for the handle and pull down. As the door creaks open, the caustic smell of chemicals flows up my nose, pouring from a corridor beyond. We step in and begin moving down a short interconnecting tunnel, before reaching yet another door.

I know that this is it, the final one. I know what's beyond it.

I open it up, and step inside, the place lighting up bright as I enter. Above, lights blaze on the ceiling, some of them broken, other flickering. The place appears dank, not like the other rooms, unused for years and growing stale. I scan the large facility as the visions I've had come to life before me; the tables with utensils, the medical and science equipment and machinery, the large tubes, fixed against the far wall.

My eyes swing around the room briefly but focus on the tubes, and the shadows inside. I inch forward, my breath caught inside my lungs and unwilling to leave, staring at the strange chambers as I go. They're filled with dark green liquid, pipes running out of them, long defunct electronic screens at their base.

But it's the shadows that interest me most. I move towards them, and they begin to take shape, and my heart starts to thud even harder. The tubes are covered in dust and grime, obscuring my view. I reach out and wipe my hand across…

And right before my eyes, I see two others staring back.

Within the tube, the face of a boy looks out, grey eyes staring, empty and lifeless. Behind me, I hear one of the girls gasp at the sight, at the child, barely seven or eight years old, floating motionless within the sickly green liquid.

I step back, and turn my eyes to the next tube, wiping my hand across it. More eyes stare, the same as the first, an identical face looking out with a blank expression.

To my left and right, I look and see the same. Boy after boy, all the same, preserved inside their chambers. But not all are filled with green liquid. Not all are filled with shadows. As I look at them, several stick out, different from the others.

Empty of liquid. Empty of shadows.

Behind me, I hear Velia whispering, her voice brittle.

"What is this place?"

I turn to her, and now it's my eyes that are blank. "It's a facility," I say.

She looks at me, eyes stark. "A facility for what?"

I turn back to the face of the nearest boy and look into his empty eyes.

"A facility for growing clones…"

# 30
## Legacy

"Mini Knights," whispers Ajax. "They've been cloning Augustus Knight."

My mind searches back to the day of President Stein's funeral, to the description of the assassin who killed him. Tall and graceful, dark hair and thin lips, keen grey eyes. It had reminded my mother of a shadow from her past, of High Chancellor Knight, and now I know why.

It was his clone.

I look again at the empty chambers, and see that there are four. Only four that survived, the others all dead in front of us. They must have been training down here since they were kids, living in this subterranean prison. Turned into weapons.

Ajax's eyes are also staring at the chambers, his head starting to nod.

"Four…" he says. "Four clones survived. It makes perfect sense."

"What do you mean?" asks Vesuvia.

"There were four targets," I say. "President Stein, General Richter, your father, and my parents. Four targets, four assassins…four clones."

"My father battled one of them," says Ajax. "We were there, we saw it happen. The guy was powerful…strong enough to go toe to toe with him."

"And the others…they managed to infiltrate Eden and Petram and Fort Warden, all of them by themselves. It makes so much sense now. Knight was the most powerful Watcher ever. If they have his genes, then who knows what they could do."

I look at Velia, at the file tucked under her arm, and quickly march over to her.

"The Seekers of Knight," I say. "It's gotta be about these clones. We have to get this file to Drake immediately."

Together, we all turn and begin moving towards the door, rushing off down the tunnel. At the end, a light shines down from the training room.

*But we never put the lights on…*

As we reach the open door and burst through, I look upon the giant hall, now bathed in a bright yellow glow. I squint at the sudden brightness and shield my eyes. And through the cracks in my fingers, I see the shapes of two men in the distance, standing near the far doorway.

"Well, well, well," comes a voice, echoing from the distant wall. "I must say, I am impressed by all of you. You have been busy, haven't you?"

I blink hard, my vision clearing, and there I see the form of Baron Reinhold ahead of us, dressed in his dark maroon cloak. And next to him, lithe and adorned in black, stands Knight's Terror, a smirk on his gaunt face.

The two of them begin walking towards us, moving deeper into the hall. I see the Baron hold up his arms ahead of him in a mocking gesture of surrender.

"Well, you got me," he says sarcastically. "You found our little secret…"

"You're cloning Knight," Vesuvia shouts. "You're obsessed with him. You're mad!"

His laughter rumbles towards us, bursting from his lungs.

"Madness is but a point of view, dear girl. I'd say what all of your parents did was madness. Changing this country from what it was…that was madness. Why would you alter such a perfect system? I'd call that madness."

"Perfect," shouts Ajax. "You think *that* was perfect?!"

"Oh yes, it *was* perfect. We had the perfect city, and the perfect country, and the perfect *leader*. And now we have none of that, thanks to your parents, and Aeneas Stein and Drake Drayton and all of the rest. Of course, some of them have got their comeuppance already," he says coldly. "Oh that was a wonderful day. I've had to wait so long for it…"

I feel Velia and Vesuvia brimming with fury beside me, their chests heaving and eyes burning.

"Don't react," I whisper calmly.

I take Velia's hand, and her eyes come to mine.

"Don't react," I repeat.

I see them soften a little, her breathing starting to calm. She turns to her sister and takes her hand, doing the same as I did.

"Well isn't this sweet. Look at you all, so young, so ignorant. You truly have no idea what's coming your way."

He laughs again, his attack dog at his side, staring at us through black sockets.

"It wasn't you then," I call out. "Knight's Terror…such a frightening name. We were sure that you were one of the assassins. But no, a bunch of boys like me were sent out instead. You were probably too scared in case you ran into Athena, I suppose."

I see those black sockets fire up, the furnace inside them burning. Baron Reinhold holds out an arm to stop him from charging.

"That's it…down boy," I say.

"I'm not sure that's wise, young Theo," calls the Baron. "You've seen just what he can do in the arena."

"Yeah, fighting substandard Watchers. I'd love to see him quiver in the face of Athena or Link. They'd slaughter him with one hand tied behind their backs."

Velia turns to me with hooded eyes.

"What the hell are you doing!" she whispers harshly. "You're going to get us all killed."

"Trust me, he's gonna try to kill us anyway. I'm trying to make him mad…if he loses focus, we might just stand a chance."

She seems to understand, and decides to get in on the act.

"You were probably too scared of Troy as well," she shouts suddenly. "Our father would have torn you to shreds."

The Baron's eyes fix on her, turning things back on us.

"Ah yes, the prodigal twins," he says. "I've had my eye on you for some time. Did you think those silly outfits fooled me in the arena? I knew who you were all along."

"Why do you care so much, anyway?" calls Velia, ignoring his gibe. "You have more power out here than you ever did on Eden. You were nothing to Knight…"

"What do you know of it," the Baron bites, his voice turning raspy. "Eden was my home…and now I have to live out here in the dust and heat. Augustus was a great man, and your parents ruined everything."

He takes a deep breath, and I see his face calm again, his composure regained.

"But great men always leave a legacy, and soon you'll find out just how destructive Augustus Knight's legacy will be. He was never going to let his death stop him. Soon, all of you will be dead, and the world will turn to ash…"

A silence follows his words, the air so tight and tense it could be cut straight through with a knife. I glance at my companions, bodies fixed in place, eyes searching the sides of the walls for weapons. I can see Knight's Terror itching to attack, just waiting for his master's command.

Baron Reinhold takes a couple more steps forwards, peering at us from the distance.

"I see you've found my file," he says. "Do you understand what it means?"

None of us answer. He takes another step.

"It means the Watchers are dead. These clones don't watch for danger and pain and suffering...they seek it out. They inflict it. They have been bred for a single purpose, to see out the final wishes of their father..."

"And what's that?" I ask.

"To tear this world of yours down. If Augustus cannot have it, then no one can...his Seekers will see to that."

He smiles coldly, and takes a step backwards, eyes still on us. Then, I watch as he turns to Knight's Terror, and speaks quietly, his words drifting towards us in the silence.

"You have five minutes," he says. "Take them out quick."

Then he turns back to us, and dips his head.

"Goodbye, children," he says. "Know that I am only a messenger. I will take no pleasure in your deaths."

"Why are you doing this!?" shouts Vesuvia.

"Because it is my duty," he says, "to carry out my master's wishes…"

With that, he nods at Knight's Terror, turns and steps out of the room, leaving us alone with a monster.

We turn to each other, eyes gritty and jaws firmly clenched shut.

"We go for weapons," whispers Ajax. "All of us, as one."

We all nod, and as we're about to separate, the raspy voice of Knight's Terror fills the room.

"You didn't face me in the arena," he growls, eyes manic now as he comes forward. "But down here there's no escape. It's just a shame that there's no one to see you fall…"

And as he walks towards us, red lights around the room start flashing, and a loud voice reverberates from all four corners as a siren starts to blare.

"Five minutes to self destruction."

The countdown is on.

# 31
## Countdown

The four of us split, rushing towards the side walls as the huge training cave echoes with the sound of an alarm. It beeps incessantly and loudly, red flashing lights pouring down from the high ceiling.

I move left with Velia, charging straight at a collection of automatic weapons on the wall. I glance up as we go, and see Knight's Terror coming straight at me, eyes glinting red as they catch the light. I scoop up a gun, turn it on him, and immediately start to fire. Next to me, Velia does the same, our guns chattering loudly as they spew out a deadly barrage of bullets.

Across the room, two more guns explode into life, Ajax and Vesuvia firing at our enemy from another angle as he comes forward. The bullets crisscross in front of us, creating an almost impenetrable barrier. *Almost…*

I watch in awe as Knight's Terror makes his way through the barrage, his lithe and agile frame able to sneak past bullets better than most. Like Athena, he's well built for such a thing, able to get through gaps that Link or Drake would struggle with due to their size.

Soon, he's coming right at us, rushing up onto me and throwing his lightning fast fist towards my jaw. I see it coming just in time and duck through the attack just as he swings a pistol from his cloak.

He brings it right up to my head, about to fire, as Velia rushes in and knocks his arm away. Across the room, the others stop firing as we tangle together, unwilling to send bullets our way.

Instead, they come dashing forward, Ajax's powerful body eating up the ground like a charging bear. He gets to us first, joining the fray and adding his meaty fists to the fight. Soon, Vesuvia has completed our quartet, all of us surrounding Knight's Terror in a vice as we swing our fists right at him.

He moves like a snake, flashing this way and that, his motion so fluid. I'm reminded of when Ajax and I began fighting Athena in the training cave, unable to touch her and never getting near. Athletic and flexible, he's able to contort his motion and weave through our attacks, sending out his own in sudden strikes.

One hits Vesuvia in the stomach, knocking her back and onto her knees. I see the flash of anger in her sister's eyes as she darts in too close and gets the same treatment. Wheezing together on the floor, the girls catch their breath before rushing to grab more weapons nearby, scooping up swords and coming back in.

But Knight's Terror is alert to the danger, alert to everything. He slides through a gap between us and moves away, firing at us with his pistol as he goes. We duck through the bullets in pursuit, chasing him down as he heads towards a weapons cache on the wall. As he does, the voice sounds again from all corners of the room.

"Four minutes to self destruction."

He reaches the weapons and scoops up a machine gun, spraying the room with bullets. Now it's our turn to duck and weave as we advance on him, our progress slowed.

"Fight us like a man you coward," I shout as I come, trying to goad him once more.

I see his eyes burn as he drops the gun to the floor. He begins walking towards Ajax and I, the girls a little way behind with their blades. We meet in a clash of fists, his speed rising with every attack. Up close, he turns to a blur, catching me with a hit to the chin. I clatter backwards, my head spinning as the girls rush past me, screaming like warriors as they slice down with their swords.

A mist descends briefly over my eyes as my brain settles inside my skull. In front of me, bodies are tossed this way and that, the girls dealt with easily. Ajax puts up more of a fight, causing Knight's Terror a few problems with his speed and strength.

But it's not enough. Soon, we've all been sent to our backs, blood dripping from split lips and cut eyebrows. Knight's Terror stands above us all, panting slightly as the voice calls once more: "Three minutes to self destruction."

"How best to kill you I wonder," growls the Watcher. "I don't have time to beat you to death. Such a shame. I'd love to make this slow…"

He pulls out his pistol again and aims it at my head.

"Maybe I should just let the flames swallow you. We don't have long."

As he speaks, I see him fire. I dodge to the right and let the bullet ping off the floor.

"You still have your wits about you, I see," he says.

He turns his gun to Velia, defeated on the floor.

"What about you?"

I feel a fresh surge of adrenaline pulsing through my body, launching me to my feet. Just as he's about to pull the trigger I throw my full force at him, knocking him back. The gun explodes but the bullet fizzes off into the distance, missing its target.

Fuelled by fury, I focus hard and see deeper into the Void, all else blurring but for the man before me. My fists whip in quick, faster and faster, Knight's Terror's eyes showing concern for the first time. He dodges and parries and seeks an opportunity to fight back, my strikes beginning to get near, inching closer to their mark.

The sight of Ajax's large frame comes into view on my left, once more joining me. We battle on as we hear the countdown continue, only two minutes remaining now before the room is engulfed in flame.

We don't have much time.

Between strikes I call out to the girls.

"Get the file and get out of here. Get it to Drake…"

"We won't leave you," shouts Velia, still slightly dazed on the floor and unable to fight.

"DO IT," I shout, still in the heat of battle.

I'm losing focus now, my mind wandering elsewhere. I know that someone needs to get out of here alive…someone need to warn the others of what we've seen.

As my thoughts tumble, Knight's Terror once more seizes his chance, connecting with a strong hit to my jaw and knocking me backwards to the floor. He does the same to Ajax, panting harder than ever now as he looms above us.

"You think I'll let any of you leave," he says through his breaths. "You're all going to die down here…even if I have to stay to make sure it happens. I am willing to die for this cause."

I look across at Ajax on the floor, his left eye already turning black, lips dribbling blood. Then to the girls, next to each other, doubled over in pain and holding their stomachs.

"You're weak," taunts Knight's Terror. "These clones…I've trained them for years. You really have no idea what you're up against. There's one…oh he's truly something special."

I look again at the girls. My eyes flash, telling

them to get the file and get out of there. Then I stand up tall and straight, and stare my enemy in the eye.

A smile rises on his face.

"You've got some heart, I'll give you that. But it won't save you. It's time to finish this."

He shuts his eyes, takes a breath, and suddenly comes flashing forward again. Ignoring the others, he darts for me, lifting a knife from his belt as he comes. I see the blade glint under the light, his arm thrusting forward, driving straight for my heart.

Mustering my final shreds of strength, I stop his hand before it reaches me, my left arm gripping his right wrist tight. The tip of the knife scratches along my chest, drawing blood as it cuts through the skin. Holding him firm, I reach down with my right hand and draw up Athena's knife, the black grip fastened between my fingers, extending the dagger with a single click as I thrust it at my enemy's heart.

Like me, he sees it coming, and his left hand wraps about my wrist. Now, locked together, we push, his blade creeping a little deeper into my flesh, sending stabbing shards of pain through my body.

I can smell his breath now, so close, see into those cold eyes, full of hatred. As his blade moves a little deeper, his smirk grows. And then, suddenly, his eyes open wide, shock and pain filling them. His chin drops, and he looks down at my dagger.

Only now, it's no longer a dagger.

It's a sword.

And it's plunged right into his heart.

Now it's my turn to smile as I watch the blood tricking from the corners of his mouth, see the light fading in his eyes. His arms hold firm for a few seconds before going weak, his knife falling to his side, leaving only my extended sword embedded in his chest.

With my finger hovering on the button on its underside, I press down hard, and the sword withdraws, slicing back out of his black heart. He never saw it coming. Never heard it over the blaring alarm as I double clicked the button and sent the sword cutting through his chest.

For a moment, he just stands there in place, staring right at me with blank eyes. And then, with a final thud, his body collapses to the floor, the colour of crimson gathering around him.

I look to the others as they weakly get to their feet. And at the moment, we hear the voice calling from the ceiling once more.

*One minute to self destruction.*

# 32

## The Looming Shadow

I'm charging towards the rear of the training room, clipping my extendable knife back to my belt as I go. On the floor to one side I see the file marked 'The Seekers of Knight', discarded by Velia during the battle with Knight's Terror. I scoop up the file and turn back. At the other end of the room, the others have gathered at the door, urging me on.

All around the room, the voice sounds on the speakers, calling the countdown.

"Fifty seconds to self destruction."

The beeping and blaring of the siren seems to grow deafening now as I sprint as fast as I can towards my companions. I can see them calling me on, mouths moving, but can barely hear them over the din.

Heart burning, I finally near them, passing by the body of Knight's Terror and charging through the open door as the countdown reaches 40 seconds. I turn to look into the classroom, still filled with files and documents we never got a chance to look at. There might be so much information in there we could use, information that could help us.

But there's no time. It's too late now.

We cross the circular room fast, the metal doors ahead hanging slightly open. Ajax leads the way, kicking through with a powerful leg, opening up our passage into the dark tunnel ahead.

The sound of the alarm begins to grow a little quieter as we rush into the darkness, the tunnel almost pitch black after the glaring light behind us. We reach the stairs, and in the background I hear the countdown reach 30 seconds.

Up we go, legs pacing, the door into the shrine room for Augustus Knight lying ahead. It sits ajar, light spilling through from the other side. I can hear the sirens calling from ahead now too, speakers in the house blaring out as the countdown continues.

I thought it would be kept to the facility, but clearly not. Clearly, Baron Reinhold has seen fit to have a fail safe for the entire compound, the whole place about to go up in smoke. As we burst through into the light, and see the many faces of Augustus Knight around us, I wonder if we have enough time.

"Twenty…nineteen…eighteen…" comes the call.

We rush through, down the corridor, into the next room. I look upon the window we came through as Ajax pulls out his spear at a gallop and thrusts it straight through. The entire window shatters, the spear cutting through and embedding itself into the perimeter wall outside.

He's first there, leaping through the window, now blown apart and big enough to jump through.

"Fourteen…thirteen…twelve…"

The girls go through next, one after the other, throwing their bodies into the open air and hitting the ground with a thud. Ajax waits at the wall, pulling his spear free. The girls immediately run towards him as he vaults them straight over to the other side with his powerful arms.

I hit the earth outside the house, just as he sends Velia over, and run towards him fast. He cups his hands together, giving me a foothold, and launches me straight to the top. I swivel round as he jumps up, taking his arm and hauling him to the summit.

"Ten...nine...eight..."

We drop to the other side and begin running through the outer buildings. As we go, I feel it coming, feel the explosion about to rip through the earth, tearing the subterranean facility apart, decimating the compound up above.

We don't move around the side this time, but turn and head straight for the front. There are no guards now, no souls to be seen. I glance at the plot where the armoured vehicles were parked and see that several of them have gone, tracks leading off in the dirt, heading out of the clearing among the hills.

"Five...four...three..."

The countdown is distant now, hardly audible as we pant and run.

"Brace yourselves," I scream, mere seconds before the compound is engulfed.

Then, suddenly, I feel a deep rumbling beneath my feet. It bounces beneath us, making us stumble and fall. We hit the floor in a heap and look back at the house and the hills behind it. For a split second nothing happens, and then, bursting like a volcano, a ball of fire comes erupting out of the earth.

The flames quickly spread, rushing down the corridors of the house and into every room, smashing through doors and blowing out windows. As the hillside erupts, tonnes of rock and dirt are cast into the air, raining down from the sky around us.

"MOVE!" shouts Ajax as we leap back to our feet and make for the exit.

Deadly projectiles come fizzing from the heavens, pieces of fiery rock landing right at our feet. I see Ajax tackle Vesuvia to one side as a large chunk almost flattens them, saving her life. Her eyes glow with thanks as she looks at him, Ajax pulling her back up and dragging her on.

I try to focus as we rush, the danger all at our rear and coming out of the blue. The fire continues to spread, galloping from the main compound and into the outer buildings. They explode as the flames reach them, wrapping them up and tearing them apart. All around us, the world turns apocalyptic, fire and stone hunting us down from all angles.

I see them coming before they hit, cutting up the ground to the left and right. Some rocks hit and burst into flame, forcing us to swerve around them. Others are much smaller, little bits of shrapnel from the blast deadly enough to slice straight through flesh and bone.

Ahead, the two large boulders loom, showing us our passage from the carnage. I spare a glance back and see the fire abating, its progress halted. Above, more debris falls, the hillside decimated and spewing out a toxic column of smoke.

"Theo, come on!" shouts Velia beside me, taking my hand and pulling me forward.

With a final surge we reach the exit, diving around the side of the boulder as the mountain attempts one last assault, tossing a giant chunk of rock right down on us. It hits too late, crashing into the boulder and splintering as we reach safety.

We fall into a huddle in the low shrubs, panting and sweating and covered in soot. Little cuts and bruises litter our flesh, more than what Knight's Terror was able to inflict. But nothing more serious than that.

*We're safe.*

I suck in a huge breath of clean air and look back around the boulder and into the compound. The entire place is blanketed in flame, every building destroyed, much of the ground now crumbling and sinking into the earth. Every shred of evidence has been destroyed, save one.

I hold out the file in my hands once again, old and discoloured, but intact. The others stand and hover around, looking at the words printed on the front once more.

*The Seekers of Knight.*

We look to one another, and then our eyes stare

out towards the low valleys, stretching away into the vast desert. The morning is still young, the heat just beginning to rise. But we know, now, that our journey is just beginning. This is bigger than any of us could have imagined.

"They're out there…" I whisper, staring towards the endless desert. "And if we don't stop them, they're going to tear this country apart."

I feel Ajax's paw come to rest on my shoulder. I turn my eyes to his.

"We will stop them," he says. "Whatever it takes, we'll stop them."

And with that, we move away to the bushes nearby, find our bikes and bags, and set back out into the endless tundra.

Knowing that, from this day onwards, our lives won't ever be the same again.

**THE END**

*The story will continue in Book 2 – 'The Seekers of Knight'*

To hear about the author's latest discounts and new releases, sign up to his newsletter at www.tcedgebooks.com